THREE KISSES
OF THE COBRA

D1519440

Best wishes,

L. J. Bah

THREE KISSES
OF THE COBRA

A NOVEL

✤

Z. T. Balian

Three Kisses of the Cobra

Vakr Books
ISBN 9780997111606

ISBN: 0997111607
Library of Congress Control Number: 2015959498
VAKR BOOKS

Front cover image – View of Singapore (ca. 1830's) – reproduced courtesy of the
National Maritime Museum, Greenwich, London
Armenian calligraphy reproduced courtesy of Ruben Malayan
The English translation of Vahakn's birth poem by Robert Bedrosian is reproduced
here by kind permission from the translator.

Author's photo by S. Ozen

Z. T. Balian's compelling narrative of the transcultural odyssey of Vartan unfolds this Armenian hero's transcendental struggles with childhood adversities, exile from the homeland, and sacrificial love. A positively engaging novel!
Shahe S. Kazarian: Professor of psychology, author, and poet

Z. T. Balian's *Three Kisses of the Cobra* is a first-person narrative by a fictional early 19th Century Armenian entrepreneur caught up in the intrigues, loves, and treacheries of the expanding Armenian trading diaspora. The fictional characters are intertwined within the historical backdrop of the slowly-decaying Ottoman Empire through the warehouses of Georgetown, Madras, and Canton to the newly-established, bustling Singapore entrepôt. The panoramic sweep of space and time is filtered through the actions and emotions of the maturing hero, from the nostalgia of early childhood through the adventures and setbacks of youth and early middle age. *Three Kisses of the Cobra* will appeal to lovers of historical fiction of all ages.
Robert and Jolene Gear: Academics and authors

Without reservation, Z. T. Balian's *Three Kisses of the Cobra* is one of the few "real" pieces of literature I've had the good fortune to read in recent years. The conciseness of detail, sense of place, shaping of character all merge into a texture I've not experienced for a very long time. This novel has restored my faith that authentic literature exists in our time.
Michael Heenan: Academic and Grandmaster of the Bei Koku Aibujutsu Ryu

This book is dedicated to the memory of my parents, without whose guidance I would not be who I am today. My special thanks to Barbara Luffman, who read and commented on the very early versions. I would also like to thank Annie and Tom Hoglind for their suggestions and encouragement. I owe a debt of gratitude to Michael Phelan for editing the manuscript. I am grateful for the advice and encouragement of my two siblings. This book would not have come to fruition without the support and love of my husband.

PROLOGUE

⚜

The email, through one of the social networks, reads:

Dear Ms. / Mr. Nayri Bantukhtian,

My name is S. C. Yow (Mr.) and I am one of the wardens of the Armenian Church in Singapore. I would like to inform you that you have a next of kin, Miss Flora Bantukhtian, who lives in Macau. I was introduced to Miss Flora on a recent trip to Macau. She believes she has relatives in Lebanon, the USA and Australia, but has been unable to contact them. And as she is nearly 86 years old, she is concerned that she will never be able to pass on the inheritance to her next of kin. When I mentioned the fact that I work in the field of information technology, she asked me to trace her relatives. I have thus taken the liberty of contacting you and one other person in Australia on Miss Flora's behalf. If you wish to get in touch with me, I'll be glad to provide you with further details concerning Miss Flora.

I'M STUNNED. HOW IS IT possible – a relative in Macau? No one in my family had ever mentioned relatives in the Far East…

The email is indeed one from Singapore and Mr. Yow's story seems very credible. I'd been to Singapore on holiday years earlier and knew that the Armenian Church of St. Gregory was one of the first churches built there in the early 19ᵗʰ Century. There was a thriving Armenian community way back then, mainly Armenian merchants and their families, including the Sarkis brothers who had built Raffles Hotel later in the century. But after the Second World War, the community dwindled and only a handful of Singaporean Armenians remained for decades. I have since learned that the community has grown as a result of recent newcomers.

When I visited St. Gregory's, I was told it came under the jurisdiction of the Armenian Catholicos of Cilicia in Beirut, head of the Armenian Apostolic Church, who oversees the needs of a great majority of Armenians of that faith in the Diaspora, the Armenian communities dispersed all over the world. At the time of my visit, a young Chinese man, who was replacing the old orchids with fresh ones in the church, told me about Miss Agnes Joaquim. He showed me her tomb in the church yard. He said that she was a prominent 19ᵗʰ Century Singaporean Armenian and Singapore's Vanda Joaquim orchid, which was her creation, was named after her. As the Armenian Church was a historic landmark in Singapore and as there was no longer a sizeable Armenian community there, he and four other Singaporean youths had taken on the task of looking after the daily upkeep of the church. Could he or one of the other four have been Mr. Yow?

I avoided thinking about Miss Flora Bantukhtian for a couple of hours. The news had not sunk in yet.

I am an only child. My parents passed away years ago. In my mid-forties and single, I live in a comfortable flat in Beirut. I work in the banking sector and have a good position in a reputable bank. I did not witness the major part of Lebanon's barbaric civil war; I spent most of those years at university abroad and then worked in a European country that granted me citizenship. The nostalgia of my birthplace and the warmth of Middle Easterners brought me back to Beirut three years ago, but the novelty of my situation has worn off. It was exciting to smell the old aromas, eat the delicious food and see old friends – those who hadn't immigrated to far-flung places. Somehow, though, I do not feel I fit in anymore. Things have changed. The poor are poorer and the rich are the '*nouveaux riches*' of the civil war. As a result, the middle class, which gave Beirut its unique cosmopolitan feel, has vanished into thin air.

I have come to the realisation that one of the negative outcomes of the civil war has been the stagnation of Lebanese society in all its aspects. I cannot reconcile my life experiences in the West with my situation in a society which still labels me a 'spinster' even though, as far as the laws of the country are concerned, I am a 'respectable professional'. The news of Miss Flora couldn't have come at a more uncertain time in my life. I was contemplating leaving Beirut for good at the end of my work contract – but to where I did not know.

Both my maternal and paternal grandparents had come to Lebanon at the end of the First World War, having survived the systematic killings of the Armenian population of the Ottoman Empire which had begun in the 1890's; it culminated in April 1915 with a planned extermination, perpetrated by the Young Turks. My grandparents had lost their lands, property and most of their family members during the genocide, but had made a new life for themselves in Lebanon like other survivors. Most of the survivors of the genocide had been assisted by the French who had given them safe passage to Syria and Lebanon, or the Swiss, Danish, and American missionaries who had saved the Armenian orphans from certain death.

My maternal grandparents came from Adana on the Mediterranean in Southeast Turkey; my paternal grandparents were from Kayseri, the old Caesarea. I remember my father saying that his grandparents were not natives of Kayseri, but that they were originally from Erzerum in North-eastern Turkey. I am linked to Miss Flora through my father's name, I thought, a most unusual and uncommon family name amongst Armenians – '*bantukht*', meaning 'a person in exile'.

Finally, my curiosity got the better of me. So I decided to contact S. C. Yow (Mr.) immediately, not forgetting to write 'Ms.' next to my name – as he had indicated his gender.

Over the next few days, I discovered a fair bit more about Miss Flora.

"She's a typical bohemian," is how he described her.

Her place was full of books and all sorts of curios – an indication of a well-read and travelled person. He'd been taken to meet her by a friend, a member of a Christian youth organization in Macau and was told her door was always open to young people of all persuasions. Heated discussions could be heard amongst students on topics relating to literature and politics in her *salon*. They helped her with her shopping and food as she'd had health problems recently. She'd never married but had mentioned a couple of 'fiancés' from her younger days. Greatly admired by all, she was addressed always as 'Miss Flora'.

Her constant contact with young people had given her an awareness of technology and the workings of electronic mail and social networks. So when she met Yow – that's how he wishes to be called – she had found the opportunity of accessing the world with the hope of finding her lost relatives. She said: "Yow is the person to trace my relatives. Who can do better than he with his knowledge of the computer?" Yow was flattered and totally taken by the old lady. He could not refuse her.

Two and a half months have passed since Yow's message and I'm now finally on my way to Macau.

The fast ferry from Hong Kong feels like a freezer although the Chinese passengers don't seem to mind the full blast of the air-conditioners. I wrap my shawl round my shoulders, feeling apprehensive at the thought of meeting Miss Flora.

I feel as apprehensive as at the time when I had decided to write my first letter to her. Yow had sent me her address not long after our first contact, but I hadn't plucked up the courage to write to her immediately. How was I to introduce myself? How was I to address her? What things should I tell her about my family and myself? I didn't know her, and yet felt drawn to her. Was it ties of kinship, or perhaps just curiosity, or the glamour of some exotic 'aunt' living in the Far East?

After Yow's email, I had agonized for several days before writing a very simple letter to her. I avoided trying to impress her, as one sometimes does when one meets a new person. I gave her simple facts about myself and my family and said I would like to visit her in Macau as soon as I could. I received a no-frills letter from her three weeks later. The message was that she was in possession of something that belonged to the Bantukhtian family, which she had to give me in person and was looking forward to meeting me.

It's dark when I get to my hotel in Macau. It's in the night-life district of town, but its immediate vicinity is strangely devoid of the usual downtown bustle. I can see bright lights and the famous all-lit-up hotel/casino from my window.

When visiting friends or family abroad, Armenians always take it for granted that they can stay with the hosts. Most traditional Armenian families around the world would have a couple of spare mattresses for visitors even if they don't have a spare bedroom. I'd booked a hotel room prior to my arrival as I hadn't wished to disturb Miss Flora late at night and, in this instance, wasn't sure whether both of us would fit the traditional mould.

My train of thought is suddenly interrupted by a phone call. I immediately recognise Yow's voice.

"Hello, Yow!"

"I hope you've managed to unpack and are comfortable."

"Yes, thanks. The hotel is very centrally located and I think I'll be able to get to Miss Flora's on foot tomorrow morning."

"Great! I've got good news for you and Miss Flora – that relative of yours in Australia? Well, she contacted me today. I gave her your contact details and she said she'll probably call you tonight."

"That's wonderful news, indeed!"

"I know you're anxious about meeting Miss Flora – don't be – everything will work out alright. And do let me know what's happening at your end, okay?"

"I'll call you when I'm back at the hotel tomorrow evening, I promise. And thank you again for all your help, Yow."

"My pleasure!"

Five minutes later, the phone rings again. It's Olivia Bantukhtian calling from Sydney. She speaks with an unmistakable Australian accent and the warmest voice imaginable.

Olivia tells me she is a bullion dealer. How strange that we should both be in related professions. And she's roughly my age. She apologizes for not having contacted Yow before but says she had taken three months off work to do a bit of travelling with her partner, John, an Australian of Irish descent, and their 6-year-old son, Joseph.

"Everyone calls him Joey," she says. "That was my father's name, Hovsep in Armenian. And Joey carries my surname – he's a Bantukhtian, too!"

She tells me her father arrived in Australia at the end of World War II, having survived internment in a Japanese civilian concentration camp as a teenager. His family was one of a handful of Armenian merchant families who were still living in Ambon in the Mollucas Islands of Indonesia when the Japanese took over and imprisoned them together with the Dutch civilians. Olivia's grandfather had died just before the war, and after the war, her grandmother and her three children – two daughters and Olivia's father – had opted to make a new life for themselves in Australia. Neither of her aunts had married or had children. I ask Olivia if she has any siblings. She says she's an only child like me, born of two Armenian parents. Her father married an Armenian girl whose family had immigrated to Australia from India just after independence. She didn't know of any other Bantukhtians in Australia.

"I'm delighted to have found another Bantukhtian," she says after I finish giving her a resumé of my own side of the story.

"We have to plan and get together soon, I hope," she says.

I promise to work something out and that I'll keep her posted on the meeting with Miss Flora.

It's a lovely morning in Macau. I walk past the old Leal Senado and cross the square towards the old quarters of town. I find Miss Flora's address. It's an old Chinese building, all in marshmallow green with interesting wrought iron railings. I climb the stairs to the second floor apartment and knock. A young Chinese girl gestures the way to a living room even before I finish pronouncing Miss Flora's name. Miss Flora stands up from an armchair and walks towards me with open arms.

"I'm so glad you could make it. I'm so happy to see you! Do sit down, please," she says, holding my hands and leading me to an armchair. She is a petite woman and frail in appearance. She is of a very fair complexion, and has huge, dark, unmistakably Armenian eyes.

Over the next few days, I become part of the armchair I first sat in at Miss Flora's. Miss Flora is one of those beings who enjoy an ease of expression, and words flow from her with no particular effort.

I go to the hotel, but only for a few hours sleep, a shower, a change of clothing and a brief chat with Olivia and Yow. I prefer to do this although Miss Flora has offered to put me up.

"My family settled in Hong Kong after leaving Singapore," says Miss Flora. "We were fortunate to leave Singapore just in time, before the Japanese takeover, and spent the war years in the United States. When the war was over, my father, Hagop or Jacob as he was known in the business, and my brother Jack decided to move their business operations to Hong Kong. They built an even more successful business than the one they had in Singapore although my father was getting on in years by this time. I moved to Macau after my father's death and then the death of Jack in a car crash."

A long pause followed. Miss Flora was clearly trying to hide the pain of losing her only brother; then, recomposing herself she said, "Let's get something to eat. Do you like Chinese food?"

"Yes, I do."

"Great! And tomorrow we can have a *real* treat – I'll cook you the only Armenian dish I know how to – chickpea and cracked wheat pilav!"

We both laughed.

After lunch, and after many questions about my family and life, and about Olivia and Joey, Miss Flora got up from her armchair and walked slowly towards an old rosewood cabinet. Reaching in, she carefully took out an old book with an embossed and partially crumpled leather cover.

"This is what I wanted to give you in person," she said in a tone of voice betraying great emotion.

"Here are the memoirs of my great-great-grandfather, Vartan. I desperately wanted to find you as I have no one to leave this to. Besides, I don't know how to speak or read Armenian, and it's about time someone read all this properly. My knowledge of the family history is through my father. You see, Vartan was one of the first Armenian merchants to settle in Singapore. He spent many years trading all over India and the Far East. He was given the honorary title of 'khoja' by his compatriots, which was reserved for the notables or dignitaries of the community. My great-grandfather was his eldest son and perhaps that explains why the memoirs were in his possession. I also know that Vartan had three other sons, and according to my father, all three left Singapore after Vartan's death. That's where you come into the picture," she said with a smile.

"But how did you know that you had relatives in Australia, Lebanon and the USA?"

"Well, as I said, the eldest son, my great-grandfather, stayed in Singapore. The second son went to Java and then settled in the Mollucas Islands. Knowing this, my father made inquiries after the

war and was told that some Armenian survivors of Japanese concentration camps were allowed to immigrate to Australia. So, I just
hoped there might be a Bantukhtian somewhere in Australia and I
was right. The third son went to America. I knew for a fact that there
were Bantukhtians there. During the years we spent in America, on
the West Coast, my father again made inquiries and was told by the
Armenian Church authorities that there was indeed a Bantukhtian
family living in New York. Unfortunately, my father never got round
to contacting them because of our move back to the Far East and his
death shortly after that. Perhaps now you could look for them and
find out what happened to them. As for your great-great-grandfather, Vartan's youngest son, he went back to his father's birthplace,
Erzerum."

"Oh, yes! My father always said his grandparents came from
Erzerum, but they eventually settled in Kayseri. The family was nick-
named '*Gharibenk*', meaning 'the strangers', most likely because they
were newcomers both in Erzerum and in Kayseri later on. But how
strange – we didn't know anything about Vartan and the existence of
relatives in the Far East."

"It doesn't surprise me, really," Miss Flora remarked. "Vartan
Bantukhtian died more than a hundred years ago and, with what your
family went through during World War I and family members that they
lost during the massacres, it is to be expected that the old family history
would never have reached you."

"That's true. As a child, all my grandparents were interested in telling me was their story of surviving the genocide. It's as if they had lost
the memory of how things were before those tragic events, as if nothing
had existed before then. But how did you guess that my part of the family had ended up in Lebanon?" I asked.

"In the 1960's, I spent some time in France, where, as you know, there was and still is a large Armenian community. Most of them had come to France from Anatolia in the early 1920's after the horrors of the genocide. During my stay, I earnestly looked for Bantukhtians, but to no avail. I was disappointed but came to the conclusion that the descendants of the youngest son of Vartan, if they existed, would have most likely ended up in Lebanon, the country with the largest Armenian community in the Middle East. It was a good guess, wouldn't you say? Otherwise, I would never have found you."

"It was meant to be," I said.

"Indeed," she said and handed me the old book with the crumpled leather cover.

Back in my hotel room, I eagerly opened the book. It was more like a leather-bound notebook. It was handwritten in beautiful Armenian calligraphy, the type used in the old illuminated manuscripts. The first page had a date, 1858. Reading the text, it wasn't long before I realised I couldn't grasp it fully. I knew then that I faced a challenge created by history: The language used was a mixture of ecclesiastical Armenian (*krapar*) and what I assumed to be local Erzerum, or an Anatolian Armenian dialect (*kavaraparpar*). Modern Western Armenian, used by the descendants of Anatolian Armenians in the Diaspora, was only adopted in the 1860's and Modern Eastern Armenian was adopted by Armenians living in the region of the Armenian Republic of today and the rest of the Caucasus, Russia, and Persia at about the same period; the relationship between the two is somewhat analogous to that of British English and American English, or French and Canadian French.

When I went back to see Miss Flora for the last time, I recounted what I could make out of the memoirs of Vartan. She listened to me intently and smiled now and again, encouraging me to carry on with Vartan's story. When I said I had problems deciphering parts of it, she said:

"I'm sure you can find someone to help you in Lebanon. I was never part of a large Armenian community to be able to get that kind of assistance. I'm certain there are competent Armenian scholars there who will help you."

"I will certainly try," I said.

As I took my leave, Miss Flora said, "Now, look after yourself and write to me."

"I'll come and see you again very soon," I promised.

Miss Flora stretched out her arms and I hugged her to say goodbye. As I did, her body stiffened and she gave me a blank look, but she held my hand tightly until we got to the door.

Going down the stairs, I wondered why she was so seemingly unemotional when I hugged her. Perhaps she had known she wouldn't see me again.

My audience with the Catholicos of Cilicia, whose Holy See is in Antelias, just outside Beirut, was fruitful. His Holiness assigned a priest, Torkom, to help me decipher parts of Vartan's memoirs.

Torkom *Vartabed* (learned priest), is a celibate Armenian clergy-man. He is a young, dynamic lecturer at the seminary in Antelias, and an expert in Medieval Armenian literature and Armenian dialects of Anatolia.

"This is fascinating, very fascinating!" he told me when I first showed him Vartan's manuscript.

Over the next month, I met Torkom *Vartabed* on a regular basis and his knowledge was invaluable. He not only deciphered the text, but also taught me things I never knew about Armenian history, traditions, and customs.

"What do you intend to do with this manuscript?" he asked at the end of our last meeting.

"I have no idea yet. I'd be honoured if you were the one to publish it in Modern Armenian. But first I have to translate it into English for myself."

"Why?!" exclaimed Torkom *Vartabed,* astonished at my urgency to translate the manuscript into a foreign language before publishing it in Modern Armenian.

"I have to," I said firmly, thinking of Miss Flora, Yow, and Olivia. "I owe it to three people very dear to me."

CHAPTER 1

⚜

I, Khoja Vartan Bantukhtian, started writing this account of my life, which my Lord has bestowed upon me, in the year of our Lord Jesus Christ, 1858.

I WAS BORN IN THE ancient Eastern Anatolian town of Garin on the day of the Armenians' most venerated saint, Saint Vartan, in the year 1800. I was my mother Azniv's second and only surviving child. Her first born, a girl, had died in her first year, but no one knew why. "She just stopped eating and passed away like an angel returning to the Almighty," my mother would lament, slapping her knees in grief. Perhaps because of this grief and because she couldn't conceive another child, my mother doted on me. I was everything to her and she would do everything for me. My mother was a small, frail woman, quiet and good-natured, who gave me free reign of the household. She never scolded me like other children's mothers and gave me a coin for boiled candy and sweetmeats every Sunday afternoon, knowing how impatiently I waited all week for it.

We were a very close pair, my mother and I. My close relationship with her was also due to my father Hagop's absence for months at a time. He was a merchant of the old order. He travelled to Persia at least twice a year where, Uncle Krikor, his younger brother and business partner had settled. Both my father and uncle were called *Mahdessi* on

1

account of having performed pilgrimage to Jerusalem, and each had the Armenian cross tattooed on the inside part of the wrist to attest to this. My father was a stocky, well-built man, but had a weak heart and sometimes behaved grumpily. I loved him dearly and enjoyed the stories of his travels. But Uncle Krikor was my favourite person in our extended family. I awaited his yearly visits with great excitement. He arrived with gifts for all my aunts' children, but I would get extra sweets and silk embroidered hats upon our return home, as he always lodged with us. "You're my special boy," he would say, patting me on the head.

Garin was the name the Armenian folk of the city used; the Turks called it Erzerum. It had a huge bazaar with hundreds of shops selling everything one could think of: silk, wool and cotton cloths, felt, hand-woven piled carpets and flat-weaves, silver jewellery and snuff boxes, copper and brass utensils, iron tools, wax, candles, lanterns, foodstuff and spices. Garin was also the trading hub, as it had been for hundreds of years, for merchandise coming from Persia and places further east. Most of the goods destined for Constantinople had to pass through my city.

The travelling merchants of Garin were mostly Armenian and had es-tablished their own mercantile associations to facilitate their movements and the transportation of goods. My father and Uncle Krikor were part of this 'brotherhood'. My uncle, who was based in Isfahan, procured textiles, silk, spices, tea and Persian carpets, and my father provided the link of transporting them to Garin and then on to Constantinople, from where other Armenian merchants would dispatch the goods to Europe – to Plovdiv, Venice, Genoa, Marseilles, Amsterdam, and as far away as cities in England and Spain – where many of their countrymen had settled and traded successfully.

One night, whilst they thought I was asleep, I overheard a conversa-tion between my Uncle Krikor and my father.

"Look, my brother," my uncle was saying "the boy is eight years old. You're not here for long stretches of time. Who is going to teach him how to read and write?"

Addressing my mother he said, "You've got to pardon me Azniv, but you can barely read your Armenian prayer book and your writing is poor. So you can't teach him. We'll have to find someone. If he's going to be a merchant like us in the future, we've got to get him a teacher."

My mother stood silent for a while. I had never before heard her meddle in the conversation of my father and uncle. But this time, she muttered shyly, "I've heard some local Armenian merchants and trades people are planning to start an Armenian school. They have asked Father Sahag to run it. They say they are waiting for the permission from the *Qaimaqam* (regional governor) and will admit girls in the future if things go well. They say permission has already been given in the western cities. The Church will be in charge, they say, but the merchants and the guilds will finance it. I've heard it's an arrangement everybody is satisfied with."

"So the Sublime Porte has finally given us permission to have Armenian schools. I never thought I'd see the day!" my father exclaimed.

"We'll go to the bazaar tomorrow morning and find out the latest" were the last words I heard before I fell asleep.

Father Sahag I knew well. He was a married priest in charge of our parish. He wore the black priest's robe and a conical black velvet hat. He was a big man with a grey beard and a thick moustache. He would visit each household twice a year – near Christmastime and at Easter – to 'bless the house' as my mother would say. He came equipped for the task: a small brass incense burner with a cross on it, small bits of incense, a tiny piece of charcoal, and a small silver cross encrusted with semi-precious stones and wrapped in a white kerchief with embroidered edges. Once the incense started burning, he took the incense burner to every room in the house, and wrapping the handle of the cross with the white kerchief and holding the cross up, repeated a customary prayer. When he'd finished, both my mother and I would bow to kiss his hand as a sign of respect. He would always pull back his hand as he didn't seem to like the gesture very much. I liked doing it because I could have a good look at his ring. He had a huge silver ring with a dark amber stone in the middle. My father and uncle both had similar rings. The stone was carved with the name of its owner and could be used as a signature stamp or seal on an official document. Father Sahag's intrigued me because the writing looked more elaborate than my father's and uncle's and there were two small crosses carved at either end.

Before he left, my mother would give him some food or Easter biscuits to take to his family. If we were the last of his rounds, he'd sit and talk. He would take off his conical hat and I could see his snow-white head contrasting with his sun-drenched forehead and hazel eyes and felt great affection towards him.

I wasn't the only youngster who liked Father Sahag. He had a way with children. He had six of his own, and now he had 46 pupils at the new school. The school was a huge room that the Armenian merchants and trades people had built very quickly next to our church. It was furnished with small tables and benches made by carpenter Mesrob.

The next four years were happy times for me. I enjoyed school and my parents and uncle were very proud of my achievements as I became Father Sahag's favourite pupil. He taught me reading, writing, history, geography, and arithmetic – all in Armenian. Master Massud, a

Turk, taught us Turkish. Father Sahag so enjoyed running the school that he also started a Sunday school, which all the children attended after church. We all enjoyed these Sunday morning sessions as, unlike church mass, Father Sahag recounted Biblical stories that we could understand.

One day, after school, Father Sahag asked me to stay behind. When everyone had left, he said: "Would you like to inspect my ring? I've noticed how intrigued you are by it." He took it off and handed it to me.

"I love the Armenian script on it. I can read very well now, but I still can't read this one," I said.

"It's engraved in an Armenian abbreviated calligraphic style. It says: *The servant of Christ, Sahag.* The letters are all intertwined. Would you like to be able to write like this?" Father Sahag asked. I said I would.

"Vartan, you know how much I love you – as much as my own son. You are my best pupil, but I can't teach you any more than I have. If you want to learn more, you'll have to go to one of the Armenian monasteries. That means leaving your mother and Garin. The Golden Monastery is nearby and has a scriptorium and nunnery but no school. You will have to go to a monastery quite a way from here. You should think about this carefully and let me know how you feel about it."

I told him I didn't need to think about it. I wanted more education but was afraid my mother would not let me go. Father Sahag said, "In that case, leave it to me. I'll take care of it."

The next day, Father Sahag's wife, the *Yeretzgin* ('the elder's wife') appeared at our door with a couple of *neshkhar* as gifts for my mother. My mother loved these blessed, small, circular unleavened breads with embossed religious figures on them. They were similar to the bread used for the Eucharist, and she regarded them as having the power of "protecting the household from evil."

Yeretzgin, whose first name I never knew, was a huge lady and always seemed out of breath. When she'd settled in her seat, she told my mother how lucky she was to have given birth to such a gifted child.

"You have seen, I'm certain, how wonderful his writing is. Father Sahag says he can get him a place at Saint Garabed Monastery in Erzenga. He is sure Vartan has the ability to study there. Did you know that seven of their graduates have become bishops and four are famous notables in the west of the country? There's a future there for the boy."

"Thank you, *Yeretzgin,* for your kind thoughts. However, you must be aware that the final decision is my husband's and he'll be here in a month's time," said my mother in a neutral tone.

When the *Yeretzgin* left, I felt my heart pounding hard. I was uncertain of how my mother would react to the idea of me going away to study. Over supper, she said, "Do not think I'm a fool and haven't noticed how keen you are on studying. You want to go to the monastery, don't you?"

"Yes, mother, but I don't wish to leave you here on your own. It's going to be very difficult for me not to be with you every day," I muttered.

"What needs to be done must be done," she said wryly. "We Armenians must always be better, more educated, and more competent than those Mohamedans who rule us. It is not by chance that you were born on the day that our venerated Saint Vartan, in the year 451 of our Lord Christ, turned certain defeat into victory when he resisted the pagan Persian army of sixty thousand with only a few thousand men. And even though he was martyred, it was his courage, his tenacity, and his faith that made the enemy retreat," she said, adding, "I'll talk to your father when he comes back."

That night I lay in bed looking at the purple moon through our window and realised how proud I was of my mother and how fortunate I was to possess her unconditional love. But sadness engulfed my teenage heart at the thought of leaving her.

It was early evening when they brought my father in a carriage. He had fallen ill on the journey from Tabriz. Other merchants accompanying him said they cautiously avoided stopping anywhere en route as Russian troops were encroaching on areas near the Persian and Ottoman borders.

My father was in a bad way. Doctor Hampartsum arrived immediately. He was the most esteemed doctor in the city and the Turkish *Qaimaqam* swore by him, even though he was Armenian, and, therefore, a Christian *giavour* (unbeliever).

"His heart is weak. I have done what I can for him. Put your trust in God," he told my mother before he left.

When my father passed away six days later, my mother's world fell apart. Her words 'My world is finished', which she repeated over and over, still ring in my ears. To shield me from her intense grief, she sent me to stay with my youngest aunt and cousins for a week. Her two other sisters stayed at our house to receive the townspeople who came to offer their condolences. Word was sent to Uncle Krikor in Persia.

Uncle Krikor arrived two months later. On the second day of his arrival, while my mother was at church, he called me into his room and asked me to sit down.

"I have invited your mother to come and live with me and my family in Persia, but she refuses to leave her homeland and kin. She tells me you have set your heart on studying at Saint Garabed Monastery."

I nodded.

"Very well, your wish will be granted. I will take care of you and your mother from now on."

The loss being too painful to describe, both of us avoided mentioning my father.

A few minutes later, it was Uncle Krikor who broke the silence.

"Just tell my special boy that his uncle wouldn't want to see him turn into a *vartabed* (learned priest, celibate) and live his life in a monastery. I need him in the business," he said jokingly and proceeded to tell me about his recent trip to the land of the Hindus.

CHAPTER 2

✤

A YEAR AFTER MY FATHER'S death, a requiem service in his memory was conducted at our local church by Father Sahag. After the church service, Father Sahag paid us a visit.

"I received an official letter from Saint Garabed Monastery saying that Vartan is accepted. He is to arrive no later than Wednesday week," he said, looking apprehensively at my mother.

"I've already prepared his clothing – only some provisions remain to be bought. He'll be ready in a couple of days," was the reply.

Indeed, my mother had things ready for me, and without my being aware of it. When Father Sahag left, she brought out two sets of fine woollen undergarments, two sets of pantaloons, a pair of soft leather boots, woollen socks that my aunts had knitted, three shirts, a couple of hats, and a new *badmujan* (long overcoat) made of good quality wool.

"Your uncle paid for this one before he left," she said with a smile as she stroked the *badmujan*. "Now that you're almost a grown up, he insisted you had one of those."

On the morning of my departure, I went to my old school to see Father Sahag before the pupils arrived. It was very early and Father

Sahag was reading at his desk. I thanked him for his help in getting me a place at the monastery.

"The only way you can thank me is by being a good student and by writing letters. You know that Father Moses carries letters quite often. Now run, they must be waiting for you."

The ox-driven cart was in front of the house. My mother and aunts had prepared two *bohja* (travel parcels made of cloth): A large one to hold my clothing and a smaller one to hold food for my journey. When it was time to leave, one by one my aunts and cousins hugged me and started to cry. My mother was last.

"Take these, my son," she said. "This is your father's favourite silver and niello Van belt, and this is from me."

She placed a necklace made of thick thread around my neck. It had a small triangular pouch at its end. This was made of cloth and covered with embroidered crosses.

"It contains the traveller's prayer. I copied it myself from the prayer book as best I could. Wear it around your neck at all times. It will keep you safe, my son."

I hugged my mother tightly and tears came rolling down my cheeks.

I arrived at Saint Garabed Monastery near Erzinga, west of Erzerum, in the heart of Anatolia, three days later. I must have looked tired for Bishop Boghos, the abbot and head of the seminary, quickly ordered hot soup and water to be brought for me and ensured I was not disturbed for two days by anyone – students, novices and monks alike.

The monastery stood in the middle of nowhere. It was a majestic, typically Armenian, stone structure, surrounded by rugged terrain. Next to the ancient monastery and church was a newer structure, the living quarters, which incorporated the school. Encircling the immediate circumference of the monastery was a fruit orchard and some small vegetable growing patches. The monks kept a few sheep, goats and chickens in the vicinity, and there was a well. Bread, I soon found out, was rationed to a small piece of *lavash* (thin, soft bread) per day on account of flour being brought from Erzinga Town only once a month.

I quickly made friends with everyone and Little Arakel became my best friend. And although I was homesick the first two months and missed my mother dearly, I soon settled into the monastery lifestyle. I didn't enjoy the daily chores in the kitchen so much but was fascinated by my lessons. There were fourteen pupils: Little Arakel, who was a year younger than me, was the youngest, and Sarkis, who was 16, was the eldest. I shared a small sleeping cell with the two of them and one other boy by the name of Menatzagan.

"Will you be my good friend?" Little Arakel asked me the first time we met. "I so long to have a good friend, like the brother that I will never have for I have neither a mother nor a father," he said in a firm manner as if he was certain I was not going to reject his request. I nodded without uttering a word. But I didn't need to since we were inseparable from that day onwards.

Bedros *Vartabed* taught us literature and grammar. He was very old, but had the memory to recite an endless number of verses with his eyes closed. Another monk, Gomidas *Vartabed*, taught us arithmetic, logic and music. All of us admired him as he was so clever at such a young age. Bishop Giragos taught us catechism and church history, but on account of his old age, he would sometimes fall asleep whilst giving his lecture. This amused us all no end and prompted Sarkis to produce his deck of cards, which was not allowed at the monastery, and start teaching us a simple game or two. Antranik *Vartabed*, the most entertaining and able of the monks, taught us history and geography. It was he who also taught me Armenian calligraphy.

At the monastery, there were a dozen monks and three bishops. In addition, there were seven novices who had initially come to study there and had chosen to stay and become celibate priests. Early on, I had realised that becoming a priest would not be my vocation even though I enjoyed the monastic life. My great admiration for my uncle and the memories of his stories of faraway places were ever present in my mind. And with the passing of time, the idea of following in the footsteps of my father and uncle intensified. This is why, after Sunday mass, when Little Arakel and Sarkis and some of the other boys begged me to recount the stories of my father and uncle, I gladly obliged. And when I exhausted my store, they would ask me to repeat their favourites.

During the winter months, it was terribly cold at the monastery. I missed the warmth of our house in Erzerum and, sometimes, my mother's cooking even more so. Unlike the monastery, which was built of massive stones and stood facing the wind and cold, our house in Erzerum was built to shield us from the cold, half visible from the road that led to it and the other half constructed below ground. This was done intentionally so as to protect us from the cold and snow. We kept our sheep and chickens in the underground area in the winter, both to shelter them from the harsh cold and to bring warmth to the house. The *tonir* (stone/clay oven) was also built adjacent to the underground section and every morning my mother would bake our *lavash* bread there. The heat of the *tonir* would rise and keep our house warm all day.

Each summer, I went home. Uncle Krikor always made sure he saw me when I was there. Sometimes, he would delay his departure to Persia or change his plans so as to spend at least a few days with us in Erzerum.

And every summer, Little Arakel came along with me. Although he was an orphan, he did have a wealthy uncle, a busy flour merchant in Bursa who, for some reason unbeknownst to Little Arakel, did not wish to see him or spend any time with him. My mother was so content to have us there that she doted on both of us. I do not wish to forget to mention the attention we received from my aunts; and Little Arakel felt loved and adopted by our family.

Both of us enjoyed running around the green meadows surrounding Erzerum and would get up to all kinds of antics with my cousins. Erzerum bloomed in the summer, being as it was in a valley of fertile land and protected by magnificent high mountains. Little Arakel and I were also well fed and loved the nuts, apples, apricots, pears and plums of the warm season, and especially the cherries.

"If you eat very well during the summer, then you will be able to face the cold at the monastery in the winter," my mother would tell us at almost every mealtime.

In the autumn, when the wind started blowing and the rains came, we were glad to be going back to the monastery, full of excitement at the thought of seeing the teachers and our classmates again.

During my years at the monastery, Antranik *Vartabed* took extra special care at teaching me calligraphy. At first, I was afraid I might disappoint him, but as the years passed, I gained a lot of confidence and slowly mastered it. On the first day of Lent during my third year at the monastery, Bishop Boghos called me to his quarters. He handed me a letter he had written and asked me to copy it in my best calligraphy and bring it back to him when I'd finished. As I left the room, I noticed the letter was addressed to the Armenian Patriarch of Constantinople. When I raised my head, I caught Antranik *Vartabed* waiting just outside the Bishop's door. I understood then that he must have known about the letter and it was he who had put my name forward to do the copying. He smiled as if to say he trusted in my ability to do the task correctly. I did not disappoint him and earned Bishop Boghos' praise. From then on, he called upon me whenever an important document had to be copied in calligraphy.

Around the end of my fourth year at the monastery, I was called to Bishop Boghos' quarters again. When I entered the room, my Uncle Krikor was standing there solemn-faced. I immediately sensed something bad had happened.

"Your mother is very ill. We have to go to Erzerum," he said in a sombre tone. "Go and get your stuff and we'll be off immediately," he said.

When I went out of the room to collect my things, I saw Little Arakel standing on the side of the door. "I heard everything," he said. "I'm coming with you."

On the journey to Erzerum, I discovered my mother had been ill for months. A terrible illness of the lungs, my uncle said. As we approached our house in Erzerum, my youngest aunt ran out of the house towards our carriage, crying out, "She's gone, she's gone..." For the first time in my life, I lost control of my body, my senses, and I collapsed.

We buried my mother on a sunny, spring morning. My aunts had dressed her in her finest clothing – a richly embroidered apron, a favourite head cap flanked with strings of silver chains and coins, and a treasured silk headscarf.

"She wanted to see you one last time," my eldest aunt said, "but it was never to be. It's God's will."

The profound sadness and guilt I felt then has never left me.

After three days of mourning and receiving condolences from all the townspeople, I felt exhausted both physically and emotionally. The most comforting face I can remember is that of Father Sahag. Without his consoling words I would never have got back on my own two feet again.

On the fourth morning, I saw Uncle Krikor sitting on the threshold, lost in thought.

"I have taken the decision to join you. Will you have me?"

My uncle looked straight into my eyes and said, "Are you sure you want to become a merchant like me? Are you willing to undertake long and arduous journeys? Listen, you may not return to Erzerum for a long time. I say this because, apart from the Sultan raising our taxes, the Erzerum route is becoming too dangerous to use. The Russians are increasing their presence in the area and so, too, are the Persians. We can surely expect the Sultan to wage a war against them." He paused and then said, "And what's going to become of your father's house?"

I told him that I was sure my decision was the right one and that it had become more and more obvious to me that my future was not in Erzerum but with him – wherever he went. I told him I wanted Little Arakel to have the house so he would no longer be dependent on his uncaring uncle.

"Very well," he said. "We leave in five days."

CHAPTER 3

⚜

I LEFT ERZERUM IN THE spring of 1816. The last image of Erzerum engraved in my mind is that of Little Arakel in front of our house and Father Sahag's tearful eyes. "God willing, I will come back," I remember shouting as our carriage began to move. When we reached the outskirts of town, my heart was filled with sadness for having left Erzerum and my loved ones, but also with expectations of wonderful things to come. A new world was opening up on the horizon of the plain of Ararat, whence we were heading.

My uncle had hired a horse-drawn carriage in town and this was to be our mode of transportation for a few days until we were united with his new business partner, who was waiting for us near Lake Van. We travelled a fair distance in the vast and empty plains for three days. Every day, the carriage driver broke the journey either early in the evening or at nightfall at small villages on the way. We slept at whatever lodgings we could find or accepted whatever the carriage driver suggested.

It was on the third day, in the early morning and from a good distance, that I saw the most magnificent sight I had ever seen and one that I shall forever carry in my heart. It was that of Mount Ararat ascending to the skies from the vast, cypress-dotted plains of Shirak.

Amazed at what I saw, I turned to my uncle and said, "It is at the peak of Mount Ararat that Noah's Ark finally rested."

"That is indeed what is believed, Vartan. And remember my words my boy, Ararat is the image of the Armenians. It represents the essence of our soul, our strength. Never forget that – wherever you are in this world – for it is this mountain that gave birth to our people," he said, and placed his hand on my shoulder affectionately.

We continued our journey under the watchful eye of our mother mountain, which guided our path and remained always in sight until darkness fell on that third day.

We had to sleep for a few hours in the carriage. Our journey had taken us into an area where there was no habitation. The carriage driver gave us shaggy woollen mountain blankets and told us to rest. He said that we would reach our destination in half a day if we moved on at daybreak.

The next day, the morning and almost all of the afternoon had passed before we finally reached our destination. It was a caravanserai at the northern edge of Lake Van. I was familiar with caravanserais as there were several in and around Erzerum. I had visited a few with my father to meet tradesmen or merchants from Constantinople or elsewhere. But this caravanserai was so much bigger and vaster that I was flabbergasted as I entered it. There were vaulted sections and a huge central area with a corresponding arched mezzanine.

"This is the biggest one you'll ever see," my uncle said. "The only other one like it is in Baghdad. Come, it's getting dark. We need to sleep for we have to be up very early."

In the morning, with daylight, I discovered the great number of merchants who stayed in the caravanserai. And there were an even greater number of horses, mules, and camels. Watching the movements of a camel for the first time in my life, but from a far distance, and munching on a few raisins and walnuts from my pocket, I heard my uncle say:

"Finish eating quickly. We need to find horses for the rest of our journey. We can't continue with the carriage. It's quicker and safer to use horses."

After making the rounds, my uncle bought three horses, and a couple of mules, from the stables of the caravanserai. From here on, we were to travel with two Armenian merchants from Isfahan. One had the title 'khoja', or notable, like my uncle, who was quick to explain that it was this khoja that had made it possible for him to reach the monastery so hastily to take me back to Erzerum. In fact, he had stayed at the caravanserai all the while, waiting for my uncle's return.

Khoja Shahmir was my uncle's new business partner. He was an Armenian from Isfahan and was a good few years older than my uncle. I was not sure, but I guessed he was perhaps in his early fifties. The moment he saw my uncle, he greeted him with warmth and told him he had taken care of the transportation of the goods he had bought on behalf of both of them. He said that a caravan had left the day before and it would take a good two months for it to arrive in Isfahan. He expected us to reach Isfahan before the goods arrived if we travelled on horseback. Then, turning towards me, he said softly, "I wish we could have met in better circumstances. Your uncle is very dear to me, indeed. Forgive me for not having been able to attend the funeral in Erzerum but please accept my heartfelt condolences on the passing of your dear mother."

I thanked him and thought that I would enjoy his company during the rest of our journey as I had complete trust in my uncle's judgment when it came to choosing his friends and his business associates. In spite of this, I had my doubts about Khoja Shahmir's son, Markar, who was the fourth member of our small group. And although only a couple of years older than me, he seemed indifferent and distant to me. When I first met him he greeted me politely, but all through the journey to Isfahan he kept himself to himself.

Upon leaving the caravanserai, the four of us travelled along the banks of Lake Van and so began our journey to Persia. Since I was a child, I had so longed to see a lake or a sea, and Lake Van was everything I had imagined. Its calm, clear, turquoise waters brought peace to my turbulent heart; it still hurt for having left Erzerum. The calming sight of the lake must have had its effect on my uncle, too. He turned to Khoja Shahmir and suggested we make a pilgrimage to the famous Black Church once we crossed into Persian territory.

"Khoja Shahmir, what do you say? We may never have the opportunity to travel in these parts together again," he said.

"You may be right, Khoja Krikor." Khoja Shahmir paused for a moment and said, "Another thought just came to my mind. Why don't we visit at least one Armenian church in every town we travel through in the north of Persia in addition to visiting the Black Church?"

"A brilliant idea – that would be the pilgrimage of all pilgrimages! What a blessing it would be if we could do it, and on the first voyage my nephew is making with me!" my uncle said, and looked at me with a smile.

No sooner had we left Lake Van behind us then we were ambushed by a group of horsemen who appeared as if out of nowhere.

"Kurds! Kurds!" my uncle shouted.

Their leader was a giant of a man in his twenties and wore the Kurdish-style turban and billowing pantaloons. With casual arrogance, he slowly placed the blade of his sword on his right shoulder; two sharp daggers, which hung from leather straps attached to his belt, on either side of his torso, completed his defiant pose. He asked if we were carrying any valuables. My uncle said we had nothing but food and bedding mats as we were returning home to Persia.

"I am Apo Bey, the chief of this area," the giant roared, menacingly. "You are trespassing and you must pay a tribute of two gold coins each!"

My uncle said that we didn't have that sort of money to spare. We had only enough for the long journey ahead of us, all the way to southern Persia. Then, with a firm, confident tone he said:

"We can give you one gold coin each."

Apo Bey frowned and gestured to one of his men to inspect our mules and horses to ensure that we had no valuables and to get the gold coins from my uncle. The rest of us were frozen in our saddles. With a hoarse voice, Apo Bey threatened:

"You merchants are very rich and I know you have a lot of money. Next time you come this way, I will kill you before I let you through without paying two gold coins each. Do not forget my words!"

Then he and his men were gone as quickly as they had appeared.

My uncle and our travelling companions were silent for a long time, and I'd had my first brush with death. My uncle was the first to break the silence.

"We got out of that pretty lightly," he told Khoja Shahmir. "I took this route to avoid the skirmishes between the Russians and Persians further north, in Persian Armenia. And now the Kurds are at it – a bunch of brigands calling themselves beys, lords, filling their own pockets by living off others. I am disheartened with this sad situation. I told you

our days are numbered. Trading in these circumstances is impossible.
This will be my last journey to Anatolia, I swear!   It is difficult as it is,
paying more and more taxes to the Ottoman Sultan and his acolytes because we are *dhimmi*, Christian infidels at their mercy. I am sick of having to pay protection money all my life and being considered a stranger
in my own land."

"It's not getting any easier in Persia with our taxes there either, my
friend" said Khoja Shahmir. "Markar thinks we should eventually relocate the business to France or Poland."

"I'd rather relocate further east – to Hindustan or beyond," said my
uncle and continued his monologue. "But what's really distressing me is
the condition of our Armenian countrymen. Our villagers in Anatolia
are suffocating under the yoke of the Sultan with the massive taxes im-
posed on them from Constantinople, and rumours have it that many are
being harassed by Kurdish brigands, the likes of Apo Bey. The Russian
incursions on the Armenian regions of Yerevan, Genje, and Karabagh
don't augur well either for the future. What's going to become of our
Armenian homeland?" And he answered his own question. "More foreign rule, death, or exile," he said angrily.

My uncle's words sent shivers down my spine. I would remember
them down the years, and even now, in my old age, I still do.

I didn't imagine we would reach the Black Church so quickly after having entered Persian territory. It was dedicated to Saint Thaddeus, one
of the two apostles who had brought Christianity to the Armenians, the
other being Saint Bartholomew. It was difficult to get to it though, it
being in such a desolate and arid area. It had been a church and monastery complex and that explained the reason for its isolation. I say

this because I soon realised the whole complex was in ruins, although Armenian folk still came on pilgrimage as they had done for centuries.

"What did you expect? This holy place was built in the 6th Century. No one lives around these parts anymore. The nearest Armenians live in Khoy," my uncle said.

The Black Church of Saint Thaddeus was missing its cupola, which had collapsed, but its massive walls were still standing. *Khachkars* (stone-carved crosses) were strewn all around it. Some were still standing but others were lying broken on the ground. We entered and reverently said our prayers facing a bare stone altar upon which sat a single silver cross. Our prayers, I was certain, were more fervently said since each of us was grateful to the Almighty for having spared us from harm by the Kurdish monster. When we had finished and were heading towards the horses, we came face to face with an old man. It was the caretaker.

"Greetings to the pilgrims! May the Lord bless you and may He bless you doubly. You are the first pilgrims I've seen in months and the first ones I am happy to give the good news to. The notables of our community are gathering the finances for the second renovation of this holy site. It's about time. It was first renovated in the 14th Century. I was told the work will start in the summer," he said.

"We are indeed blessed. We are pilgrims from Erzerum and Isfahan. We are heading to Khoy and will inquire there about how we can contribute to the renovation," my uncle said before we left.

It was then that my uncle and Khoja Shahmir decided to take a route that took us through all the Armenian settlements on the west side of Lake Urmia instead of taking the route further east through Tabriz. They had both been to all the six churches in that city on previous journeys, and, to complete the pilgrimage, they believed it would be more auspicious to visit churches they had never visited before.

Thus, we first visited the Church of Saint Sarkis, one of the seven Armenian churches in Khoy and were able to offer the bishop there our contribution to the renovation of the Black Church. We continued our journey further south and reached Salmas next. Many Armenians lived in this area and had built 26 churches in all. Here, we visited the Church of Saint Hagop in the locality of Aslanik. Our next stop was Urmia, where we learned there were no less than 28 Armenian churches, and it was at Saint Bedros in the locality of Chahar Gusan that our pilgrimage was completed.

"Tomorrow we'll be heading further south, to Kermanshah, and from there south again, all the way to Isfahan. Are you happy with this journey?" my uncle asked.

I told him my first experiences of Persia had been all blessings. I had prayed in old and new churches that I had not thought existed. I had met Armenians who had given us food and shelter, and with warmth and friendliness I had not expected. The lands we had travelled through so far were of amazing natural beauty, especially the abundant cypress, hornbeam, and mulberry trees, and the vast lake of Urmia. But most of all, I was just content to be his companion.

CHAPTER 4

✦

WE ARRIVED IN ISFAHAN ONE hot, sunny afternoon. The rest of the journey from Kermanshah had been striking for both the intense heat of the day as we moved to the south of Persia and my amazement at the variety of people that I observed in the different regions through which we travelled. There were Azerbaijanis, Turkic tribes, Kurds, Luris, Arabs, city dwellers, village people, and nomads. All had their own unique facial traits, type of clothing and food, and manner of behaviour.

What struck me first about Isfahan was the wealth of the city, with its ornate mosques and buildings, a palace, a fortress, several gates and bridges, and the river Zanderud dividing the city into northern and southern districts. Isfahan was also greener than I had expected it to be, with trees and flowers in every district. I was particularly attracted to the beautiful willow trees along the banks of the Zanderud. Many Christians and Jews had settled in Isfahan over the centuries. There were at least four European churches in the city, built by the Augustinians, the Capuchins, the Jesuits and the Carmelites. The Armenians, being the largest number of Christians, had erected a dozen churches and a cathedral. Some lived in the neighbourhoods of Huseyniye, Shamsabad, Abbas-abad, Gabr-abad and Tal Vazgun, but most tended to prefer New Julfa, southwest of the Zanderud.

My uncle lived in New Julfa, in the locale known as New Yerevan, situated just behind the Armenian All Saviour's Cathedral. To my great surprise, this cathedral's architecture did not resemble those of typical Armenian churches. It had rather the look of a Persian mosque, with a circular dome. Inside though, it was the most ornate church I had ever seen. Colourful tiles with Biblical themes adorned the walls. There were wonderfully sculpted silver and gold church crosses, candle holders, and chalices. There were also a myriad of exquisitely embroidered ritual curtains, chalice covers, and ecclesiastical costumes.

The Armenians in Isfahan called themselves *Jughayetsi*, those of Julfa. They had named their area of Isfahan *Nor Jugha*, or New Julfa, to evoke the memory of their original town, Julfa, in Armenia, from where they had been forcibly deported by Shah Abbas in the early years of the 17th Century. In order to create a buffer zone between the Persian Empire and that of the Ottomans, Shah Abbas had ordered all the Armenians from the region of Julfa to be removed to his capital, Isfahan. The Armenians of Julfa had been immediately and ruthlessly deported. More than half of them perished while crossing the river Araxes as they had not been given time to prepare for such a journey. Those who had survived the journey to Isfahan were reluctant newcomers, having lost their lands and wealth and left behind their ancestors' tombs with their *khachkars* (stone-carved crosses). But Shah Abbas, aware of these Julfa Armenians' reputation as excellent tradesmen, skilled craftsmen, textile manufacturers, and weavers, was farsighted enough to offer them unprecedented privileges in order to develop his own capital city.

These initially reluctant Armenian settlers also had help from the Shah in organising their community. He allowed them to re-establish their businesses, build homes and churches, and worship freely. The Julfa Armenians very quickly flourished and became prominent in the manufacture of silk textiles and carpets of rare quality, and they established the trade between the East and the West. They, thus, became instrumental in making Isfahan one of the most prosperous trading centres in the Eastern World.

By the time of my arrival in Isfahan, its glory days were long gone. This was the result of a succession of unwise shahs and the invasion by the Afghans, who had ransacked the city some fifty years earlier. Although the Armenians of Isfahan had experienced hostility from some of the shahs after Shah Abbas's death, they had persevered and still managed to trade successfully with both the East and the West.

The story goes that my uncle had met an Armenian merchant from New Julfa in Erzerum in his younger days and had once accompanied him back to New Julfa. They had become such good friends during the journey that, upon arrival in Isfahan, this merchant had offered my uncle his daughter's hand in marriage. Having accepted the new friend's offer, my uncle had decided to make this magical city his home.

Uncle Krikor's wife, Zarouhy, or Zaroug Khatoun as people called her, was some 12 years younger than my uncle. She was a lovely young lady with a plump, round, open face which expressed her affectionate and easy nature. I got on very well with her from the minute I first walked into the house. Uncle Krikor and Zaroug Khatoun had twin daughters, the nine-year-olds, Hripsime and Kayane, named after the first Armenian Christian women to be martyred in the early 4th Century.

"The Lord has not given me a son yet but has blessed me twice with twin daughters," I had heard my uncle say to people who had asked him about his children.

The birth of the twins had been very difficult and had almost cost Zaroug Khatoun her life. Since then, she had been pregnant several times but had suffered miscarriages before the completion of the third month. This I had overheard in discussions between my mother and aunts in Erzerum. At first, the twins were aloof, possibly jealous of the attention their father gave me. But after a few weeks, I began to enjoy a good rapport with them, and we soon became the best of friends. They even started calling me 'our big brother'.

My uncle's house was grand and very comfortable, to say the least. Everything was opulent compared to the modest houses in Erzerum. There were silk cushions, magnificent carpets, fancy drinking vessels, expensive European cutlery and crockery, as well as clocks and chairs. Typical of the Armenian houses in the area, the entrance of the house was purposely kept narrow to shield it from prying eyes, but, inside, it was very spacious with many rooms. There was also a large garden at the back of the house with a very large and old pomegranate tree, which I was told was grown a long time before from seeds brought back from the Old Julfa. The back of the house also had a half-covered courtyard where the twins played while Zarong Khatoun did her carpet-weaving and sipped her tea in the afternoons.

It was three weeks after my arrival when my uncle asked me what I wanted to do next with my life. I told him I wanted to go to school, like he'd promised.

"You don't forget anything I've said, do you?" he said with a smirk on his face. "Tomorrow, we'll go to Master Constant's Institute, the famous Armenian merchants' school. You will see, the school employs very good teachers who will teach you geography, book-keeping, weights and measures, trade law, and Persian and English."

"Will they also teach me the Armenian dialect you use here? It's so different from that of Erzerum. It's almost like a foreign language for me and I am still struggling to understand what the twins are saying," I said jokingly, triggering my uncle's laughter.

I very quickly became fully conversant with the Armenian dialect spoken in New Julfa and, for the next three years, I thoroughly enjoyed my studies at the Institute where all the future merchants of the city were trained. I was so completely immersed in my studies that, although I was friendly with most of the other students, I never forged such a close friendship with any of them as I had done with Little Arakel. Moreover,

I reasoned that since I corresponded with Little Arakel on a regular basis and was living with my uncle so happily, I did not feel the need to start a new friendship.

On my graduation day, the school honoured me for being the best student in English. My prize was a book in English. During those three years at the Institute, my uncle continued his travels to India, often with Khoja Shahmir, leaving me 'in charge of the household'. It was while my uncle was away that he asked me to do some of the copying of his accounts under the supervision of his book-keeper, Mr. Ashod, a soft-spoken and gentle man, with whom I got on very well.

My Armenian calligraphic skills were very much appreciated by the local Armenian community. If the Archbishop had to write a formal letter to the Catholicos or some other church dignitary in Echmiadzin, or to the Armenian Patriarch of Jerusalem, he would call upon me. It didn't take long for some of the master craftsmen in the city, making ex-quisite jewellery or metal vessels, to ask for my assistance in writing the commemorative script on an item that was commissioned for a special occasion. These craftsmen were able to transfer the script that I had written on paper onto the object they were making. Sadly, I was also asked to write the elaborate scripts for many a tombstone, an ancient Armenian practice, and to aid the few master stone carvers still thriving in the city. Out of respect for their dead, and also because of my uncle's good reputation in the city, I dared not refuse people's requests.

As much as I had enjoyed my years of study and the city of Isfahan, I had become impatient to join my uncle on his travels. Towards the end of June, a couple of weeks after my graduation, I broached the subject with my uncle.

"You will go with me next time I leave," he said. "But that will be in October, when the monsoon season is over in the Far East."

Unable to hide my excitement, I said, "I can't wait that long!"

With an over-earnest manner, my uncle began: "Look Vartan, I've been talking to Zaroug Khatoun about you, and both of us think you should get married before we leave Isfahan. She reminded me that you are 19 years old now – a man – although in my mind's eye, I will always see you as my special boy. Have you noticed anyone at church that you like?" he asked.

I was obviously aware of the young ladies at church mass, but no one in particular had caught my attention. They all seemed a lot more elegant to me in their fineries than the womenfolk in Erzerum and I was too shy to be caught staring at any of them.

"They all seem attractive here uncle, and you know there is no way of speaking to any of them when they are chaperoned by their mothers or aunts all the time. So, it's difficult to choose one," I said.

My uncle laughed.

"You're right. Well, what about Anoosh? What do you think of her?"

Anoosh, whom in my earlier pronouncement I had not considered as part of the other Armenian womenfolk because I had already been introduced to her, was the prettiest of all the girls I had seen in Isfahan. She was Zaroug Khatoun's cousin. I now quickly realised why, while my uncle had been away recently, and every time I came home from the Institute, I found Zaroug Khatoun chatting with her in the house. Zaroug Khatoun wanted me to notice her, and I *had* done. Anoosh and I had exchanged shy nods and a couple of greetings.

"Er,...I think she's very pretty," I said.

"You know she's an orphan, like you. She lost her parents when she was a very little girl. They were living in Feridoon at the time. She has lived with Zaroug Khatoun's parents since then. She's got a good dowry and will inherit land in the Feridoon area, where her older sister still lives. But that doesn't matter as much as the fact that we can vouch that she's a good girl. If she accepts to marry you, it will be a good match. Don't say anything now, Vartan, and we'll talk about this again in a couple of days. One piece of advice from me – only say yes if you feel a spark in your heart when you think of her," my uncle concluded.

I had heard that Armenian expression before. Matchmaker Anna in Erzerum used it every time there was talk of an imminent engagement. Once at my aunt's she'd said, "I never let a matchmaking arrangement go through if the young ones haven't felt that 'spark in the heart' for each other. God would punish me if I did."

That night, in bed, I thought of Anoosh – her pretty face, her elf-like body, her delicate features and her inviting manner – and the little spark in my heart grew stronger.

CHAPTER 5

✦

Two weeks later, Anoosh and I were engaged with the blessing of Father Abraham, who also married us a month later. My uncle organised one of the biggest feasts New Julfa had seen in a long time. All the Armenian folk were invited and Anoosh's sister and relatives from Feridoon came for the week of celebrations.

On the night of their arrival, there was a huge banquet laid out by Zaroug Khatoun and my uncle in honour of Anoosh's relatives. On the second day, as is the tradition, we were invited to view Anoosh's dowry at Zaroug Khatoun's parents' house, where Anoosh lived. On display were all her fineries and all the exquisite embroideries she'd made. There were also a couple of handsome carpets and four smaller rugs that she'd woven under the supervision of Zaroug Khatoun, who was an accomplished weaver. We were then invited by Anoosh's relatives to an evening banquet. Weddings were the rare times when the Armenian men and women got together in Isfahan as, traditionally, they led a segregated existence much influenced by the Muslim tradition which engulfed them. Wine flowed freely at wedding celebrations though, and, as the night progressed, I felt I had had too much to drink and could not take my eyes off Anoosh until my uncle nudged me to say it was time to go.

The third night of celebrations was the traditional *henna* night – the eve of the wedding – when the two families exchanged gifts. We started with a feast at my uncle's house in honour of all our friends, and a couple of hours later, I received my groom's gifts from Anoosh's family. There was a silk brocaded coat together with an intricately worked silver belt. Soon afterwards, our party began their walk towards Anoosh's residence, laden with the gifts for the bride. There were silk cloths and jewellery. Zaroug Khatoun and my uncle had bought Anoosh a full set of head jewellery, two matching necklaces, and a ring. My gifts to Anoosh included an emerald stone of the purest quality that I had chosen myself on a visit to one of the city's best dealers in precious stones. I had it set in a gold ring and had both our names engraved on the inside in Armenian. I knew Anoosh liked it the minute I presented it to her. When she put it on, she tilted her head shyly and thanked me. And I thought she looked ravishingly beautiful, but I was too embarrassed to say this to her in front of all present. *Henna* bowls were passed around and each of the guests smudged their little finger with the paste. The *henna* colouring lingered on little fingers for quite a few weeks afterwards, a remembrance of the occasion. And after much singing and eating, we retired to prepare for the next day.

On my wedding day, everything was in order. The men folk came around to 'dress the groom'. They would circle each item of clothing around my head three times before I could get hold of it. In the meantime, they would slap my shoulders or arms jokingly to mark the end of my bachelorhood and also to wish me good luck. Eventually, I was dressed in my silk pantaloons, shirt, and the coat and belt that Anoosh's family had gifted.

My uncle had hired local Armenian musicians – players of dhol (large drum), duduk and shvi (wind instruments). They started playing with such enthusiasm that the whole neighbourhood was soon out on the streets. The musicians led our wedding party all the way to Anoosh's residence. We were going to 'fetch the bride'. When we got there, the bride's carriage was waiting. The music intensified and so did the chant-ing, claiming the bride.

Anoosh appeared wearing a beautiful red velvet coat embroidered with gold thread flowers over a white silk dress and pantaloons. Her head and face were veiled in the finest white lace, flanked by head jewel-lery on either side of her face. Upon seeing her, the whole party cheered. After she had seated herself gracefully in the carriage, it moved away; the crowd, led by myself, marched behind it.

At the church door, I held Anoosh's hand for the first time and led her towards the altar. The sound of the wedding *sharagan* (hymn) and the smell of incense overwhelmed my already intensified senses. I want-ed to weep as I envisioned my mother's and father's faces, wishing they were there. All I remember after that is my head and hers were joined at the forehead and prayers were said to complete the sacred union.

For three more days after the wedding, neighbourhood banquets were laid out by my uncle and reciprocal ones by Anoosh's family. Apart from me poking my head and arm out of our room to receive the of-fered food, which we barely touched, we were left undisturbed in our little cocoon. There were many times I cupped Anoosh's elf-like small face in the palms of my hands and felt an immense joy.

Barely two months after our marriage, Anoosh announced that she was with child. I was overjoyed and felt proud for us both. My uncle had talked to me about building my own living quarters on the plot just behind his house, which he had bought he said from an Armenian mer-chant who had moved permanently to Calcutta. As soon as he heard our good news, he wanted to begin the building work immediately.

"Go tomorrow and see Markar, Khoja Shahmir's son, and tell him he is to supervise the work himself. You and I will be leaving for India in less than a month's time," he said.

Markar, the son of my uncle's partner, and with whom I had first journeyed from Erzerum, ran the offices of both my uncle and his father. He did most of the legal paperwork involved in the business. I did not enjoy his company whenever I went in to offer my copying services to Mr. Ashod, the book-keeper. Markar had a very cynical streak in him which, together with his obnoxious personality, did not make him naturally appealing to people. The morning I went to see him, he was not pleased with the task my uncle had given him and said with venom in his voice:

"I think your house might just be ready by the time you return because you will be gone for a long, long time," and surreptitiously added, "They married you off you know so you won't succumb to all the low-life temptresses you will encounter in those foreign lands."

He then left the room not waiting to hear my angry response.

I did not report this conversation to my uncle that evening, but he had sensed my unease in dealing with Markar.

"Don't worry about him. The young man has a habit of suffering from bouts of jealousy but he always does what he's told, and, more importantly, his father is one of the most trustworthy men in our community and, thus, the best partner I can have."

A fortnight later, I was ready to depart with my uncle on my first journey to the East. Armenian merchants were reputed for their self-sufficiency while travelling. To this end, every small detail was carefully planned, especially when dealing with provisions for the journey. There were light meals of cooked fine cracked wheat held together with chilli paste as well as lentil patties. These would suffice us for the journey from Isfahan to the port of Bandar Abbas, the main departure point to the East. For the sea journey, there was cured meat wrapped in a thick casing of ground chilli paste and spicy dry sausage; these could last up to a year if kept hung in a dry place. There was dried strained yogurt which could be used to make a hearty soup if mixed with water. There were walnuts and chick peas, dried apricots and figs, raisins, grape and date molasses, and flour and sweetmeats. Most importantly, there was the thin Armenian *lavash* bread, dried to last for a couple of months. A limited amount of wine was also carried from Isfahan, but drinking water for the journey was obtained from wells nearer the port.

The Armenian merchants of Isfahan never undertook long journeys alone. They always arranged to travel in groups, which resulted in a substantial reduction in travel expenses and protection for both goods and people. Thus, a small group of merchants would synchronise their departure and charter a ship to carry them to India. Some were even the owners of the ships. My uncle and I were to begin our journey with six others; one of them was my uncle's partner, Khoja Shahmir. The other four were all related to the sixth person in the group, Melkon Khan, an energetic man in his forties who had inherited the ship, the *Anahid*, from his father.

I wrote about all this, expressing my excitement about my maiden sea voyage, in a long letter to Little Arakel. I also told him about my marriage to Anoosh and asked him to convey my regards and my news to Father Sahag next time he was in Erzerum. In the last letter I had received from him a few months earlier, he had said that he was contemplating staying on at the monastery and becoming a novice as his studies were coming to an end. I was eager to find out what he had decided and in my heart wished he would not choose priesthood so he could join me in Isfahan.

✥

When the day of my departure came, it was difficult to say my goodbyes to Anoosh, all the more so because she was carrying our child. Hiding my anguish and pain on seeing her tears, I assured her I would be back in a few months' time, planting a kiss on her sweet lips before leaving our bedroom to meet my uncle in the forecourt of the house.

The journey to Bandar Abbas was relatively shorter than I had imagined, but the hot, sandy winds of the southern deserts were unlike anything I had experienced and made the journey almost unbearable at times. When we got to the port, the *Anahid* was waiting. She had massive sails and looked very sturdy. I had never seen a ship before, although I had seen several etchings of ships at the Institute library. The *Anahid* was a brig of two high masts. Years ago, she had belonged to the East India Company and had cannon placements. When she got too old, she was sold to Melkon Khan's father. He modified her and turned her into a merchant vessel, giving her a new life.

On board ship, I was a complete novice. Everything had to be explained to me. I was the only one in the party on his maiden voyage. I soon got to know the crew well which was made up mainly of Indians from South India. Some were even Christians and had crucifixes tattooed on their thumbs. It took me some time to get used to their naked torsos and their *lungi*, a checkered loin cloth wrapped around the waist, but I quickly began to admire their confident gestures and nimble bodies. There was also a Persian cook and three hired helps to do the cleaning and hauling. The Persian was skilled in catering for the variety of culinary tastes and requirements on board; the Hindus, however, insisted on catering for themselves. The navigator was a gregarious Greek old-timer who came from Izmir and sang beautifully sad songs in his native tongue.

It wasn't long before land disappeared and we were alone on the open sea. Bittersweet thoughts engulfed me as I looked at the horizon at dusk. I thought of Anoosh and the baby she was carrying and dearly hoped I would be reunited with them before too long. At the same time, I felt a sense of well-being and was in awe of the beauty of the vast sea.

There was a tap on my shoulder.

"You have your sea legs – you can hold down your food! You're bound to make journeys like this one many times," said my uncle. "Just remember to stay out of the sun. Oh, and one more thing – you must learn how to swim well. The sea is deceptive. Today, it's as calm as a sleeping beauty, but it can get as vicious as an evil witch," he remarked and sensing my apprehension, he added, "The crewmen will teach you how to swim like a fish!"

I had indeed managed to swim and keep myself afloat in Bandar Abbas. At the beginning of the journey, when the sea was still and very calm, the crewmen would jump from high up into the water and encourage me to join them. I enjoyed this so much that soon they jokingly gave me the nickname 'the smooth fish' which pleased me no end. Later, when the sea became a vast ocean, it did not disappoint and led us quietly, like a protective mother, to the port of Bombay.

CHAPTER 6

⚜

BOMBAY PORT WAS A SIGHT to behold. Tens of ships, perhaps a hundred, were anchored there. It was teeming with thousands of men loading and unloading goods. As I walked on the pier, I saw porters, sailors, Indians, Europeans, and a great number of British officers, and sepoys, those local Indian soldiers in the service of the British Crown and the East India Company. On the way to the inn where we were to stay, I felt oppressed by the crowds on the streets of this sprawling city. There were street vendors, women in their traditional colourful costumes, children, animals, and paupers, the appearance of whom shocked me; some were lepers with missing limbs and noses and others had heart-breaking deformities.

"You'll get used to the crowds and the smells. These are peace-loving people on the whole with a peaceful religion," my uncle remarked.

He was right. It did not take me long to like being in Bombay. I soon found it exotic, full of life, and endlessly fascinating; but most of all, I loved the excitement of meeting all kinds of people from the four corners of the world.

Every day, I accompanied my uncle on all his business dealings and met other Armenians, as well as Persians, Jews, Englishmen, Italians, and Parsis; these last were Persian Zoroastrians who had fled Persia a

long time ago and had settled in Bombay. I put my negotiating skills
to work fairly quickly as my uncle encouraged me to clinch deals. This
surprised me at first because of the risks he was taking, but, eventually, it
gave me the self-confidence I lacked to do things on my own. The event
that was instrumental in bringing this about was my uncle introducing
me to Khoja Manas, a descendant of Khoja Owenjohn Jacob Gerakian,
the Armenian notable who had originally established the present
Armenian community of Bombay in Surat. His descendants, and other
Surat Armenians, had later relocated to Bombay when the city gained
importance as the main trading hub of western India.

Khoja Manas, a very good friend of my uncle's and a close business
associate, took me under his wing. He introduced me to the world of
merchants who traded from India. In Bombay, my uncle operated from
Khoja Manas' premises. This gave me the advantage of learning the
day-to-day executing of business transactions and let me feel more comfortable and emboldened in carrying on in my uncle's footsteps. A few
months had passed after our arrival in Bombay when, even to my uncle's
and Khoja Manas' surprise, I negotiated a particularly complicated deal
with three English merchants from whom I bought a substantial amount
of Ceylon cinnamon and cardamom from south India using the English
I had learned at the Institute in Isfahan. Both my uncle and Khoja
Manas were impressed and congratulated me on my first important
business deal and, thus, I was welcomed into their fold.

A couple of days later, two of Khoja Manas' young sons and his book-
keeper invited me to a celebratory outing. It was an enjoyable night out
in town with a lot of eating and drinking at one of the inns frequented
by merchants. We had copious amounts of delicious, spicy food cooked
in coconut milk and washed it all down with an alcoholic beverage from
the Portuguese colony of Goa. I can't remember how I got to the Parsi
inn, where I was staying with my uncle. All I remember is that it must
have been in the early hours of the morning and my uncle was already

up. I cannot forget the disapproving look on his face, and next thing I knew the world was spinning and I was violently sick. In the following hours I developed a fever and it worsened as the evening drew in. My uncle was beside himself. He immediately got the English doctor that Khoja Manas consulted to come and examine me.

"He's got the dreaded Bombay fever," was the doctor's diagnosis. "Monitor him carefully and give him this medicine every 5 hours. He's a young man. Let's hope he gets over it," he told my uncle.

My complete recovery took well over three weeks and my uncle was there looking after me, day after day, as my mother would have done had she been alive. I felt terribly guilty for my carelessness that night which I was sure had brought on the illness. I felt even guiltier for having disrupted my uncle's schedule. His plan had been to first sail to Calcutta from Bombay and then to Madras and further east from there. I was to go with him, but now, the ship that was to take us had already sailed.

A few days later, my uncle found a sloop sailing to Madras and then onto Calcutta the following week.

"It won't be as comfortable as the ship Khoja Shahmir had booked for us though. I intend to join him in Calcutta as soon as possible to help him with the shipment of our goods to Europe on a British ship. But I'm afraid if I do that I might not be able to make it in time to join Melkon Khan on the *Anahid* that will set sail for Penang, the Prince of Wales Island, from Madras very soon," my uncle said in a sad tone.

"There is another way out of this, Uncle Krikor," I said. "I spoke to Khoja Manas this morning and he told me about a ship sailing to Calcutta tomorrow but it will not be docking at Madras – she will be stopping elsewhere, can't remember the name. Anyway, will you agree to take it and I shall sail on the sloop to Madras next week and try to delay Melkon Khan's departure until your arrival? Please, let me do it. I would like to make up for my un-gentlemanly behaviour and I promise I will never ever get drunk again," I said.

"I can see you have realised that you can't hold down your alcohol," my uncle said with a smirk on his face.

By suppertime, my uncle was persuaded to let me go to Madras on my own. I was entrusted with two missions: one was to delay Melkon Khan's trip to Penang until my uncle's arrival and the other was to contact a business associate of his, an English merchant by the name of John Atkinson.

A week after my uncle's departure, I, too, set sail on the sloop to Madras. We sailed south to the Malabar Coast stopping once at the port of Cochin. And then, when we had reached the most southern tip of India, we swung back north, along the Coromandel Coast, to Madras. The beauty of the sea and lush green coastal areas compensated for the loneliness I felt – none of the people I had met in Bombay were on board this ship and I was glad when we finally reached Madras. As soon as I disembarked, I went in search of Melkon Khan and his *Anahid*. I felt relieved to see her docked at the far end of the port and my fears dissipated when Melkon Khan told me he would not set sail for Penang before my uncle's arrival from Calcutta.

John Atkinson, Esquire, had been a high ranking employee of the East India Company at its Madras settlement for years until the Company lost its monopoly of the Indian trade in 1813. A few years later, he had established his own private trading company and had prospered in Madras with a reputation as an experienced trader in almost every kind of commodity, and in precious stones in particular. When I visited his offices, he welcomed me with extreme politeness. He was tall, quite heavy, with a thick neck and a double chin. He had ginger hair and beard and large freckles all over his thick fingers. What struck me most were his quick wit and his conversation, which was devoid of the usual over-formalities. In no time at all we came to an agreement on the lot of precious stones that my uncle had asked me to purchase.

The deal done, he invited me for tea. A little while later, there was a knock on the door and in came a tall, blond, elegantly dressed young man.

"This is my son, Lesley," John Atkinson said. "And this is Vartan, Khoja Gregory's nephew – you remember." Turning towards me he said, "Your uncle has mentioned you to Lesley many a time. I understand you are of the same age. Lesley has recently joined me in the business and I'm sure he would like to hear about your life in Isfahan." And excusing himself, he left the room.

Lesley Atkinson and I got along extremely well – from the first conversation we had. Initially, a mutual sympathy and easy communication ignited the friendship. Not long afterwards, we discovered we shared a love of travel stories and English poetry. Lesley immediately helped me find lodgings in town and introduced me to the other traders, including the Armenian ones. He even took me to the Armenian Church on Armenian Street to attend mass on Sunday morning. Lesley also told me that, some time ago, as in other settlements of the East India Company the Armenians had been given the right to build their church in Madras because their numbers had exceeded 40. I found out later that evening that the church had been erected in 1772 and was dedicated to the Holy Virgin Mary.

Whenever we met European traders, Lesley would introduce me as "My dear friend, Vartan, an Armenian trader from Isfahan." When he introduced me to Armenians, he would praise my knowledge of the Armenian language and my calligraphic skills; Lesley was fascinated by the shape of the Armenian letters and would often ask me to write words he uttered in English in Armenian script so he could see what shape they took. This, together with the interest that a newcomer generated in the Armenian community, encouraged requests for writing the calligraphic epitaph on a tombstone and a wedding invitation on several occasions within the first two weeks of my arrival in Madras.

Lesley and I became such good friends that we ended up eating together and spending most of our days in each other's company.

"The only difference between you and me is that you're a married man and I'm still a sought-after bachelor," Lesley joked.

And I replied, "There's another difference. Don't forget my oriental attire – my pantaloons, my headdress, my large tunic, and my pointed shoes."

Some weeks after my meeting the Atkinsons, Uncle Krikor finally arrived from Calcutta. He was pleased with the deal I had made with Lesley's father and immensely happy that Lesley and I had become friends. To show his gratitude to John Atkinson for treating me so well, he invited Lesley to join us on our trip on the *Anahid*.

"I understand you will venture into Dutch territory," John Atkinson said.

"Yes, but don't worry about Lesley – I'll look after him. No Dutchman is going to find out he's an Englishman," said my uncle half-jokingly, conscious of the sometimes fierce rivalry between the two nations for the spice trade.

"The young man has to have the experience of those faraway islands," said John Atkinson.

A few days later, we were ready to embark on Melkon Khan's *Anahid*. Both Lesley and I were excited about the journey ahead of us, and Lesley had already adopted our style of oriental clothing even though he didn't need to wear them until we were in Dutch controlled waters.

"I like these," he said pointing to his pantaloons, "they're so comfortable compared to my usual trousers."

We first docked at the Prince of Wales Island, or Penang, where for the first time I met Chinese people. I was instantly impressed by their instinct for trade. The Armenian merchants living there also impressed me with their unrivalled confidence in trading. What surprised me about these Armenians was the fact that they even had their wives and children with them. Although this was nothing out of the ordinary in India, somehow I didn't expect to find Armenian families so far east. I thought, if I was successful in trading, Anoosh would perhaps one day venture to accompany me to these faraway places.

The *Anahid* took us next to Surabaya in Java and then all the way to the islands of the Maluka, the famed Spice Islands. The Dutch gave us very little trouble as both Melkon Khan and my uncle had friendly relations with a prominent Dutch official named Johannes Van der Hoeven. Both Lesley and I marvelled at the beauty of the islands and the friendliness of their men folk and the wild beauty of some of their women.

"Ah, it's like Kubla Khan!" Lesley kept on repeating.

He loved to recite the poems of Blake and those of the poets Shelley and Keats. And on a quiet night on deck when the stars felt so close, I heard him whisper:

"Tygre Tygre, burning bright / In the forest of the night..."

The poem reminded me so much of the ancient Armenian epic poem and the description of the birth of Vahakn, the legendary Armenian god of thunder and lightning that I too recited:

"Erkner erkin, erkner erkir / Erkner ev dzoven dzirani..." and then made a great effort to translate it for him.

The sky was in labour, the earth was in labour,
The purple sea also was in labour.
In the sea was a red reed, also in labour.
Out of the stalk of the reed, smoke emerged.
Out of the stalk of the reed, flame emerged,
And running out of the flame was a fair/flaxen lad.
He had hair of fire.
He had a beard of flame
And his eyes were suns.

Months passed before we got back to Madras. We had left that port laden with Coromandel cotton textiles and silk and now returned laden with spices of all kinds.

"So, are you ready to go back to Anoosh?" asked my uncle one morning when I had just awoken.

"Yes, I am. I long to see my child – we left over eight months ago," I told him.

"Well, very early this morning, when you were still asleep, a kinsman of Khoja Shahmir, who has just arrived from Isfahan, gave me the good news. Congratulations, Vartan! You are now the father of a girl and Anoosh is doing well and in good health!" he shouted with joy and hugged and kissed me on both cheeks.

I was overjoyed and could not wait to go home. We sailed back to Persia on the *Anahid* a couple of days later.

During my last meeting with Lesley he said, "I shall miss you my friend. Come back soon!"

"I will," I said and gave him a book of Shakespeare's sonnets which I'd had the fortune of finding that very same morning and which I knew he did not possess.

The sight of my child – a sweet and fragile little being – filled me with immense happiness and my love for both her and Anoosh blossomed.

"What's her name?" I asked Anoosh.

Surprised at my question, she said, "When you were away, people told me you would probably want to name her after your late mother, as it is the custom."

Wrapping my arms around her I said, "What would you like to call her? After all, she is your daughter, too."

"I'd like to name her after the Mother of God, Mariam, so she would protect her," Anoosh said.

"So be it," I said and pressed my lips to her smooth forehead.

CHAPTER 7

⚜

MARIAM'S CHUBBY CHEEKS AND HUGE, round eyes, reminded me of my happiness every day I was in Isfahan. Everybody said she had my eyes and light brown hair. Deep in my heart I wished my dear mother and father could have seen her. I still often missed them and was sorry they were not alive to be part of my new life.

Anoosh told me countless times how Zaroug Khatoun had helped her immensely with the coming of the baby and also with everything else in the household.

"I don't know what I would have done without her. Not even once did I feel the urge of wishing my mother was alive to help me with my newborn," she'd said on one occasion.

As a token of our appreciation, Anoosh and I thus gifted Zaroug Khatoun one of the three Burmese rubies of rare quality that I had purchased from Lesley's father.

Zaroug Khatoun was delighted with her gift. The twins, giggling like teenagers often do, were so excited at seeing a stone of such a distinct purple-red colour that they began hovering around their mother and were now jumping up and down for her to permit them to hold it in their own hands.

Seeing their delight, I said, "Young ladies, I have two more of this type of stone. They are slightly smaller in size than this one. They are yours but you'll have them when you're a bit older." As I said this, I was watching Anoosh for her response. She nodded discreetly but approvingly.

The jolly atmosphere that engulfed everyone in the room soon turned sour when my uncle asked me if I had checked on the building of my house that Markar was supposed to supervise whilst we were away. I told him it was only a quarter finished. I also told him that I had bumped into the builder by chance that very same morning.

"Well, what did he say?" my uncle demanded.

I told him the builder had said that Markar had stopped paying both his and the workers' wages over a month ago for no valid reason; the builder had assumed we didn't want them to continue the work. I didn't tell my uncle that I'd been very angry at the news and had thought of confronting Markar immediately. But that first reaction had led to another a few minutes later, a thought that had stopped me in my tracks: It had been my uncle's wish for Markar to work on my house, not mine, and I did indeed value both my uncle's judgment and that of his business partner, Khoja Shahmir's; it would have been unwise of me to jeopardize their relationship over Markar's behaviour. So I had turned around and gone back to my uncle's house where the sight of Anoosh, holding Mariam in her arms, had calmed me down.

My uncle was furious. It was the first time ever that I'd heard him utter a curse. He grabbed his coat, ordering me to get hold of the builder to restart the work, and then said, "I'm going to see Khoja Shahmir about his good-for-nothing son." With that, he was away.

I found out afterwards from Mr. Ashod, my uncle's book-keeper, what had transpired. My uncle had gone to our business premises, walked straight into Khoja Shahmir's office and told him exactly what Markar had done. Mr. Ashod heard my uncle say, "I don't know what Markar is up to, but he's not up to anything good." Khoja Shahmir, whom everyone had known for a long time was deeply hurt and disappointed with his son's general conduct, had never criticized his son publicly. So what followed next was beyond anything I could ever have imagined. Khoja Shahmir got up, went to the door of his office, and bellowed Markar's name. By the time Markar came out of his office at the back of the premises, Khoja Shahmir was standing in the middle of the lobby, fuming with anger. He gave his son a humiliating dressing down, not only in front of my uncle but also in the presence of Mr. Ashod, Yohannes the office assistant, and two local Armenian merchants who had just arrived in the waiting area for a meeting. Raising his finger at his son, and with a stern face, Khoja Shahmir accused Markar of having neglected his responsibilities towards his friend and partner. He then insisted on an apology from Markar. Markar hesitated; Khoja Shahmir repeated his demand. Markar finally murmured an apology to my uncle and left the room, his face flushed with resentment.

In no time, every single Armenian merchant in the city had heard about the incident, thanks to the two Armenian merchants who had witnessed it, and Markar's humiliation went far beyond the four walls of our business premises. Mr. Ashod said he heard people saying they felt sorry for Khoja Shahmir, whose only son, with all the wealth his father could offer him, had turned out to be such a useless member of the community. His frequent visits to the local brothels did not help his reputation either and fuelled the Armenian gossip-mongers of New Julfa.

I found myself secretly relieved that Markar had not completed the work on my house. I had never liked him and felt my new house would be haunted by the spirit of his resentment. So, I gladly took over the supervision, paid the builder and his workers higher wages to encourage them to work faster, and in very little time the house was completed.

When the day arrived, even the twins were offering to help Anoosh move her personal belongings into the new house.

Our house was of modest size – one big sleeping room, another small room and a large sitting area. Since it was built on an area of land just behind my uncle's house, I had the reed fences, which had been originally placed there for privacy, pulled down and connected the two half-covered yards, mine and my uncle's. This way, the twins, who were now 14 years old, could practise their recently discovered interest in embroidery, while Anoosh and Zaroug Khatoun carried on working together at their weavings. The space would be ideal, too, for Mariam, along with our future children, to play under the watchful eye of their mother.

Waking up in my new home the next day, I lay there a while in contentment. At last, we had our own home – Mariam, Anoosh, and I. I savoured the moment, knowing the time was fast approaching for my second voyage to the Far East.

Anoosh and Zaroug Khatoun had decided that the cooking would be shared between them and that, as ever, we would all eat together. My uncle said he was very pleased with the quality of the building work of my new house and offered to pay for the furniture I had bought. To mark this happy occasion, Zaroug Khatoun prepared a feast of barbecued skewered meat, marinated in thick, sour pomegranate juice. The fragrant rice was covered with jewels of nuts, dried apricots and plums, and raisins. The guest of honour was Khoja Shahmir, who turned up with a handsome Chinese porcelain urn. He offered the gift to Anoosh, delighting her with this addition to the new house.

I quickly sensed that Khoja Shahmir was trying to apologise for his son's behaviour. I had long guessed that he was a lonely man; he had lost his wife over a decade ago and his relationship with his son Markar was far from affectionate. I cast my mind back to when I first met both at the caravanserai near Lake Van, and then my trip with them to Isfahan. During that long journey, I could not remember one single instance when they exchanged pleasant words. Their conversation was restricted to practical matters of food, horses, and the like. If my uncle had not mentioned their relationship as father and son, I would have assumed they were but companions, and that, out of necessity.

Preparations were underway for my second trip to India and the Far East when I received a letter from my dear Little Arakel. I had not heard from him since my marriage to Anoosh. As always, his letter began in a jolly tone with all the good news about my aunts, their children, and other folk in Erzerum. He assured me once again that whenever he stayed in the house in Erzerum he would do all that was required for its upkeep; he had even asked one of the neighbours to keep an eye on it when he was away at the monastery. Father Sahag, who sent his greetings, was getting on in years, but was still running the school. Whenever Little Arakel was in Erzerum, especially in the summer, he took over the running of the Sunday school to relieve Father Sahag of some of his responsibilities. Little Arakel conveyed his best wishes on my betrothal and said the day he heard of my wedding he visited my parents' tombs and prayed that they would bless the happy event. I shed a few tears upon reading this and thought of Little Arakel as my true little brother – honouring my parents in my place as I would have done had I stayed in Erzerum.

Little Arakel proceeded to tell me that he had finally taken the decision to seek ordination. I knew right away that this was the reason why he had delayed his correspondence. He said he had been a novice at the monastery for some time. He was hoping to be ordained a *vartabed* and become a learned priest of the Armenian Apostolic Church in three years' time, after finishing his higher studies. Following our church custom of taking a new name upon ordination, Little Arakel was to be known as Nareg, after one of our renowned priests of the Middle Ages who was also a mystic poet and whose prayer-poems, I can still recite from memory.

Sensing that I might be disappointed that he had chosen a different life to mine and would never join me in Isfahan in the future, he wrote the following:

My dearest brother Vartan, do not be sad. This is our Lord's path for me. It is my calling and the ultimate way of serving the suffering Armenian people. We have been under the yoke of foreign rulers for hundreds of years and things are worsening. More and more, our people are crushed by heavy taxes and injustice, and there is no hope in sight of liberty. Have you not yet heard of the insurrection of the Greeks against their Ottoman rulers? It is happening as I am writing to you. Our people yearn for that same independence from the Ottomans as the Greeks – something that has been denied us for too long. How much more deprivation, exile, and humiliation must we endure? My dear brother, I am ready to help, advise, and guide our people in these troubled times, and the only way I can see to do it is through the priesthood.

Little Arakel's words both troubled and saddened me. Deep down, I had somehow known that he would never come and live with me in Isfahan. Perhaps that is why I'd left him with the care of my father's house in Erzerum in the first place. I also instinctively felt that, with his sharp mind and quiet and collected temperament, he was perfectly suited for the priesthood. And despite being called 'Little Arakel' by everyone at the monastery, he exuded such confidence that even the older students sought advice from him with their worries and problems. It was his confidence in my future, his encouragement and reassurance that had made it easier for me to leave Erzerum when I did. At that time, I cannot deny that I had felt guilty for leaving my people behind in Erzerum, though I'd had no choice but to follow my uncle.

I envied Little Arakel for being there. I could go back to Erzerum with Anoosh and Mariam, I initially thought. But how could I disappoint my uncle? Hadn't he taken care of all my needs? Hadn't he filled the void left by the absence of my father and mother? Hadn't it been my idea to join him in the first place? And could I abandon Anoosh's people, and the Armenian folk in Isfahan? The people who had adopted me – weren't they my people, too? I took pride in being part of the Armenians of Isfahan. Hadn't they been forcibly exiled from their homeland? And yet, they had survived, generation after generation, and prospered and excelled in what they undertook.

Little Arakel was right. Every one of us had to play his own part in ensuring the survival of our people, as our ancestors had done for centuries – and against all odds. I intended to do the same in my own way.

"Khoja Shahmir will not be travelling with us this time," my uncle said in a matter-of-fact tone. "His health is not as it was. He's not robust enough for this trip. But not to worry," he added, as if to reassure himself. "He'll be in charge of the business here instead of that good-for-nothing Markar of his."

Mr. Ashod, the book-keeper, gave me the details of Khoja Shahmir's condition. His health had been poor the past few weeks; high blood pressure, the physician called it. Khoja Shahmir had always had high blood pressure, Mr. Ashod said, but the condition had been aggravated by yet another argument he'd had with his son. After the humiliation inflicted on him by his father, Markar had learned that he was the latest item of gossip in town and the laughing stock of many. The argument had taken place in Khoja Shahmir's office. Markar told his father that he was so humiliated that he could not show his face to anyone in Isfahan. He wanted to leave for Russia, he said. Khoja Shahmir pleaded with him not to go – after all, he was going to lose his only son. Markar banged his fist on his father's desk and shouted at the top of his voice "I'm leaving, whether you like it or not."

"I don't know if he can leave without the consent of his father," said Mr. Ashod. "He doesn't have a single penny to his name."

That evening when I returned home for our family supper, and as soon as I had greeted my uncle, he knew I had heard about the latest row between Markar and Khoja Shahmir.

"Such a shame – his only son – something is broken in that man and it will never mend. I just wish him well and hope he will regain his health," my uncle said with sadness clouding his face.

I nodded, but to change the subject, led him to focus on discussing the details of our next trip.

CHAPTER 8

♣

SINCE RETURNING TO ISFAHAN, I had accomplished several things – finished the building of my house, copied a vast number of documents for Mr. Ashod, and arranged the shipment of all the goods destined for Constantinople, some via Erzerum. This had meant spending many months in Isfahan; and yet I felt there hadn't been enough time with Anoosh and Mariam, who was growing up with noticeable changes every day. Time disappears ever so quickly in the company of loved ones. It felt as if I had arrived only yesterday, and tomorrow I would be leaving them. A dread gripped my heart for days from the time my uncle advised me that we would be away for at least a year. Several trips to the Far East were planned, and one especially to the Maluka Islands for spices. Weren't the Armenian merchants most prominent in the spice trade? We needed to be unrelenting in order to obtain the best results, my uncle said.

I knew him to be right, but I kept on asking myself, "How many more times will I have to leave Anoosh and Mariam behind?" Then a thought that I'd had on my first journey resurfaced – the idea of taking Anoosh and Mariam with me. I could be based in Madras with my wife and child, where my dear friend Lesley was, and still be useful to my uncle. I could still go on journeys to the Maluka Islands or wherever else. It would be easier and quicker to be reunited with my family in Madras than journeying all the way back to Isfahan. After all, I'd seen so many

Armenian families in Madras, and further east, in Penang, on my first journey. I had just finished building my house in Isfahan, but, surely, that could be sold. But here things tangled up in my mind – what about my uncle, Zaroug Khatoun and the twins? And would Anoosh accept leaving Isfahan? I needed to untangle all these knots in my head but to do that I had to talk to my uncle. He had indeed mentioned several times that, if he had to, he had no aversion to settling in India or further east where there were Armenian communities. But this was not the right moment to approach my uncle – not with Khoja Shahmir's condition, and only a few days before our departure. I decided to leave broaching the subject until arrival in Madras; at an opportune moment, I would have to have a sincere talk with him.

We set sail on the majestic *Anahid* once again, on a bright morning and in high spirits. The Armenian merchants who had sailed with me on my maiden voyage were our companions again, and, although Khoja Shahmir's health had improved slightly, my uncle had resigned himself to the idea that his partner was not going to join him this time.

We arrived in Madras on a hot, humid morning after several stops: Bombay, Portuguese Goa, and Cochin. During all three stops, we had to either procure goods for our journeys further east or order goods for our journey back to Isfahan.

In Goa, what interested me most was the locals' devotion to their venerated saint, Saint Xavier; I hadn't realised Catholic fervour could be found in a place so far away from Rome. In Cochin, I was fascinated by the sight of the Chinese fishing nets the locals used. These were large, shore-operated, fixed nets some ten feet high. Each of them was operated by six men who balanced the net to lower it into the sea or to hoist it. I also witnessed a local religious ceremony of Hindus, which was a revelation to me. The ceremony was a mixture of dance, masks, music, and colours. At first, it seemed so alien, but upon further observation I became aware of its uniqueness and how vital it was for the locals to enable them to express their beliefs.

I'd mulled over this during the rest of the journey. Thus, the minute I set foot in Madras, I headed for the Armenian Church of the Virgin Mary to say my prayers, engulfed by the smell of burning incense. That scent, and the ancient Armenian *sharagan* the priest was singing softly, created the mystical atmosphere so typical of my church and gave me the comfort I was looking for.

Blinded by the sunlight as I came out of the dark church, I was startled by someone grabbing my arm. It was Lesley.

We embraced. "Welcome back, my dear friend!"

"You found me too quickly, you rascal," I said jokingly.

Lesley wanted all my news of Isfahan and I happily obliged by telling him about my new house and Mariam's cute little gestures.

"So, tell me, what have you been up to all this time?" I asked him.

Lesley began by telling me about his first venture to Burma. I knew the best rubies and other precious stones came from there, but didn't know much else. Lesley was so excited about his trip that he could speak of nothing else all that afternoon and evening, non-stop – how wonderful a place it was, how lovely the rivers, how rich in precious stones, how good for trading, and how opulent the court of the king.

"Unluckily for me, they don't like the British very much and I'm afraid your Armenian compatriots there don't like them much either;

there's intense rivalry in trade between them since your compatriots have special privileges at the king's court," he said.

This indeed intrigued me and I thought I must find out more about those Armenians in Burma; I could ask my uncle or his friends. But the thought went right out of my mind as soon as Lesley and I sat down for dinner.

A couple of weeks later, we were ready to embark on our long journey, which was to take us well over a year to complete. Having to spend long months at sea didn't dampen my spirits; I could look forward to the pleasure of Lesley's company. We set sail on the *Anahid* and took a south-easterly direction from Madras. The journey itself was to be broken into several stages, stopping at various ports along the way as was required by the commercial needs of our fellow traders on board.

Our first voyage took us to the island of Sumatra, stopping only at Penang on the way. We headed for Bencoolen in South Sumatra, mainly to deliver supplies ordered by local merchants. Only one of our Armenian companions had been there before and he'd said it was an insignificant little place with only a single fort. Before we departed Madras, Lesley had explained to everyone that the local British governor, Sir Stamford Raffles, had encouraged local Bencoolen merchants to use Armenian merchants, and, if possible, Armenian-owned vessels to deliver supplies to this area under his jurisdiction as his liberal policies of governing were not appreciated by the East India Company. Sir Stamford kept his dealings with the Company to the minimum.

Bencoolen was, indeed, a sleepy little place, but a happy one, and we were all impressed by the decent way the locals were treated by their British ruler. My uncle so liked the lush green of the surroundings and the quiet, easygoing feel of the town that he even ventured to say, "This would be an ideal spot to bring over one's family from Isfahan."

The owner of the *Anahid*, Melkon Khan, said he remembered Sir Stamford when he was the assistant governor of Java during the Napoleonic Wars. And turning to my uncle said, "You must surely recall. That's when we lost our ship, the *Arshag*. The French simply took it over." He then insisted on us getting an audience with Sir Stamford, 'to establish good ties', he said.

Lesley did try to get us an audience the next day but came back disappointed.

"He's gone to Singapore for a short visit," he said.

This was the first time I'd heard of the existence of Singapore.

"Your father recently told me about how Sir Stamford is establishing a new port there, Lesley," my uncle said. "I believe he has a reputation as a solid man of learning and progress, and a young man still – not past his 40th year," he added with admiration.

Lesley agreed and said Sir Stamford was a true scholar and had written a book on the culture and history of Java which had earned him his knighthood. I promptly urged Lesley to join me in my search for this book. Thus we purchased the last copy available of *The History of Java*, published 1817, from one of the local stores. Armed with the comprehensive information contained in this valuable source, both of us were confident we would be ready for our next journey.

Jakarta, or Batavia as the Dutch called it, the capital city of Java, aroused both negative and positive feelings in me as soon as we set foot in it. I did not know much about the island of Java as, previously, I had only made a brief stop at the port of Surabaya. Batavia was a much larger and more impressive city, with a Dutch-built central square called 'Koningsplein'.

The main mode of transportation, water-buffalo drawn carts, was a novelty to me. The harbour was not as large as that of Bombay but could accommodate a myriad of vessels, from large schooners and modified galleons to the smallest barques and sampans.

The crowded and dirty port areas and alleyways turned my stomach. I also saw human deformities I didn't know existed. There were men with bald patches because of bloody head scabs much like those of wild dogs suffering from scabies. The origin of these nasty wounds remains a mystery to me. I observed others with large holes in their cheeks and some others had half lips; Lesley explained that they were the result of the betel nut and lime – a concoction far more powerful than the Indian 'pan' – that the locals had the habit of chewing all day.

The more days we spent in Java, however, the more positive my feelings became. Both Lesley and I were as fascinated with the local culture as Sir Stamford must have surely been. This was made possible through an acquaintance of my uncle's, a Javanese grandee by the name of Hari. Hari was related to one of the important noblemen on the island, the now deposed Sultan of Banten. When the Dutch had taken over the island and the Dutch East India Company turned it into their main rice-producing colony for all the territories they controlled as far as the Spice Islands, the rulers of Java were all vanquished but not before they had put up a good fight. Their political power had evaporated, but they still maintained their noble status amongst the local population.

Hari had us sample some of the local cultural delights. Both Lesley and I were mesmerized by the sound of the 'gamelan', a group of percussion musicians, accompanying the finest ancient legendary dramas. These were performed by male dancers with colourful masks and wide-eyed female dancers whose dance focused on eye and finger movements. Equally gripping was the shadow theatre, which used delicately carved and painted puppets. Their shadows, which were cast on a cloth screen, told the stories of legendary characters.

The garments of Hari and his entourage, together with their intricately made daggers called *kris*, also fascinated us. We found these men of such elegance and refinement in their silk loin wraps and headdress that in the end we had to congratulate ourselves for selling them the fine silk from India in the first place. The cotton we supplied was also the raw material for their master craftsmen; these talented men used a special technique with wax for printing and drawing. With this skill, they were able to produce complicated designs of flowers and birds on cloths which were then worn as *sarongs*, body wraps, by both men and women.

It was also Hari who introduced us to the very few Armenians who lived in Batavia, amongst them the Manuks, who were descendants of the noble Zorabians. Gevorg Manuk, who was a merchant like the rest of us, had made my uncle's acquaintance in Madras many years before. Manuk sent us regular invitations to dine with his family. We also met his sister, Takoohy, who was a partner in the business. Some of our travel companions were surprised at the presence of a female Armenian merchant, having never previously encountered one. Their uneasiness was quickly dissipated when Takoohy appeared at our first dinner, accompanied by her two handsome young sons, who both seemed barely older than sixteen. We later learned that she had lost her husband the year before and was still in mourning. She wore black, European clothing of exquisite taste, and a long, black pearl necklace. Her fine appearance was complemented by her refined and confident manners and excellent command of Armenian, Dutch, and English, enhancing her air of nobility. After that first meeting, every single one of our companions looked forward to seeing Madam Takoohy, for she dominated the conversations with her vast knowledge on a range of subjects and because she was abreast of all the latest news.

"Can you tell us more about this new epidemic, Madam Takoohy," Melkon Khan asked her on one occasion.

"Gentlemen, we are all fortunate that this cholera disease is dead and gone from here. It struck this island only recently and took the lives of a hundred thousand men, women, and children. I've heard that it originated in a remote place in China and has spread even to some of the cities in India. May the Almighty spare us from such a calamity in the future," she said.

On another occasion, when I asked her if she knew any of the Armenian families who lived elsewhere on the island of Java, she was able to list all those who lived in Surabaya and in other, smaller locations on the island. She knew their professions and the number of children each family had.

"Her name fits her like a glove," Lesley said later when I explained that Takoohy means 'queen' in Armenian.

Lesley, in fact, got on extremely well with the Manuks, who, like his father, traded mainly in pearls and precious stones. They spent hours discussing the precious stones business. When they found out that Lesley had recently been to Burma and was planning another trip in the near future, they urged him to contact their younger brother, Sarkis, who was based there and had been trading in precious stones from Burma for years.

"It's been a very exciting place, culturally and all the rest of it," declared Lesley on our last day in Batavia. "I'm glad I joined you and didn't pay heed to my father's latest warnings about the Dutch here," he added.

"Some of our travel companions are more interested in the local women than the local culture," my uncle remarked. Neither my uncle nor Melkon Khan were impressed by their night-time antics, nor were the two of us.

"I cannot be with a woman I'm not acquainted with, or rather, I'd prefer I was in love with her," Lesley said with conviction. "I'm the eternal romantic!"

After leaving Java, we journeyed through to the Sea of Celebes, stopping once in the Celebes port of Macassar for fresh food supplies. We were overwhelmed by the number of Dutch schooners at this port, by the delays of disembarking because of the chaotic port procedures, and by the number of uncouth sailors that we came across. We also witnessed brawls amongst drunken and unsavoury characters whose nationality we had difficulty in determining. At the inn where we dined and the market where we bought supplies, rumours were circulating of pirate ships in the area. Hence, we decided not to linger in Macassar for longer than necessary and set sail as soon as we could.

This proved not a very wise decision as most of us were too tired by the time we reached the Maluka Islands. Three of our travelling companions and five of our crewmen came down with a nasty illness – fever, chill, and vomiting being the main symptoms. We therefore had to stay put for more than two months – until everyone was in good health and we were able to procure the necessary amount of spices; that, after all, was the purpose of our journey to these far-flung islands.

The hub of these islands, which number in the hundreds, is a place called Amboyna on one of the tiny islands of the Maluka Archipelago. This is where we anchored the *Anahid*. We were greeted by two Armenian merchants, who were based there and had been trading in spices for over five years. The two, who were first cousins and from Calcutta, were our middlemen. They had already a large quantity of spices stored for my uncle. There was nutmeg and mace, but the bulk of our spice procurement was cloves, my favourite.

Other than for the abundance of spices, the islands are remarkable for the clear blue waters that surround them. Although this was the second trip to these islands for both of us, Lesley and I still marvelled at their beauty, especially the crystal-clear waters teeming with a wealth of fish of all kinds and colours.

"This is a poet's paradise," Lesley sighed as we walked along the sandy shore barefoot one afternoon.

"I wish I had the talent to draw this God-given beauty," I said looking at the vast sea in front of us. It was indeed with sadness that we left the Maluka Islands, not certain if we would ever be back there again. The *Anahid*, laden with spices, bore us safely back to the shores of Madras.

CHAPTER 9

✥

"Is that really what you want to do?" my uncle said.

"Yes, I'm certain. It's what I need to do. I want Anoosh and Mariam here with me. Lesley has been a great help. We checked out some of the lodgings in the quarter where Armenian families, the majority from Isfahan, live in Madras. We found a couple of places that are perfectly suitable," I said.

"Alright then, I have no objection. I myself would rather come and live here too, Vartan. I told you this many times before. I have the feeling that Anoosh would love to join you. I'm not so certain Zaroug Khatoun would agree to the move though. I know what she will say – that all her kin are in Isfahan, and now that the twins are nearing marriage age, I can just about hear her say 'But how can they find suitors when there is such a small number of Armenians in Madras?' I tell you, I did marry a woman who thinks and I'm proud of her. She does have a mind of her own. Look, Vartan, I'm a practical man. We can sort out our business dealings in a slightly different manner. Come to think of it, it would be just the right move for us now – to have you based here in Madras," my uncle concluded.

I was so happy and relieved that for the next week I kept on badgering Lesley with my plans for bringing Anoosh and Mariam over – how we would travel, where we would live, what kind of furniture we would need to purchase, and so on and so forth.

Lesley took the badgering quite well and, in one of his jolly moods, said, "I'm happy for you, Vartan, but I guess I'm happy for me, too. I'll have my best friend here in Madras at all times."

A week later, the *Anahid* took us on two more voyages: one to Macao and China, ending in Calcutta, and the other, the fateful trip to Malacca.

On board the *Anahid*, Lesley and I were entrusted with the task of keeping the two main logs, one for the supplies for the journey and one for the cargo. The supplies log had to be updated every day, and the one for the cargo, at departure point, at every stop on the way, and at the final destination. For the journey back, we would have a new cargo log with the same rules. Precise records had to be kept of the cargo as we would transport goods belonging to merchants who were not necessarily making the trip. Thus, with, say, eight travelling companions, we would have the cargo of at least eight others who were not on board. I was responsible for the supplies log but I always kept a cargo log written in Armenian, which was useful for our book-keeping later. Lesley was in charge of the cargo log. This was written in English for official purposes and customs' officials.

The cargo the *Anahid* carried varied. On one journey she might carry silver, copper, indigo, textiles, cotton, silk, precious stones, diamonds, oil, and Benares opium, and on another, she might be laden with gold, musk, spices, wood, gunpowder, camphor, rice, sugar, and Chinese tea. These goods were usually procured from the region and transported to a location in the same region or to Europe via Persia or Constantinople. But the *Anahid* sometimes also transported goods dispatched from Europe or the Near East which eventually ended up in places like Siam or China. The cargo could consist of European furniture, cloths, toiletries, toys, French delicacies, glassware, spoons, perfumes, oils, seals, and jewellery.

I should also add here that we were equipped to ward off any pirate attacks and thefts. We always had on board our 'handyman' and our 'giant' as we called them. Melkon Khan's Greek navigator could never be found on board whenever we anchored the *Anahid*; he had a knack of slipping away to spend whole days at some watering hole near the port. Thus, the 'handyman' and the 'giant' were 'the guardians' of the *Anahid*. In fact, they lived on board permanently. Maam, the handyman, was an Indian 'warrior' from Cochin. Although of very small build, he was the most agile man I had ever seen. He called himself 'a warrior', and this was true. He had mastered the traditional art of fighting, *Kalaripayattu*, well-known in his homeland, and had practised it since he was a boy. He was the one who fixed this and that on board and supervised the loading and unloading of bales and crates of goods. The lower-level crewmen and porters were weary of him – he was very moody; he could hire or fire them and did not tolerate laziness or nonchalance. Bab, the dark giant from the Malabar Coast, had arm muscles the size of my thighs, a set of gleaming white teeth, and a child's smile. And although he looked physically menacing to strangers, all the crewmen liked him, and there was nothing he could not carry or move. Both men got on very well with their patron, Melkon Khan, who paid them handsomely and who regularly enjoyed partaking of their specially cooked Indian food. Indeed, Melkon Khan spent more time on board with Maam and Bab than with his own Armenian compatriots in any given town when the *Anahid* docked.

As for defending ourselves against pirate attacks, we were well armed on board. Lesley was good with pistols and muskets. He was trained, from a tender age, by his father, who had been in the British Navy in his youth. I would not be lying if I said that my knowledge of firearms was nil despite several attempts by my uncle to get me interested in them. It was with Lesley that I finally learned how to use a pistol. There were a number of pistols and muskets on board the *Anahid*, supplemented by machetes that the senior crewmen carried. Every Armenian merchant, without exception, possessed at least one traditional dagger. Some of these were purchased in Persia; but the best silver, hand-crafted ones, made by Armenian master artisans, came from the Lake Van region of Anatolia. Whenever I sailed on the *Anahid*, I wore mine strapped to my father's silver Van belt, the one my mother had given me as a teenager.

The trip to Macao was to fetch a tea cargo to Calcutta. This belonged to Aratoon Apcar, a well-known Armenian merchant, and a quarter of this large tea shipment was owned by my uncle. Our other goods were waiting to be picked up in Calcutta; these were principally precious and semi-precious stones from Burma for Lesley's father. Half of the amount had already been purchased from him by my uncle and was destined for a jeweller in Bombay.

Just before we boarded the *Anahid*, my uncle informed Lesley and me that there was a slight change of plan. We were not only stopping at Portuguese Macao but also continuing on to China, to the port of Canton. He said he had just got word that the tea shipment had to be loaded in Canton, not Macao as was originally planned, and we were to collect four passengers from there who would journey with us to Calcutta.

This was the longest period at sea I had experienced so far because, in order to save time and energy, we purposely did not stop at any port, save for one, until we reached Macao. And we all knew that we needed to make haste as the monsoon season would soon be upon us. The

Anahid thus took us southwards and, sailing along the coast of the island of Sumatra, finally docked at Bencoolen, where we discharged our cargo. Then, sailing the narrow strait between Sumatra and the island of Java, she took a northerly direction and was soon plying the waters of the South China Sea.

Upon docking at the port of Macao, we were met by a Portuguese official by the name of de Melo, a very pleasant older gentleman who had befriended Melkon Khan's father years ago and who was able to converse in good English, albeit with a thick Portuguese accent. For the few days we remained there, we were treated as his guests. He offered us comfortable lodgings and abundant food and wine. The relaxing, sleepy nature of the town pleased all, and Lesley and I made a point of visiting the old, beautifully ornate Portuguese cathedral. It was also in Macao that we all witnessed for the first time a marriage union between a junior Portuguese officer, who worked under de Melo, and a young, Christian Chinese, the daughter of a well-known scribe, also employed by de Melo. Although they came from different worlds, the young couple seemed so full of life and happy that even hardened hearts were softened and none found the union objectionable. Two days later, de Melo arranged for an experienced sailor to accompany us to Canton for Melkon Khan had never before taken the *Anahid* to that port.

We first navigated the China Sea until we reached the mouth of the Pearl River. It was smooth sailing up the river, the banks of which were covered in lush vegetation. As we advanced, we saw an endless number of small towns surrounded by fertile, cultivated land, a distinguishing feature of the area. I was surprised at how quickly we reached the city of Canton. I had not seen such a neatly configured and welcoming city before with wide avenues and countless marketplaces although I was told, as a foreign trader, I would never be allowed to venture into the densely populated, poor Chinese neighbourhoods where some of the local population lived in dire conditions. Nevertheless, this was the city of the Qing Emperor, who had proudly turned it into one of the most important trading hubs of the region, rivalling those run by the English, the Dutch, and the Portuguese. The Canton Viceroy secured an enormous sum of money for his emperor from taxes collected on every single trading activity. In addition to the many foreign vessels that docked here, more Chinese sampans and junks could be found in this port than any other in the region.

As we approached the harbour of Canton, we were greeted by the flags of all the countries whose ships docked there. These flew on very high poles and included those of the British, French, Portuguese, Danish, Dutch, and even the States of America. In the background, one could discern the distinctive, large new buildings known as 'the thirteen factories'; these were the trading companies that corresponded to each flag and operated from the city. The buildings also formed the foreigners' quarter of the city. Since foreigners were segregated from the rest of the city, each of the buildings housed living quarters, shops, and warehouses. It was in one of those that our tea cargo was kept, and it was loaded onto the *Anahid* in just one morning. This surprised none of us for, instead of the usual ten or twenty porters at any other port, the trading companies here used no less than a hundred porters to load and unload goods.

The four passengers who were to journey with us to Calcutta arrived shortly afterwards, seated in tiny, open-top carriages – each pulled by one man. Three of the passengers were Chinese. I greeted the fourth one, a man of around forty whose garments resembled mine.

"Hovannes Ghazar," he announced in Armenian, "but I go by my official name of Yohannes Lassar." He then added, "I am journeying with my old Chinese teacher and two master Chinese printers. I must apologise on their behalf for none of them speak any other language but their own native Chinese."

His three companions, sensing that the conversation was about them, greeted me with a nod and a bow. I immediately gestured that they were welcome to board the *Anahid*. As they embarked, I noticed how delicately they moved and how regal they looked in their Chinese silk robes held at the waist with a wide belt. Each was coiffed in the same manner. The head was shaved from the forehead to the middle; the rest of the hair was gathered in one long plait that reached the end of their backs.

Yohannes Lassar, I soon found out, was born in Macao. The son of a wealthy Armenian merchant, he had learnt to speak Chinese like a native while in the care of his numerous Chinese nannies. His father taught him Armenian, Portuguese, and English when he was just a boy. As a young man, he was sent to Canton to perfect his Chinese. The old man who now accompanied him had taught him how to read and write it. Following in the footsteps of his late father, Lassar became a trader and moved to Calcutta, but success in business eluded him and he lost most of his assets. It is then that luck smiled on him and he was offered the position of translator and teacher of the Chinese language at the New College of the English Baptist Mission in Serampore, a small town just north of Calcutta, which was at the time still under the administration of the Danish East India Company.

"I was encouraged to translate the New Testament into Chinese, which I completed more than six years ago," he said when both Lesley and I showed much interest in learning more about him.

"I hope to be able to publish the first Chinese translation of the entire Holy Bible. I began the task a dozen years ago with the scholar Joshua Marshman, to whom I taught all the Chinese he knows. He is a man of sound mind and discipline. My knowledge of the Armenian language has greatly assisted us since the Holy Bible in Armenian is one of the very few early translations from the original, an important endeavour accomplished by our Revered Translators of the 5th Century."

"What you have embarked on is surely a feat very few humans are capable of succeeding in," Lesley remarked.

"Indeed, it is so, and I am very concerned that my translation may not accurately represent Chinese thoughts. That is the purpose of taking my old Chinese teacher with me to Calcutta. He is the only one who is able to correct my errors."

"Will you be publishing the Holy Bible in Chinese in Calcutta once you have finished the task then?" I enquired, turning my gaze towards the two Chinese printers.

"We are fortunate that The Mission in Serampore possesses a printing press. But for printing in Chinese, we require the skills of experienced Chinese printers. Chinese characters have to be carved on metal or wood using a special method. Hence, I volunteered to find suitable printers in Canton and the two who are accompanying me will remain in Serampore until the task is completed and will be paid handsomely for their effort."

The rest of our long journey, in the company of Yohannes Lassar, was most enjoyable and educational. I showed him samples of my Armenian calligraphy, which he appreciated, and in turn, I admired his ability to write the complex Chinese characters. These he drew with great natural ease as if he were writing in his own native tongue.

Two weeks later, the *Anahid* was plying the waters north, towards the Bay of Bengal when we were suddenly confronted by a heavy downpour of rain. The rains lasted for three days and nights and there was no relief in sight. Fortunately, they did not develop into a full storm and we safely docked, glad to be on the firm ground of Calcutta.

I bid Yohannes Lassar, and his companions, farewell and prayed that he would accomplish the noble task he had begun. It was some five years later that I learned he had finished his blessed undertaking. I felt proud and privileged to have met and conversed with him; his translation of The Holy Bible into Chinese, known as the *Sheng Jing* and published in 1822, was indeed the first of its kind.

"Here," said Lesley, handing me a newspaper in Armenian at breakfast the next morning. "They publish another one as well, I'm told."

"Where did you find this?" I said, not believing my eyes.

Armenian newspapers here in Calcutta – who would have credited it? Thus it was that I discovered compatriots in Calcutta. And there were many of them. I later learned that a certain Reverend Father Joseph Stephanuse had established the first Armenian printing press in Calcutta in 1797 just 8 years after Reverend Father Aratoon Shemavon had done so in Madras.

Father Stephanuse's legacy had continued with the establishment of the Armenian Literary Society of Calcutta, in 1818. On this visit, I had the honour of meeting its members, who had recently published some of their own poems, plays, and translations. They were also in the process of publishing other works by fellow countrymen in Bombay. It was thus that I met Father Martin Megerdich of Shiraz, whom everyone considered the first writer and publisher of Armenian dramatic works among the Indian Armenians. Another member of the society was John Avdall of Bosra. He was very young, about my age, and a talented writer and publisher of works in both Armenian and English.

In a matter of days, I had visited the two Armenian churches, the almshouse, the Armenian school, headed by Aratoon Kaloo, and where instruction was given in both English and Armenian. I also had invitations to some of the local Armenian notables' homes. Such imposing mansions I had not seen before. They were built on vast grounds, surrounded by beautiful gardens and shaded by tall trees. These well-to-do fellow countrymen had been so successful that they led a life similar to their English counterparts in Calcutta. I was truly impressed and proud of their achievements.

I even took Lesley with me to see a play in Armenian that the locals had put on in a small theatre. The play featured scenes from the local Armenian life. Lesley didn't complain although he didn't understand a single word of what was being said. He was rather happy eyeing all the young ladies of the audience who had come in their fineries to the event; and the majority, he remarked, were clad in fashionable European or English style. He then winked at me, and I understood that I had taken the right decision to bring Anoosh and Mariam with me to India in the very near future.

We returned to Madras. One morning as I was getting myself ready for the journey back to Isfahan, my uncle turned up at the lodgings I was sharing with Lesley. He said that we had to go urgently to Malacca to rescue one of Khoja Shahmir's shipments which was stranded there. The ship that was to pick up the cargo had caught fire somewhere at sea, not far from Malacca, and had been completely destroyed.

"Don't worry – we won't lose more than a couple of weeks. I promise we'll head for Isfahan soon after that. I have to do this, I have to, for Khoja Shahmir's sake," he said firmly.

I dreaded this unplanned journey not so much because it would delay our return to Isfahan – I had waited so long and two more weeks would not have killed me – but mainly because Lesley would not be coming with us this time. He was readying himself to go to Burma again in a few days.

On the day of his departure, Lesley was in his usual good spirits.

"Now remember, I'll be back here in 3 months' time. Send word and I'll rent temporary lodgings promptly for you and your family, my dear friend," he said, and before leaving, placed a little square box on the table – with a note. In the box was an exquisite little gold brooch embellished with small diamonds. The note said: *Please accept this for Anoosh. I hope I will see you both very soon.*

CHAPTER 10

✤

IT WAS HARD TO NAVIGATE through the Malacca Straits. "Treacherous waters," Melkon Khan called them. At times, we were forced to advance very slowly in order to skirt either undercurrents or rock formations.

"Many people died here during the Napoleonic Wars and many ships were taken or destroyed by the British Navy or the French. I was lucky the *Anahid* was nowhere near these parts then," Melkon Khan said, scratching his head.

I was glad that I hadn't witnessed those wars and my only concern now was to get back to Madras as fast as possible so I could sail on home to Isfahan.

"Are you awake? Come, have a look, Vartan!" my uncle said with enthusiasm.

Up on deck, dawn was breaking and we were about to dock at Malacca. From here one could see the importance of this port to traders. It presented itself as a natural harbour, one that would shelter vessels from the dangers of monsoons. The sun was just rising over the horizon and I could view the town awash in an orange-pink shade. All looked quiet and orderly. A sense of appeasement fell upon me and I soon forgot my resentment for having been asked to go there. As soon as we disembarked, I went looking for a place of prayer. I knew that there were only a dozen or so Armenian merchants operating from Malacca and that there would not be an Armenian church here.

"I'll take you to a church. Come with me – you'll like this one," my uncle said.

The white-painted Christ Church was right in the centre of town. On one side, a picturesque river flowed. Its silver surface was broken, from time to time, by the popping head of a monitor lizard. On the other side of the church was a row of market stalls, neatly arranged, where locals, both Chinese and Malay, noisily sold their wares. I found the architecture of the church most unexpected.

"Old Dutch," my uncle said. "This was built by the Dutch before the British took control of this town. Come, there's something even more interesting for you to see inside," he added, dragging me in.

The church was a lot bigger inside than one could have guessed from the façade. I was awestruck after taking just two steps inside. There it was – not far from the entrance – a tombstone with Armenian calligraphy, flanked by two funerary skulls. The calligraphy was executed in a very similar manner to the one I had the habit of using myself, and I imagined it could have been me who had done this departed man's epitaph. It read:

Hail to you who reads the epitaph on my tomb! Have you news of my nation's freedom – for whose calamity I did much weep and for whose delivery I passionately longed – if someone has risen among us as deliverer or leader, which, while on earth, I earnestly desired. Vainly I expected in the world to see a good shepherd come to look after the scattered sheep. I, Jacob, son of Shameer, an Armenian of a respectable and noble family, whose name I keep, was born in a foreign land, at New Julfa in Persia. Fortune brought me to this distant Malacca, where my remains in bondage are kept. On attaining twenty nine years of age, I parted from the world on the seventh of July in the year of the Saviour 1774. I laid myself down to rest in this grave, which I myself acquired.

The words overwhelmed me and my eyes welled.

"People say he was the third son of Agha Shameer Sultanoumian, the famous Madras Armenian pearl merchant of the last century. Such a tragedy, he died in the prime of life," my uncle said, shaking his head.

I turned to Jacob's tomb again and sensed my affinity with the dead man. I could be he. I also longed for the delivery of my nation from the yoke of foreigners. Was it not because of this that I had to choose, like many of my countrymen, the path of an exile? Would I be what I am today if my homeland were free?

And I could die here, too – far from my loved ones, as Jacob, son of Shameer. What had destiny in store for me? What was the Lord's design for me? I knelt in front of the tomb of Jacob, and, facing the church altar, prayed earnestly that I would see Anoosh and Mariam again.

We sailed three days later. It was early morning. And although we had secured Khoja Shahmir's goods and everything went as smoothly as planned, I felt sad for leaving Malacca and Jacob's tomb behind; such sadness I had not felt on any of the journeys before. As the day progressed, the sky got cloudier and the night ushered in pitch darkness and fog. The *Anahid* plied the treacherous waters of the Malacca Straits with stealth for two days and two foggy nights, engulfed in an eerie silence, hinting at the grave events that were to unfold.

On the third night, I was awoken from a heavy sleep by a loud banging on the thick rosewood door of my cabin.

"Pirate ship!" Maam was shouting at the top of his voice so as to wake all who were still asleep. My uncle, who shared my cabin, was not in his bed. I quickly ran up on deck with my pistol in hand, oblivious that I had on only my undershirts.

"Keep your head down. They're shooting at us," my uncle roared.

"It's the *Corne Noire* – I recognise it from its bulbous shape – the bastards!" shouted Melkon Khan. "Here's the plan. I've rehearsed it in my head many times and may I be cursed if I don't save the *Anahid*!"

He told us to carry on shooting in the direction of the *Corne Noire*. There were six other Armenian merchants on board, and Melkon Khan ordered us to take strategic positions at different spots of the deck and to continue firing. He then ordered Maam and Bab to start dumping the heavy cargo on the deck into the sea. And when finished, he said, they should continue dumping the cargo from the lower decks. Other men were ordered to bring us more ammunition. Melkon Khan had spoken but once before of the danger that loomed in the Malacca Straits. This was where pirate ships lay in hiding, ready to strike, he'd said. If we came face to face with one of them, we'd have to have the *Anahid* as light as possible to make good our escape. Otherwise we would be dead. This was Melkon Khan's strategy and I prayed that he knew what he was doing.

My heart was beating faster and faster and then I shot my first bullet. My uncle was shooting not far from me – from the opposite side of the deck. The crewmen were frantically throwing the cargo into the sea, with Maam urging them to work faster and faster. Bab, with his superhuman strength, was hurling huge wooden chests off the deck. As I kept on firing, I could see the lights of the *Corne Noire* drawing closer and closer towards us. We were shooting blindly at a faceless enemy.

"Keep shooting!" my uncle cried.

There was a deafening barrage of gunfire and bullets coming our way. I honestly don't know how long this frenzy lasted, but it felt like a long, long time. Then I saw one of the crewmen get shot in the head as he was pulling a box close to the edge of the deck; he fell face down.

"Don't stop, don't stop, carry on!" I could hear Maam's voice. And then the unthinkable happened. I looked to the left and witnessed my uncle collapse. He dropped to the deck in a seated position, his back supported by a crate.

I crawled towards him as he shouted, "Don't, don't! I'm alright; it's just my left arm – I can still shoot – keep shooting!"

It was then I suddenly felt the *Anahid* cutting faster than usual through the water. I realised Melkon Khan had fulfilled his promise to save the ship and all on it. The *Corne Noire*'s lights began to fade farther and farther into the distance.

My uncle managed to get up and shoot once before collapsing again. The shooting stopped. I ran to his side and saw he was bleeding profusely. One of the Armenian merchants, Minas, who acted as our doctor on board, had studied medicine for a short while. He rushed over, had a look at the wound, and ordered some of the men to move my uncle to his cabin.

"We'll see what can be done. Don't worry," he said, seeing the shock and horror written on my face.

As I was going below deck to be with my uncle, I heard Melkon Khan's jubilation: "We got away! Thank you, Lord! Thank you my lady-rock, *Anahid!*"

Minas would not let me in the cabin.

"Let me do my work. It's no good you looking over my shoulder," he said as he shut the door in my face.

I was impatiently waiting for news of my uncle's condition when Melkon Khan appeared with the bad news that we had lost one of the crewmen.

"That, I guessed. I saw it happen," I said.

"Your uncle will be fine. It's just the arm. Minas will fix it, I'm certain," he said. I nodded.

The wait was interminable. This prompted Melkon Khan to tell me the story of the *Corne Noire*. She had been a French Navy ship during the Napoleonic Wars, when the French and British fought each other mercilessly. Near the end of hostilities in the region, there had been a mutiny of a group of French officers who had killed everyone on board unwilling to join them. At that particular time, the *Corne Noire* was sailing the Malacca Straits. To enable them to escape the wrath of the French Navy, the mutineers joined forces with the pirates in the area. These were mainly Chinese and Malays, but rumour had it that there were also British Navy deserters amongst them. Since that time, the ship, which originally carried a different name, was re-baptized by the mutineers as the *Corne Noire*, the biggest vessel the pirates now possessed.

"Luckily, there aren't many of them, according to reports from the office of the Governor of Penang; but the pirates are there and they hide in the coves. We are truly fortunate that I could get the *Anahid* to sail faster than usual, and my guess is the *Corne Noire* is getting too old for a good chase. The pirates will probably salvage some of the cargo we ditched and will feast on it, calling it their booty, to sate their appetite for stolen goods. We are presently not far from Penang and they won't venture out this far for fear of being captured by the British Navy vessels," he concluded.

"You can come in now," I heard Minas' voice through the cabin door.

Melkon Khan opened the door and we both went in. My uncle was lying there, unconscious. His arm was bandaged and one of Minas' helpers was clearing the bloody cloths and water.

"I was able to remove the bullet. He's just asleep. But we need to get him to the nearest port and let a proper doctor look after him. He needs to rest for a good while," Minas said as he left.

"It was not in our plans, but we need to stay in Penang for some time. We should get there by early morning. Get some rest," Melkon Khan said, putting his hand on my shoulder to reassure me.

I remained in the cabin the rest of the night, not sleeping a wink, watching over my uncle.

CHAPTER 11

⚜

OTHER THAN THE LARGE NUMBER of bullet holes that could be fixed in time, the *Anahid* was in good shape and we docked at the port of the Prince of Wales Island as Melkon Khan had planned. The crewmen were grateful for the stopover because they could have a cremation ceremony for Shiv, their compatriot shot dead by the pirates. Maam told Melkon Khan he would take care of all the necessary arrangements and said he knew where to find the local Hindu community. Melkon Khan responded by offering to take care of all the expenses and assured Maam he would pay the customary sum set as gratuity to the deceased man's family in India. Melkon Khan then took his leave to seek an appointment with the Governor of Penang in order to report our pirate attack.

Unfortunately, my uncle's condition was not good. He was lucid but in a lot of pain. With the help of Bab, Minas and I managed to move him to a comfortable inn and a room with a large bed in Georgetown. Minas and I then went looking for a certain Doctor Smith whom we'd been told was the town's best.

And Doctor Smith did provide my uncle with expert care. He was a man of great confidence and that, in turn, reassured me immensely. His assistant, Mr. Chang, came in every day to change my uncle's dressing and to administer pain-relieving medication.

"Mr. Minas did the correct thing by removing the bullet as quickly as possible," Dr. Smith said. "But I'm afraid your uncle's condition is quite complicated. He has a bone fracture in the upper arm and because the bullet lodged itself quite deep in the flesh, some nerve damage as well. The wound will take longer to heal in this tropical climate. His arm must be kept immobile for a while until the fracture heals completely. As for the nerve damage, my prognosis is that you must be prepared for the eventuality of his not being able to regain the full use of his arm and fingers."

"We must thank the Lord your uncle did not lose his life, like that poor Indian man," Minas said after Dr. Smith had left.

"Minas, it's strange. I had the premonition something terrible was going to happen as we left Malacca. I still can't believe this is happening to us and I'm dreading facing my uncle to tell him Dr. Smith's prognosis."

"Vartan, my friend, if it's any consolation, all I can say is that you can't fight fate."

That evening, I took the bowl of food to my uncle myself to feed him. I sat on the chair next to his bed. He looked pale and tired. He opened his eyes and stared at me.

"It's not good news, is it? I may not be able to use my arm again – I can read it all over your solemn face," he said. "Vartan, please take me home. I want to be with Zaroug Khatoun and my daughters," he pleaded.

All I could do was nod silently in agreement as my voice choked and I held back the tears.

I had supper with Melkon Khan a few days later. He had been very well received by the assistant to Lt. Colonel Farquhar, the Governor of Penang, who'd promptly ordered a report drawn up regarding the pirate incident, the death of our Indian crewman, and the wounding of my uncle, as well as the loss of goods that ensued. Melkon Khan said this was a good outcome since he needed the report for insurance claims for the lost goods.

"Of course, they'll have to inspect the *Anahid* and take stock of the goods that remain on board. It's going to take time to sort this out and I need to stay here for a while. Many people have lost all or part of their cargo. It puts me in an awkward situation until I make sure everyone's been paid for their losses. If your uncle wishes to head back to Isfahan, I suggest you use one of Agha Catchadoor Caloustian's ships. He's the doyen of our community here and not only runs a mercantile firm, but also owns at least half a dozen vessels. He offers both cargo and passenger services to all the main ports in the region. His ships frequently sail to Madras and you should be able to find your passage to Isfahan from there easily. I shall be visiting him tomorrow, so you can come along if you wish and I'll introduce you to him."

I met Agha Caloustian the following day. A middle-aged man of stature in European clothing, he seemed a man of considerable means, not least because he had the title of 'Agha' and his office was luxuriously decorated with European furniture and fineries. He knew the governor personally and, as I listened to him, I had the impression he knew just about everything an experienced businessman needed to know. He offered us imported French brandy and little pieces of European-style bread, topped with a dollop of butter; both Melkon Khan and I welcomed his hospitality as we had not tasted butter since we'd left Isfahan. Agha Caloustian also offered us little pieces of chocolate – hard, dark brown delicacies made from a type of nut. "I'm importing it now and everyone, especially children, love it!" he said. Melkon Khan lobbed a couple of pieces in his mouth and came back for more. I was too embarrassed to tell Agha Caloustian that I'd never had chocolate before, and as the first piece of this sweet delicacy was melting in my mouth, I decided I had to purchase some to take back to Isfahan for my loved ones.

Agha Caloustian then ordered one of his clerks to fetch the schedule of the vessels.

"Let's see – the *Sarah* is in Calcutta...the *Anna* is on its way to Burma...the *Governor Petrie* is under repair at the docks...Yes, you could take the *Covelong* to Madras, sailing next week, and that way you'd catch up with the *Ahamed Shaw*. She'll be waiting for the *Covelong* to arrive in Madras since she'll be carrying some of the cargo destined for Persia. All done then – my clerk will give you the necessary details before you leave," said Agha Caloustian and wished me a safe journey.

We thanked Agha Caloustian warmly for his hospitality and assistance and took our leave.

"Impressive character, isn't he? Useful man to know – just the right person to be the doyen of our community here in Georgtown," Melkon Khan said as we were walking back to the inn. I could only agree.

"But what I don't understand is why your uncle is in such a rush to go back to Isfahan. He's still convalescing," he said, shaking his head.

I stopped walking, turned to face him and said, "Melkon Khan, you've known him for over twenty years and you of all people should know that no one is as headstrong as my uncle."

My uncle's condition was getting better but Doctor Smith was of the opinion that he should not undertake a long journey at sea until he had recovered completely. But there was no way one could weaken my uncle's resolve to join his family. When he found out that Minas was to accompany us to Isfahan, since he too had been away from his family for

a long while, my uncle rejoiced and said that at least the burden of looking after him during the journey would not be solely my responsibility.

By the time the *Covelong* docked at Madras, I was terribly worried.
My uncle was in constant pain. Minas said it was because of the heaving
and rolling of the ship preventing my uncle from keeping his arm still.
I wished to believe him – he had been of great help to us and a loyal
friend even though we'd only recently become acquainted.

I also regretted that Lesley was not in Madras but away on a trip to
Burma with his father. I longed for his companionship. He would have
reassured me, or at the very least empathised. I was at a loss – I had never before seen my uncle in such a weak state. The day before we sailed
again, he seemed to have regained some of his strength, bolstered by
his sheer determination to return to Isfahan. The following day, as the
Ahamed Shaw set sail, we fell into silence. For sure, all three of us shared
the same hope of a short journey home to the arms of our loved ones.

It was at Bosra that the *Ahamed Shaw* docked instead of at Bandar Abbas,
our usual port of call. This created not a huge problem but an incon-
venience. I was grateful for Minas' help in transferring my uncle to a
decent inn to rest whilst we went looking for suitable transportation to
reach Isfahan. In Madras, my uncle had been able to rise and walk, although with frailty. He had embarked on the *Ahamed Shaw* on his own
two feet, using either Minas or myself as a crutch. By the time we arrived
in Bosra, he had weakened again as the sea journey had taken its toll on
him. He was too frail to walk and had to be carried ashore.

Minas and I found a well-known Assyrian in that dusty town who
organised all manner of overland journeys to Persia, Arabia, Jerusalem,
and beyond. We had the specific requirement of a shaded horse-drawn

carriage for my uncle to ensure we arrived in Isfahan in the quickest and in the most comfortable manner possible. The Assyrian quoted us a much higher price than we had anticipated, but we agreed to it; a camel caravan was too hectic and an ox-driven carriage too slow, given my uncle's frail condition.

There was a vast square in front of the Assyrian's premises at the edge of town where all the carriages, horses, camels and oxen were stationed; and we saw people endlessly arriving and leaving. While in conversation with us, the Assyrian turned away at intervals to shout something in Arabic, Assyrian, or Persian to some porter, caravan leader, or passenger.

"I cannot assure collection from the inn for your uncle. Bosra's streets are too narrow for my carriages." And pointing proudly to the bustling scene in front of his premises he added officiously, "The journey starts here."

"Is he in a comfortable position there?" demanded the Assyrian in Persian, referring to my uncle in the carriage.

I signalled that all was alright. Although my uncle felt very weak that morning, he was, nevertheless, in good spirits. Having secured the necessary supplies for the journey, Minas and I were ready to depart when a man approached us.

"You're Minas, aren't you?" said the man in Armenian. "I'm Bedros, from Isfahan. I was your older brother's schoolmate."

Minas, attempting to recognise him, and then slowly, with a dawning smile said: "Yes, of course, Bedros, the coppersmith! I haven't seen you in years. What brings you to these parts?"

Without answering, Bedros said, "You're on your way back to Isfahan from India I assume. Have you not heard then?"

"Heard what, my friend?" said Minas.

Bedros then told us, first with hesitation and then with tears in his eyes, that two months prior Isfahan had been hit by a cholera epidemic. Many had perished, young and old, rich and poor.

"What are you talking about? I hope this is not some kind of a joke or a madman's rant," my uncle said, raising his head in the carriage.

"No sir, all I'm recounting is true – believe me. I buried my wife and son with my own hands. All I have left is one son, may God preserve him. He's over there – sitting under that tree, waiting for me. We're on our way to Jerusalem on a pilgrimage – may God have mercy on us, on us all," he said and took his leave with slow steps towards the tree without waiting for our response.

"Let's move," my uncle said sternly.

Both Minas and I were shocked speechless. And thus we remained throughout the entire journey, silence broken only occasionally by Minas uttering in a bewildered tone, "God have mercy..."

CHAPTER 12

As we approached Isfahan, our first stop was Minas' house, which was situated just at the entrance of New Julfa. The sun was setting when we halted in front of the house. Minas rushed out to tell his household he had arrived and I was left to keep an eye on the unloading of his personal belongings. Barely ten minutes had passed before Minas came out of the house and stood at the threshold with both hands on his head. He was crying like a child.

I ran towards him and he looked deep in my eyes and said, "We're done with – my only son is dead and your family and your uncle's have perished."

I became weak at the knees and started to cry out – calling out for Mariam and Anoosh – and a sea of tears flooded out of me. I staggered towards my uncle as fast as I could. He was sitting upright, his eyes wide open.

"They're gone? All of them?" he said in a soft voice. A lone teardrop rolled down each of his cheeks – the first and last I was to see him shed.

I nodded frantically until I heard Minas' loud wails, and then the world went blank.

I opened my eyes. It was morning. My uncle was lying in a bed next to mine. A woman was placing a wet cloth on his forehead. Minas was opposite me, sitting in an armchair; his hand covered his eyes, temple to temple.

"I've got to go home," I said.

He looked up: "My friend, that's not such a good idea. We'll look after you – see, my wife has been helping me to attend to your uncle's needs. He developed a high fever late last night and his arm doesn't look good. He's in pain and was delirious all night. I have ordered medication to ease his pain and make him sleep; these should arrive tomorrow. I gave the last drop of sleeping potion to you last night to help you relax and sleep. I've also sent word to Doctor Arshagunian through my brother. He used to treat the Shah's officers and knows a thing or two about gunshot wounds. He's away on a mission but should be here next week."

"That's good, thank you," I said. "I need to get up and find out what happened exactly. Who looked after them? Who buried them? I must visit their graves."

"Look, Vartan. Last night when you were asleep, many townspeople turned up here upon hearing of our arrival. Amongst them was your book-keeper, Mr. Ashod, who I believe is the only person who knows exactly what happened to your family. He's coming again this afternoon to see you. He attempted to tell me things last night, but forgive me I was in no state to listen to anything."

"I understand perfectly well, my friend," I said, at which point Minas started sobbing again for his lost son.

The sight of Mr. Ashod that afternoon made me weep. We both wept as we hugged each other. "Please, Mr. Ashod, don't spare me anything – tell me all that transpired."

"Two months ago, the cholera epidemic started its savage attack on the townspeople. One after another, people became sick and most of those who caught it perished. I can't tell you how helpless we felt. Your daughter Mariam caught it first and, being only a toddler, she hardly survived a few days, may her soul rest in peace. Next was Khoja Shahmir, whose weak heart didn't help. As by this time people in the city were panicking, Zaroug Khatoun was very much afraid and sent word to me to talk to Markar to arrange for their escape from Isfahan to Feridoon where Anoosh's older sister and other relatives live. When I spoke to Markar about it, he just dismissed it by saying they were not his family and that he didn't see how he could be responsible for them. It pains me to say that Zaroug Khatoun got no help at all from Markar in her hour of need."

I clenched my teeth and said, "I shall teach that man a lesson once and for all. Go on, please, Mr. Ashod."

"I remembered that your uncle, wise as he always is, had purchased a vacant lot at our cemetery, next to Zaroug Khatoun's family burial ground. So it was I who took a couple of men with me to bury your daughter. It breaks my heart to tell you that Anoosh was devastated and was beating her chest and pulling her dishevelled hair when we came to take the little one's body to the cemetery. The malady struck her next and the twins with her. Zaroug Khatoun was looking after the three of them. I would go there every day to see if she needed any supplies but the three patients were not in good shape and Zaroug Khatoun looked exhausted. There were no doctors to be found in the city either. They had either escaped or were dead. There was nothing anyone could do to cure the malady once it struck. I knew Zaroug Khatoun's old mother was alright, so I went and fetched her so she could help her daughter with the sick ones. Zaroug Khatoun also asked me to send word to Feridoon. I did send word with someone escaping the city with his family, but was not sure how the Feridoon people could help us."

Seeing me weeping, Mr. Ashod stopped. I wiped my tears and gestured to him to continue.

"Anoosh and the twins lost their battle against the cursed epidemic within one week. I buried them too, Vartan, and may God have mercy on me. Zaroug Khatoun insisted on coming to the cemetery with the priest. I can tell you she shed heartfelt tears but in dignified silence. The next day, when I went to your house at the usual time to see if they needed anything in the way of food, I discovered Zaroug Khatoun had fallen prey to the epidemic. Her mother, poor old lady, who is alive and well, was trying to look after her as best as she could, but Zaroug Khatoun succumbed to the illness. I arranged her burial – she lies peacefully next to the others, Vartan. The day before she passed away, I went to the house and was talking to her old mother when I heard sounds coming from the bedroom. Her mother said she wanted to see me. I went in and there she was lying in bed, drenched in sweat and haggard. In her dignified manner she said: 'Mr. Ashod, please tell Krikor to forgive me. I did everything to save the family but couldn't.' I promised her I would, Vartan, but how can I tell your uncle this and still look him in the eye when I couldn't save your family either."

In tears, I said, "Do not be concerned about it Mr. Ashod. I will recount everything to my uncle when the time is right. You have done enough. You're a good and kind man, Mr. Ashod, and I shall be forever indebted to you."

The epidemic had disappeared within a month, almost as quickly as it had appeared, leaving my uncle and I without our families.

My uncle's condition deteriorated over the next few days. He was lucid one moment and delirious or semi-conscious the next – a condition I almost envied since I thought it spared him the pain of the loss I was enduring.

Dr. Arshagunian finally appeared one morning and, after having checked my uncle's arm and condition, took me and Minas aside and whispered that my uncle's whole arm would have to be amputated without delay if his life was to be saved.

"You'll need to move him to my practice. I prefer to have all the required medical instruments and medication close at hand," he said as he was leaving. We decided then that we would move him to Dr. Arshagunian's clinic very early the next morning. Minas immediately went out to ask friends to assist us.

I stayed in the room watching over my uncle. It was quiet and no sounds could be heard from Minas' household. I sat there, breaking into silent sobbing, for how many hours I cannot recall, until I noticed my uncle move his head. He was trying to get up. I hastened to his side and asked if he needed anything.

"Don't let them amputate the arm of a man who has already lost everything," he said, and then he pleaded with me over and over again, "Take me home."

The next morning my uncle and I were in our own home. Minas helped me set up a bed in the front room for my uncle and said he would come by every day at lunchtime to administer the pain-killing medication to my uncle and to bring the food his wife prepared for us. As soon as

Minas left, I busied myself with my uncle, not daring to go anywhere near the back of the house where my little house stood. Feelings of anger surged in me, followed by feelings of sadness and despair. At dusk, when my uncle had finally fallen asleep, I felt the urge to go to the little house I had built for Anoosh and Mariam. As I crossed the yard, I imagined Zaroug Khatoun sitting there weaving and the twins giggling. Their dowry embroideries would be of no use now – they would never be brides...

I entered my little house. I saw Anoosh's hair comb on a table and touched it tenderly. And then it hit me – there it was – Mariam's tiny dress. I held it up to my face and sobbed and sobbed until I couldn't bear to be there anymore.

As I ran back to my uncle's house, I thought of taking my own life...

My uncle woke up several times during that night. I could hear his groans over and over again as I fell in and out of sleep in an armchair next to his bed. Near daybreak, he tried to force himself to sit up in bed and nearly succeeded.

"Have you visited them?" he said suddenly.

"Yes, uncle, they're lying peacefully next to each other."

"Then promise you'll build them their tombstones."

I nodded and promised.

He then asked me to come closer. He grabbed my arm tightly with his right arm and looked at me fiercely: "Don't you dare think about what you're thinking. You must live for us, you must live for our people and for our next generation, you must live, my boy," he said and his head fell back on the pillow.

My beloved uncle left this world shortly after uttering these words and without seeing the sun go up that day; and on that day, I became an orphan once again.

"Stop doing this to yourself. You haven't shaved or cut your hair in months and you've lost half your weight. My wife keeps on complaining that most of the food she cooks for you is untouched. How many months has this been going on? Mr. Ashod and I are very worried about you. For Christ's sake, this must stop. Vartan, my friend, you said you promised your uncle to build the tombstones and you haven't even done that!"

These were more or less the same words I'd been hearing from Minas every day for God knows how long. Then he handed me a letter – "Mr. Ashod asked me to give it to you. It's from your clergyman friend."

Echmiadzin, September 26, 1823

My Dearest Brother Vartan,

I have today heard, from a vartabed who has just arrived from Isfahan, of the tragic passing of your young bride and child and of that of your uncle and his family. I am truly sorry for your loss and pray God for His mercy so their souls may be illuminated in Heavenly Jerusalem.

I pray for you and me too. As in the card games we used to play in secret at the monastery school, we are not always dealt the right cards, my

Vartan. I learned this at a very young age when I lost both my parents and became an orphan. This was not easy to bear, nor was my uncle's indifference. I must confess, I thought of taking my own life on many occasions even though I was only a teenager then. I am certain you have been experiencing similar feelings of despair since the tragic loss of your family.

But, dear Vartan, it was my faith in our Saviour and your friendship that saved me from such foolishness. You treated me like your own brother, and for your dear departed mother, I was a son. Thus, I dwell no longer on my lost childhood but on the good that I was offered. You offered me a place where I belonged – Erzerum.

You must be wondering why I'm writing to you from Echmiadzin, where our holiest cathedral stands. This is my last pilgrimage as a layman – for although I've been at the seminary for so many years, I am still one. I shall be ordained a vartabed next month and will soon afterwards be assisting Father Sahag in running the school in Erzerum. The school has an additional building now, next door to the existing one, and there will be a larger number of admissions, including female pupils. I volunteered and the current abbot at the monastery did not object, telling everyone that I was to serve my own Erzerum community. You cannot imagine the extent of pride I felt to be associated with serving and educating the young ones in Erzerum.

Which brings me to the point of asking you – what will you do now, Vartan? Will you follow in your loving uncle's footsteps? Will you continue, as I've heard, offering your talent as an Armenian calligrapher, bringing both joy and consolation to people? Will you stand tall as an Armenian in this world?

Write to me.

Your Little Arakel

To tell the truth, nothing was as powerful as Little Arakel's words in bringing me to my senses, and his letter, neatly folded, is kept in my Bible to this day. No other person's words could touch or console me like Little Arakel's. It was then I realised how patient Mr. Ashod and Minas had been with me. They had offered me their friendship but were only rewarded with ingratitude on my part.

When Mr. Ashod and Minas turned up the next morning, which was a Sunday, they were shocked to see my hair cut and my beard shaved.

"Mr. Ashod, I'm coming to pay you a visit tomorrow morning to sort out the paperwork that I've neglected for so long," I said.

"I thought you'd given up on the business. How long has it been? Over a year now? Empty offices can make one very lonely," he said with a smile.

"Let's head for the cemetery after Sunday service. We need to start on the tombstones," I said earnestly, and then, I am almost certain, I heard Minas' sigh of relief and his murmured 'Amen'.

CHAPTER 13

⚜

ENDLESS WEEKS OF PAPERWORK WITH Mr. Ashod consumed all my time and energy, but I welcomed it. Putting order into my uncle's business was a priority if I were to clarify my financial status and continue trading.

"All's done! The books are up-to-date and the business is in a healthy state with no debts to pay," declared Mr. Ashod, and added, "What's your next move?"

"There's one important matter we haven't tackled yet – the partnership with Khoja Shahmir. I have no intention of working with Markar now that his father is no longer with us. I want the partnership dissolved. I would like you to set up a meeting with Armenag, the lawyer. He will be able to explain the details of such an undertaking," I said.

"But dissolving the partnership could be very costly, especially with someone like Markar as the only heir to Khoja Shahmir's fortune," Mr. Ashod said with a worried face.

"Frankly, I don't care how much it costs. I have no wish to be associated with Markar a minute longer than necessary."

It thus came to light that my uncle's partnership with Khoja Shahmir was based on mutual trust and no matter who put whatever money into the business, upon the death of either, or if the partnership were to be dissolved for any reason, the business was to be split equally or 'fifty-fifty' as they say in the business. That suited me fine but Mr. Ashod kept on grumbling about Markar having drawn large sums of money, albeit his father's, from the business on a regular basis since the death of his father. He also complained that Markar only came to the premises to collect the money and hadn't done a day's work or even lifted a finger since his father's death.

"Never mind, Mr. Ashod – do not worry yourself too much. We'll sort this out soon. In any case, I prefer not seeing his face here on a daily basis. Don't you?" I said.

Our entire communication with Markar was done through Armenag, the lawyer, who reassured me that all was going well and said he had arranged a meeting with Markar for the final settlement and the signing of legal papers.

On the set date, as was customary, each of us had to produce two witnesses for the official signing of papers. We gathered in what had been Khoja Shahmir's office. Present were Minas and Mr. Ashod, who were my two witnesses, and Armenag and his assistant. Markar arrived half an hour late to the meeting, as we had expected. He was flanked by two of his henchmen – burly, unsavoury characters, unknown to our circle of merchants.

Markar sat down at his father's desk with the usual smirk on his face. He did this with an insouciance that betrayed him. He truly believed that he owned the entire premises. His two burley witnesses took up position, standing upright behind him as if he were their master. Without addressing anyone else, Markar looked me straight in the face and said:

"I object to the terms of this settlement. I am entitled to 15% of the partnership on top of my father's 50% share. It was agreed between your uncle and my father. That means I own 65% of the stakes now, my friend."

He then got up and headed towards the door. I stood up, and turning towards him, said he was lying. He looked at me intensely again and shook his head.

"Then prove it with the necessary legal documentation. And don't ever again call me your friend," I retorted.

His face changed, taking on a frenzied look. He lunged forward suddenly, grabbing me by the collar.

"Are you threatening me?" he shouted, and the next thing I knew his thick fingers were squeezing my neck in an attempt to strangle me.

I instinctively punched him in the ribs as hard as I could; he let go of my neck, startled. The others intervened to put an end to the fight. Minas and Mr. Ashod grabbed me by the arms to restrain me, and Markar's henchmen, who were clearly surprised at the turn of events, tried to push him out the door. They finally managed to get him out of the premises but we could all hear Markar shouting: "How dare you! I will break every bone in your body, you bastard!"

After I had calmed down, Armenag said, "This will not do. I didn't expect this from Markar. He's a madman. He didn't mention this 15% issue to me before. If he really had a legal document, he would have produced it by now. My advice is that we approach the Armenian Merchants' Association in Isfahan immediately to settle this before things get out of hand."

"Do what you think is necessary," I said, my head still throbbing with anger.

⚜

One evening, barely two weeks after the incident, I was sitting at my uncle's desk arranging my papers. Mr. Ashod and Minas, who had been helping me with orders, had just left. I was almost ready to leave myself when I heard a strange tapping noise. I came out of the office and to my surprise found the main door of our premises ajar. I sensed something was wrong. I turned around and saw him – a bearded, stocky man in ragged clothes brandishing a shiny dagger. I instantly knew he had come for me. I didn't have my dagger on me but I thought, if he's going to kill me, I won't make it easy for him.

The man readied himself to charge and I tensed myself to counter-attack with my arms and clenched fists. The man approached me stealthily, swinging his dagger. I ducked. Then I heard footsteps – men rushing through the door. For a split second I thought they were the man's accomplices coming to finish me off. Then I recognised them – three young members of the Armenian Merchants' Association. Before the man could swing his dagger a second time, the three were upon him. He struggled to escape but to no avail; he was pinned down. I grabbed the dagger from his hand.

"Who sent you?" I demanded.

"We know Markar did," a breathless voice said. It was Minas'. Mr. Ashod was right behind him, trying to catch his breath, too. They had come across the three young men as they were on their way to save me and had warned them about what was happening.

"We need to take him to the Association's headquarters. Those are our orders," one of the young Armenians said.

102

Mr. Ashod, with a long sigh of relief, said, "We're all coming with you."

⚜

The bearded man who had tried to kill me turned out to be a common criminal from a low-life area of Isfahan. The governing committee of the Armenian Merchants' Association interrogated him and discovered he had been paid by Markar to kill me. He was also instructed to steal anything he could grab from our premises in order to make it look like it was a burglary, thereby quelling any suspicion of premeditated murder. The only way the committee was able to extract this information from the criminal was by promising him they would not turn him over to the authorities if he cooperated. He, nevertheless, also had to put his thumbprint signature on a written statement incriminating Markar.

"Why are they letting him go?" demanded Mr. Ashod and Minas in unison just as I came out of my meeting with the head of the governing committee, Khoja Asadur Asadurian, the doyen of all Armenian merchants in Isfahan.

"Let me tell you everything," I said, proceeding to tell them the whole story:

"A couple of days ago, one of Markar's burly henchmen was in a tea house in a part of Isfahan far away from New Julfa. He was overheard boasting to someone that his patron had arranged to assassinate an Armenian merchant with whom he'd had a brawl. The Persian man who overheard him knew he worked for Markar and immediately went to see Khoja Asadur with the news. Khoja Asadur, who had knowledge of my brawl with Markar from our lawyer, promptly convened a meeting of the members of the governing committee. As this was a case of life and death, they decided to intervene. They sent the three young men who saved my life to find Markar's henchman. The three finally caught him early this morning as he was leaving a brothel. They brought him to the Association's quarters, but the man denied everything and would not talk. By this evening, he was worn down by questioning and afraid of being taken to the authorities, so he himself proposed to betray his patron if the Association offered him a sum of money. The money was brought to him and he began to talk: how the plot was hatched, when and where I was to be assassinated, and in what manner. But he didn't know who the assassin was. 'You still have time to save the man' he said before he too was asked to sign a statement incriminating Markar. It was, thus, a matter of luck and providence that the three young Armenian merchants were able, in the nick of time, to save me from certain death."

"Praise the Lord!" cried Mr. Ashod.

"While the three young men were on their way to save me, Khoja Asadur had been quick to react and had asked two members of the governing committee to fetch Markar to the Association's quarters with the pretext of an important meeting that required his presence. Markar had no inkling that the Association knew about his murder plot, so he gladly turned up at the Association's quarters. The governing committee then questioned him about the plot. He flatly denied it and got up to leave but was stopped in his tracks when Khoja Asadur produced the incriminating statements of both his henchman and the criminal and threatened to hand him over to the authorities if he did not cooperate with the Association. At this point, Markar broke down and cried like a child, asking for mercy and forgiveness. Khoja Asadur said this only compounded the contempt felt by all the members of the governing committee towards Markar. 'We do not wish to hand over one of our own to the Persian authorities. And, because we all esteemed your late father, we will not do so. But we do not think you belong with us. We have decided there is no place for you here amongst us in Isfahan. You have only brought shame upon our association and community. We will arrange for you to leave this country and settle elsewhere. It is your choice. Leave or spend the rest of your life in jail,' Khoja Asadur told him."

"And how did Markar respond to that?" asked Minas.

"He barked defiantly, 'And what of my father's stake in the company? With what money do you propose I settle elsewhere?' Khoja Asadur responded sternly and said, 'You were willing to have Vartan killed out of greed. You thought you would be able to take over everything after his death, especially now that he has no family and no heirs. It is now up to Vartan. If he is willing to give you your father's share of the partnership, it is his choice. If he does not, we will not oppose it and will back him legally on that point and not spare any effort to do so. After all, do you have the right to expect a settlement from a man you tried to assassinate?' This was the end of the conversation and Markar was completely disarmed."

"Markar is still here then?" Minas asked.

"Yes, he's in one of the rooms upstairs," I said.

"Well, what have you decided about his share?" Mr. Ashod inquired.

"Khoja Asadur asked me the same question and I told him I had high regard for Markar's late father. Khoja Shahmir had been a trustworthy man and my uncle's loyal partner. For his sake, I was willing to give Markar his share of the partnership. But most of all, I told Khoja Asadur, my Christian conscience would not allow me to keep money that was not rightfully my own even if it were my enemy's."

"Well said!" Mr. Ashod nodded.

"Let's get out of here. It's getting very late and you're not sleeping in your house on your own. You need a good night's sleep after today's ordeal. You're staying with me until this man is out of Isfahan for good," said Minas firmly.

⚜

"How are we going to get the money together in such a short time to pay that criminal?" Mr. Ashod asked the following morning.

"Stop worrying, Mr. Ashod. We have a new partner – Minas. He is investing some of his savings. It's not as much as we need, but I'm certain Khoja Asadur will assist us in finding the rest of the required money quickly. The Association will be happy to see the back of Markar."

"I'm glad to hear that. I do like Minas a great deal and can say I have great confidence in his ability to fit in with our business."

That was something I, too, had noticed. Lately, Minas had been helping Mr. Ashod and me with our paperwork and he did everything we asked him to efficiently. Minas had been there for me since I had come back to Isfahan and had always looked out for me. Our friendship was now solidly based on trust and, regardless of the attempt on my life, I had already been thinking of asking him to be my partner in the business. I knew he did not have the grand means of Khoja Shahmir, but that didn't matter to me. He came from a modest background and had diligently put money aside after every trip he'd made to India and beyond. Being of a cautious nature, he did not trust people too readily and was hesitant to embark on a business venture with someone he didn't know well. There was another matter, something that had kept him in Isfahan since our return. Having lost his only son to the epidemic, he felt the burden of guilt for having left him and his wife on their own, although he did not say this in so many words.

When I had gone to his house the previous night and was discussing the payment to Markar, he proposed the partnership himself and said he was willing to invest all his savings in order to solve the issue of the payment. I told him I would be honoured if he became my partner but dissuaded him from investing all his savings.

"I'll manage to find the rest through the Association," I said, and we shook hands and gave our word of honour to support and be true to one another.

"No, no, there is no need for collateral – certainly not your house," Khoja Asadur said and then added, "The Association will cover the rest of the money on condition you pay us back the sum within one year. After all, this is the whole point of the existence of the Association. It's merchants helping one another."

Khoja Asadur, who was a man of considerable clout and respected both within the Armenian community of Isfahan and by the Persian authorities, single-handedly arranged the departure of Markar. This happened on the third morning after the attempt on my life.

Khoja Asadur obtained travel documents for Markar in record time, arranged the payment of the rest of the money, and found two volunteer Armenian merchants willing to accompany Markar all the way to Russia, from where he'd always wanted to run his business. Markar was told that if he ever showed his face in Isfahan again, the Persian authorities would immediately be notified.

"Good riddance," said Mr. Ashod when he learned of Markar's departure.

"We must celebrate!" said Minas and added, "My friend, may God keep you safe always."

That night, I went home and slept as soundly as an infant secure in his mother's arms, relieved Markar was finally out of my life. But how wrong I proved to be!

CHAPTER 14

OVER THE NEXT FEW MONTHS I tried to raise as much cash as possible to re-start the business my uncle had left me and to clear the debt to the Association. I quickly sold a large plot of land at the edge of town that my uncle had bought years ago. A large part of the money went towards paying my debt. The remainder was crucial for the business and I thought that it would be enough to cover the day-to-day expenses and procurement of goods for well over a year. With Minas' and Mr. Ashod's help, we were getting regular orders for goods to be shipped to Constantinople and from there on to Venice and Genoa. But I soon realised that this type of trading was not going to sustain us in the long term and one of us had to resume journeying to India, and further east.

And I knew that it would have to be me rather than Minas. After all, I had no family responsibilities in Isfahan any longer. But I didn't quite have the vision of how to go about things, how to plan the journeys, and with whom to associate in business. I felt sad that my uncle was not with me to guide me. I was at a loss about what to do next. Three successive events, all occurring on the same day, helped me make up my mind.

It was a Sunday morning. I was readying myself for church when I heard a knock on the door. My eyes filled with tears of joy when I opened the door. It was Melkon Khan, the owner of the *Anahid*. We embraced and Melkon Khan expressed his deep sorrow at my uncle's passing.

"So what brings you to Isfahan?" I asked.

"I have given myself a month in Isfahan. I haven't been here in years and I thought I might be able to see some of my kin one last time before I depart this world. I'm not getting any younger, you know," he laughed.

"Have you news of the *Anahid*?" I asked.

"Oh, she's my old princess and as strong as ever. She was properly spruced up after that unfortunate pirate attack. She's docked at Bandar Abbas, and Maam and Bab are guarding her until my return," he said.

"I'm planning on resuming the journeys, such as I undertook with my uncle to India. Can I accompany you when you leave Isfahan? Will you take me to India?"

"Certainly, young man, you're always welcome aboard the *Anahid*. We'll be heading directly to Madras – my usual port of call," he said with a smile, and then added, "Oh, before I forget, I have a letter for you from Lesley, your English friend."

After we agreed on the date of travel to Bandar Abbas, Melkon Khan took his leave and I sat down to read Lesley's letter.

Madras, September 29, 1823

My Dearest Friend Vartan,

I write to express my condolences on the tragic loss of your beloved young wife and child, and larger-than-life uncle. I heard the terrible news of their passing from Melkon Khan, and I so wished I could be near you to comfort you. Words cannot express the sorrow I feel for you. I cannot but think that such a tragedy can only be overcome by your faith in our Lord, and with the love and support your friends can bring you.

I have missed you, my friend. I have missed our conversations and trips, even our meals together. It has been over a year and a half since I last saw you. Are you not planning a journey to Madras?

I have had my share of tragedy here, too. My father passed away a year ago of a sudden heart attack. I went through a period of great sadness, feeling all alone in this vast world the day he was buried.

The last six months have been a time of struggle to collect debts that were owed my father. I have now got enough capital and a load of precious stones left by my father and can start a new business in Madras. But I am looking for an associate. Will you be my partner? Let's start something new, afresh. I am hopeful that there is a brighter future out there for us both.

Your loving friend,

Lesley

Lesley's words brought much comfort to me, and I agreed with him – there must be a brighter future somewhere for us. The thought of a partnership with him planted seeds of excitement in me. A new adventure was beckoning. I was sitting there, dazed, imagining a new life for myself when I suddenly realised I had missed Sunday mass. I picked myself up and headed towards the cemetery, as I always did on Sunday after mass to visit my loved ones.

The Armenian cemetery of Isfahan stood at the edge of New Julfa, on a vast corner piece of land. Huge oak trees shaded its entrance. I walked past very old monumental Armenian *khachkar* (stone-carved cross) tombstones of notables of the community, which flanked the pathway, towards the left part of the cemetery where our family plot was located. The plot was shaded by nearby trees and I felt the cool autumn breeze on my face. Like every Sunday, in front of every tombstone that I had had erected, I stopped and said my prayers. As was my uncle's wish, the calligraphic epitaphs on the tombstones were mine. I had written them in tears and given them to the stonemason so he could reproduce them in carving.

The first tombstone was that of my daughter Mariam and my beloved wife, Anoosh; they were buried side by side: *The pure shall inherit the Kingdom of Heaven.* I had written this since I believed Anoosh and Mariam were as pure as the Virgin and her child. The next tombstone was that of the twins. Their tombstone read: *Named after Hripsime and Kayane and lived as innocently as our first female martyrs.* The third tombstone was that of Zaroug Khatoun. It said: *Loving wife and mother.* I had had a carving of a carpet comb and a spindle added on one side of the tombstone. I had thought she would have appreciated it since weaving had been her only passion in life apart from her family. The fourth tomb was my uncle's. His epitaph was thus: *Loving husband, father, and uncle. Descendant of Erzerum Armenians, adopted son of the people of New Julfa, merchant of the World.*

After saying four prayers, I stood in front of my uncle's tomb for a long time, lost in thought, until I noticed Minas coming towards me with a big smile. I knew he came to visit his son's tomb often but was not sure why he expressed such happiness in a sad location. When he got closer, he opened his arms and hugged me.

"You seem jolly," I said, somewhat disconcertedly.

"My wife is with child. And you're the first person I'm telling the good news to," he said with enthusiasm and joy. "But I've got to run; she's waiting for me." And he was away before I could congratulate him properly.

I remained standing in front of my uncle's tomb for a while longer. I couldn't see any other visitors around. Silence reigned. And then I thought I heard my uncle's voice: "Live for us" and then again "Don't look back."

"What do you mean? Selling the house? Have you gone mad? What's this nonsense about a branch of the company?"

"Calm down, Mr. Ashod. Perhaps I was not very clear. Let me explain. I am selling my uncle's house and my little house at the back of his in order to raise the money I need to leave for Madras to start a new business there."

"And where are you going to live when you come back?"

"He will always have a house here. My house is his," Minas interjected.

"Yes, thank you, Minas. Mr. Ashod, I will go into partnership with my English friend, Lesley, in Madras. It will be a new trading company with a new name. Our business here will be a branch of that new company. Minas is ready to head this branch for me. As you very well know, he doesn't wish to journey to India anymore. His wife is expecting a baby and he'd rather stay in Isfahan." Minas nodded.

"Yes, I gathered that much. Go on."

"You will help Minas to run the new company's branch in Isfahan. I will procure whatever goods you have orders for and send them to you from India and beyond, and you, in turn, can provide goods from this part of the world when I have orders for them."

"But what's wrong with keeping the business as it is. Our merchants have traded with one another for the last two hundred years. This branch thing is a new idea that I don't understand."

"Mr. Ashod, there is nothing wrong with trading and creating trade links with other merchants. The branch idea is a new strategy. The cost of transporting the goods will remain the same. But the new strategy will allow us to save on procurement costs through by-passing the middlemen. It will allow me to buy the goods directly at source and will eliminate the waste of time and effort on journeys to and from India. Another advantage is that Lesley and I could also trade in that part of the world – from India to Macassar, and beyond."

"I've been a book-keeper for over 30 years and know a thing or two about keeping costs down. So I understand what your aim is. But surely this strategy of yours means you'll be leaving Isfahan for good," said Mr. Ashod and started shaking his head.

"That is correct Mr. Ashod. I will be based in Madras, like many other countrymen of ours. I haven't got many other choices."

"We were forced into exile over two hundred years ago, settled here and built our lives in New Julfa. And now many of our young and able people are leaving for other parts of the world where they will build new lives for themselves – still away from their homeland," Mr. Ashod said in a tone that betrayed defeat.

"That is the tragic lot of Armenians, Mr. Ashod," I said, placing my hand on his shoulder to console him.

My uncle's house and my own were sold together a week before I left Isfahan. Most of the furniture was sold prior to the sale. Whatever remained was given away. I sent Anoosh's and Zaroug Khatoun's personal belongings, the carpets, embroideries, and jewellery to Feridoon where Zaroug Khatoun's mother now resided.

I moved to Minas' house during those last days in Isfahan. Both he and Mr. Ashod were sad to see me go. I was sad, too, to be leaving them and Isfahan and my loved ones' graves behind. But I knew I had no choice but to find a way to carry my life forward and be useful to both of them at the same time.

A few days before my departure with Melkon Khan, a messenger from Khoja Asadur appeared at Minas' house one early morning to say that I was expected at the Armenian Merchant Association's quarters that evening. When I turned up at the requested time, all the members of the governing committee were present and welcomed me warmly. Khoja Asadur initiated the conversation by saying that all the members appreciated the way I had dealt with the issue of Markar and the promptness with which I'd repaid the loan. He assured me that Markar was indeed in Russia and the word from Armenian merchants returning from there was that Markar had had no qualms about leaving Isfahan and no regrets for having been banished from the city. He was in the process of starting up a business venture with a minor Russian nobleman.

I, in turn, thanked all the members for their far-sightedness and the way they had handled the Markar problem. I also explained to them my plans for settling in Madras and keeping a branch of the business in Isfahan. They all listened and nodded approvingly.

"Your late uncle, whom we all esteemed, was known to all of us as Khoja Krikor of Erzerum. All the members of the governing committee are convinced that you deserve to inherit your uncle's title of 'khoja' as a sign that we all appreciate your presence amongst us. We will assist you in any way we can and expect the same from you wherever you are in the world. However, there is one thing we would like you to clarify for us. We are not certain how you wish to be formally addressed," Khoja Asadur said.

"I am greatly honoured. My uncle was very dear to me and I humbly accept his title which your esteemed association now wishes to confer upon me. Permit me to say that although I myself am a native of Erzerum and am proud of my origins, I had to leave my birthplace at the tender age of sixteen. And although I had a new, happy life in Isfahan, I have to now leave it, too. My destiny is like the destiny of our people – constantly in exile. Thus, I would like to take the surname of Bantukhtian," I concluded.

"We are honoured to welcome you into our fold as one of our equal merchant brothers," Khoja Asadur said and shaking my hand added, "From this day forward, you will be known to all us merchants as Khoja Vartan Bantukhtian."

"I can't believe they honoured you in such a grand manner," Mr. Ashod said. "I'm proud for you. Well done!"

"It's thanks to both of you and the Association that I'm still alive and well," I said.

"It's time to celebrate!" Minas shouted. "Wine and barbecued meat are in order!"

And that night, the three of us had the happiest meal we'd had in ages. That meal lasted for hours and was laced with lively conversation and laughter.

That happy meal became a bittersweet memory the moment I left Isfahan, and thus it has remained all these years.

CHAPTER 15

⚜

I WAS HAPPY TO EMBARK on the *Anahid* in Bandar Abbas. I felt safe in her welcoming arms. She looked in better shape than she ever had, with freshly painted hull and top sides, and new sails, all of which Melkon Khan proudly pointed out to me. Bab and Maam had not changed a bit, and I was grateful to them all for sharing their meals with me. This journey to Madras was different from the previous journeys I had undertaken in that there were no other travelling companions on board – only crewmen.

"I brought some goods from Madras destined for Shiraz, but have little now from Isfahan for the journey back," said Melkon Khan. "The demand for my services from the merchants of Isfahan is getting thinner these days. Not as many of them are travelling back and forth like they used to. I guess the old days are gone. Things are changing fast, I tell you," he concluded philosophically.

Not having other merchant companions around suited me well on this journey as it gave me the space to concentrate on planning my next moves. The idea of a new partnership with Lesley gave me the encouragement I needed. Every morning I would prepare my quill and portable ink set and, finding a quiet spot in some corner of the *Anahid*, I would scribble down notes in a small notebook. It was at this time that

I thought of writing to Little Arakel; I had been meaning to do so since taking the decision to leave Isfahan.

My letter was short, detailing the essentials of my new business plans and expressing my excitement about a new future in Madras. I told him we were both embarking on new lives. Upon ordination, he was to have a new name, the new title of *vartabed*, and a new clergyman's attire. I, too, had taken on a new name and title. As for the attire, I was almost certain I would not be wearing my Isfahan pantaloons and pointed shoes for much longer.

"Atkinson and Vartan Trading Company – that sounds good. My surname is too long and too difficult to pronounce," I said to Lesley jokingly.

I had met with Lesley less than an hour after disembarking at Madras. His first words to me were:

"I somehow knew you were coming. I just felt it in my bones last week. So I found new lodgings for us to share. It's a spacious house with a garden at the back. I'm certain you will like it."

Thus began my new life in Madras, and a new year – I was 24 years old.

Lesley had rented business premises next-door to his father's old place. It was not large but we both thought it adequate. We soon found an Indian book-keeper named Joseph and an office clerk whom Lesley employed mainly out of loyalty since he had worked for his father for many years.

Our house was very comfortable and we both enjoyed the balmy nights of Madras, sitting in the garden sipping tea. The house came with a resident Indian houseboy. Ram was only 17 years old but there was practically nothing he couldn't do around the house, including cooking a number of Armenian dishes which he had learnt from the wife of the Armenian engineer who had previously resided in the house.

Living in this house pleased me no end as it was located only two blocks away from the Armenian Church which it was my habit to visit regularly on Sundays.

"I've decided to adopt European clothing," I said to Lesley one evening.

"Why? Aren't you happy with your Persian attire, especially in the heat of Madras?"

"I feel my heavy headdress is too uncomfortable in the humidity of Madras. My long robe and pantaloons are too cumbersome in the narrow alleyways and my soft pointed shoes are too dainty for the sometimes muddy streets. Besides, most Armenian merchants here are now wearing European clothing – and even some of the Chinese traders in Penang, too. Do you remember?"

Soon I was decked out in cream-coloured trousers, a brown lightweight coat and sturdy leather shoes with square toes. The one item I had trouble getting used to for a long time was the top hat that Lesley offered me to complete my outfit.

"You look exactly like a fashionable young Englishman!" Lesley said every time I put the hat on, and he would then continue with a litany of comments about my looks just to pull my leg and give us a good laugh.

"I'm afraid there's bad news from Burma. War has broken out between the English and the Burmese. Many lives have been lost on both sides they say." Lesley was speaking in that high-pitched voice he had every time he was worried or anxious.

"That is terrible news for us, my friend. Weren't we expecting a shipment of rubies from Sarkis?" I said.

"Yes, I'll try to find out if the shipment has already left Burma. I'll have to check with the vessel company's manager tomorrow morning."

When I returned to Persia almost two years ago, Lesley had already left for Burma. It was his second trip to that country and he was confident enough to contact the Armenian merchant, Sarkis Manuk. He was the younger brother of Gevork and Takoohy Manuk that we'd met in Batavia and who had advised Lesley to get in touch with their brother next time he was in Burma. Lesley told me that Sarkis made such a positive impression on him with his flair and apparent influence on the merchant milieu that he didn't want to seek anyone else to associate himself with in Burma. Thus, since starting our new business in Madras, Sarkis had been supplying us with good quality rubies and had done so in a very competent and correct manner.

"We've done very well with the sale of rubies, so we should not worry too much if this last batch fails to reach us. God will open new doors for us. Just this morning I got word from Minas in Isfahan that he was able to procure the emeralds from Persia and the chalcedony from Constantinople that we had ordered," I said.

"Frankly, Vartan, I'm not really concerned about the rubies. I'm worried about the safety of Sarkis and his family. Wars are ugly events," Lesley said. "I hope you'll have the opportunity to meet Sarkis one day. I'm sure you'll appreciate him as much as I do," he added.

❧

Two months later, we received our order of rubies. They arrived on a vessel from Penang with a letter in English from Sarkis. Lesley read the letter aloud. In it, Sarkis said that he was able to escape Ava with his family to Rangoon at the start of the hostilities and that the English had allowed him to board an English vessel bound for Penang.

"Well, I thank God he and his family are safe and sound. He's a man of great talent. Apart from Armenian, he speaks Dutch and Malay like a native. Being the youngest of the Manuk family, he was born in Batavia. He also speaks fluent Burmese. He's been based in Burma for over ten years and his English, as you can see, is impeccable, too. I'm sure he charmed his way through with the English officers in Rangoon to get on that English ship bound for Penang. No doubt about it, he's a smart man," Lesley concluded.

"I can imagine. He's the brother of none other than the regal Takoohy of Java," I said.

"Indeed, the Armenian queen of Batavia!" Lesley said with a grin on his face. "Let's mark this happy occasion. I invite you to an early supper at the Parsi eatery that has just opened."

"Hang on," I said. "Didn't you tell me you were taking Ms. Whittaker to a late afternoon tea at the English Inn?"

"Oh, bugger! I completely forgot about that. Will you do me a favour, Vartan? Will you come with me? She will be chaperoned by Ms. Smith and I can't stand being on my own with those two English ladies."

I could not refuse Lesley and went along to meet the ladies. Ms. Jane Whittaker was 19 years old. She had beautiful auburn hair, green eyes, and a very fair complexion, with freckles on her face and forehead. She was the daughter of Mr. James Whittaker, one of the wealthiest English merchants in Madras. She was always accompanied by Ms. Smith, her tutor, the Christian name of whom I do not recall. Although probably in her late 20's, Ms. Smith looked a lot older, possibly because of her plain looks.

The minute she set eyes on Lesley, Ms. Whittaker turned into a lively creature and would not stop asking him questions to attract his constant attention. Lesley answered her politely but averted his gaze; I do not think their eyes ever met. Whenever Ms. Whittaker got tired of asking her questions, there were long, awkward pauses. Neither I nor Ms. Smith exchanged a single word. She looked at me with contempt and I didn't dare engage her in conversation.

"Why are you doing this to the poor girl? It's patently clear she is infatuated with you," I said after we'd said farewell to the two ladies.

"I know she is enamoured of me, but I can't reciprocate."

"Then why do you agree to keep on meeting with her? This is the third time, if memory serves me right," I said.

"I guess I'm doing it because my late father would have wanted me to. In actual fact, he wanted me to marry Ms. Whittaker. He told me several times that it would be a good match, her father being so wealthy. I have tried but I can't imagine myself wed to her," Lesley said in a sad tone.

"Then you should stop giving her false hope," I advised him gently.

"You're right. My behaviour is far from being that of a true gentleman," he said, and added with a mischievous smile, "I'm not giving *myself* false hope though. I will find the lady of my dreams one day!"

❧

Almost two years had passed since I settled in Madras and started the partnership with Lesley when suddenly orders coming from existing local clients began to diminish. We had done so well so far, and beyond our expectations, even without Sarkis' rubies, which had stopped coming after he left Burma. We were able to import from Persia woven silk cloth, dried fruit, Arabic amber and emeralds on a regular basis. We used the services of Melkon Khan for this purpose. And on the outward journey from Madras, the *Anahid* carried our spices and tea to Persia. Save for a couple of months of delays because of the terrible earthquake in Shiraz, which fortunately did not affect Isfahan, our association with Minas had worked perfectly well. He wrote several times that the company's branch in Isfahan was in healthy shape and that Mr. Ashod was very satisfied with the results. I was pleased with this news for I knew Minas' family responsibilities had grown. His wife not only gave birth to a healthy boy soon after I left Isfahan, but a year later, a baby girl. The boy was befittingly named 'Asadur' or 'gift of God' and the girl, 'Mariam', in memory of my own daughter, something that made me very proud.

By this time, Lesley and I had welcomed the end of the Anglo-Burmese War. Sarkis had gone back to Burma. He had resumed supplying us with rubies as well as sapphires, a newly discovered precious stone from Siam which was gaining popularity. There was even talk of one of us going to Burma to procure the rubies ourselves. Sarkis had sent word that his business had grown immensely and he would not have the time to do much of our procurement in the future.

But I just couldn't understand why we were not getting the same amount of local client orders. I had kept myself very busy since we started the partnership and perhaps thought I had cocooned myself in the comfort of our business premises for too long. I decided it was time I renewed my contacts with the Armenian merchant community in Madras. Perhaps they had better knowledge of the trading situation.

⚜

"So what have your Armenian merchant brothers been telling you?" Lesley inquired.

"They say business is sluggish in Madras because it's losing its trading position. The East India Company is but a shadow of its former self, they say. They reckon trading is shifting to Penang, to Georgetown more precisely, and this latest place, Singapore, with its brand new harbour."

"Ah, yes, you must recall – established by none other than the great Sir Stamford Raffles," Lesley said and then added, "Maybe we should move to Georgetown."

"Well, if things get any worse, we'll have to leave Madras. We won't have any other option. I quite like the idea of this new Singapore – 'unchartered territory' as they say. I know it's risky but we'd be pioneers in a new trading hub."

"Hmm…Let's give it a few more months and then we'll decide what we should do next," Lesley said, rubbing his chin.

⚜

Over the next few months, our trading didn't get any worse but it didn't get any better either. I noticed Lesley constantly brooding or daydreaming during this period. He often looked sad. I thought he was just worried about the business. But whenever I asked if that was what was bothering him, he would dismiss my question. This behaviour was most unlike him.

One morning I got up very early and was sitting in the back garden of the house, watching Ram sweep the leaves that had fallen off the bushes at the end of the garden, when suddenly I felt Lesley's hand on my shoulder. I looked up into his blood-shot eyes. He looked drawn, as if he hadn't slept all night.

"What's the matter, my friend?" I said. "You haven't been yourself lately."

"I've got something important to tell you."

He sat next to me.

"Go on," I said. "You have my full attention."

"I think I'm in love," he blurted out, "with an Armenian girl."

CHAPTER 16

✦

L<small>ESLEY HAD MET</small> S<small>HOUSHAN</small> L<small>ILLY</small> Apcarian two months earlier when he had gone in to Apcarian and Associates' insurance firm for the settlement of an insurance claim. All he knew about Lilly, as everyone called her, he said, was that she spoke perfect English, was the daughter of Apcar Apcarian, one of the three founding partners of the firm, and that he was by now familiar with her handwriting; this was on a receipt she gave Lesley and which he kept in his pocket like some holy relic.

"Why did you keep it from me all this time?" I said.

"Forgive me, Vartan. Firstly, although it was love at first sight, I had to be sure of my feelings for her before I told anyone. Secondly, I was too embarrassed to talk about my intimate feelings, and thirdly, I was not at all certain how you would react. I know you Armenians don't like to mingle with non-Armenians when it comes to matters of love," he said with a sheepish look.

"Normally I wouldn't approve, but since you're like my brother I would say it's alright by me," I said jokingly and added, "Go on, tell me more."

"Well, I had gone to the firm for an insurance claim and saw a senior clerk who did the paperwork for me and paid me the money. He then asked me to go to an office behind his to collect a receipt from a Ms. Lilly, stating that the money had been paid to me. I don't know why but I was expecting Ms. Lilly to be a mature matron, but lo and behold, the minute I stepped into the office, I couldn't believe how wrong I'd been. Her desk had a carved wooden name-plate – Shoushan Lilly Apcarian – and she was writing at her desk when I entered the room. She didn't quite feel my presence until I was two feet away from her. She cut a fine figure, I tell you – lovely dark shiny hair and milky complexion. I guessed she must be in her early twenties. When she looked up, her huge, dark eyes with long, curved lashes caught mine. I felt like a juggernaut had knocked me over. And that was it. I was hooked!"

I laughed and patted Lesley on the shoulder and said, "It's very unusual for a young lady to be working in an insurance firm, even if it's her father's."

"Yes, that is unusual. I went there again on four different occasions after that first meeting to find out more about her circumstances, to catch a glimpse of her, to find a way of having a conversation with her. One time I used the pretext of wanting to buy insurance. On the three other occasions, I went in to inquire about a number of conditions set forth in the insurance contract. But each time, I had to deal with the senior clerk, not her. Twice I caught a glimpse of her and once I caught her coming out of her office. Our eyes met and deep down I sensed she felt for me, too, for she remembered my name and said she was pleased to see me. 'The pleasure is all mine' I told her. Then someone called out her name, and she excused herself and disappeared into one of the offices. I tell you, my friend, I've been suffering ever since. I'm going out of my mind trying to figure out a way whereby I can have a conversation with her. I've written a whole mountain of poems for her. Perhaps I should simply send them to her?" he concluded.

"Hold your horses, Lesley," I said. "Don't rush into things. You might regret your actions later. Let me find out more about your beloved Lilly from my Armenian acquaintances first."

"I'd be most grateful, my friend," he sighed.

That very same evening, I walked to the inn which served as a regular meeting spot for Armenian men folk, merchants and others alike. It had the advantage of being located in a neighbourhood where most of them resided with their families and was situated at the rear end of the grounds of the Armenian Church. It was to this inn that I'd come when I'd wanted to find out how merchants felt about the trading situation in Madras.

"Khoja Vartan, Khoja Vartan, please come and join us," shouted Avedis, trying to catch my attention and pointing to the empty chair at his table. Avedis was a kinsman of Melkon Khan and I had journeyed twice to Madras with him on the *Anahid*. He was in his early 40's. Sitting next to him was Andon, his closest friend since childhood. The two were inseparable. The third man at their table went by the name of Setrak. I had met him before on numerous occasions and had regularly come across him in the church yard on my way to mass. Setrak, or Seth as he was known by all the merchants of Madras, was a mature fellow. The strange thing about him was that he had the body of a pubescent boy – tiny torso, wiry legs and a small head. But he was the wittiest and funniest man I had ever come across and I always had a good laugh in his company.

"So tell us young man – who told you how to find me here? Was it my sweet baklava maid?"

And seeing my perplexed expression, he chuckled and made us all laugh.

"Hey, I'm only joking. Tell him not to punch me, Avedis. With this tiny body I'd be laid out on this floor like a flat piece of Armenian cured beef."

Seth entertained us for a good ten minutes until he tired and turned to sipping his tea. I thought it was an opportune moment to ask about Apcar Apcarian, for I didn't dare mention his daughter. Adressing Avedis, I said:

"I was thinking of buying insurance for my goods and people have recommended Apcar Apcarian's firm. Is he a trustworthy man? What do you know about him?"

"As far as I know, he has a very good reputation and so does his firm," Avedis said. Andon nodded in agreement.

"Now you ask me, young man. I can tell you Apcarian's 'in and out' as they say in Turkish – his whole life story!" Seth butted in.

"We're dying to hear it. You're such a gossip-monger," Avedis said, teasing him.

Ignoring Avedis, Seth continued.

"Hear this – Apcar Apcarian, who is a native of New Julfa, was one of the wealthiest Armenians in Calcutta. He had a well-established insurance firm there and led a life of plenty. He lived in an opulent residence in a neighbourhood populated by moneyed English merchants. He has no son – only two daughters. Both were born in Calcutta. People say he doted on them and gave them the same education as he would have if they were his male offspring. The girls had an English governess for years, and tutors galore. He was also a generous donor. He was the main benefactor of the Armenian Church and almshouse in Calcutta. Unfortunately, a few years ago a swindler, an Englishman, took him for all he had. Court cases followed, and in essence, Apcarian lost most of his assets. If two of his former associates hadn't come to his rescue, he would have eventually ended up penniless, they say. So, to cut a long story short, he and his two associates decided to move to Madras three years ago and operate from here."

"No one seems to have seen his daughters. They don't attend church service. His wife does though, now and again. If I recall correctly, my wife said she's in poor health," Avedis said.

"My wife says both his daughters, the elder of whom is 23 and the younger, two years her junior, wear European-style clothing and work with their father at the firm. Who's ever heard of such a thing!" Andon said indignantly.

"Watch your words Andon! I know where you're going," Seth retorted. "You're talking about two young Armenian girls whose reputation is irreproachable. For your information, the older one is engaged to one of the associates of Apcarian. You're such an old-fashioned ignoramus, Andon!" Seth said with a grimace expressing his contempt.

"All right, all right," said Andon sheepishly to calm Seth down.

"Look, these are educated girls from Calcutta, not your common-or-garden types from Madras," Seth continued. "And what is wrong with the girls helping their father if they can do the job better than anyone else? Let me explain to you what I mean by that. From what I hear, Apcarian's daughters are as sharp, if not sharper, than you and me. They know the ins and outs of the insurance business like the back of their hands. The older daughter, they say, is the main auditor of the firm's overall accounts, and the younger one supervises all the clerks they employ. I wish only my son were half as intelligent and could help me in my business."

We all could only but agree with Seth.

I left the inn, grateful to Seth for having spared me the effort of asking for specific details about Apcar Apcarian. Lesley was even more grateful when I recounted the story to him, word for word. At the point where I said the older daughter was engaged, his eyes widened and in a matter of seconds, sweat beads formed on his forehead.

"Don't worry, Lilly is definitely the younger one," I said and carried on.

When I'd finished, Lesley said, "This is not going to be easy. From what you're telling me, I gather that the father is very protective of his daughters. I must be certain of Lilly's feelings for me before I make my move."

"The idea of sending her one of the poems you wrote for her is a reasonable one. Give her a couple of days and then go to the firm and ask to see her in person regarding your insurance contract since now you have the knowledge that she supervises all the paperwork. But my advice is don't embark on this if your intentions are not honourable, my friend. It will get you nowhere."

"But my intentions are *very* honourable," Lesley said. "I told you I would find the lady of my dreams!"

Lesley agonized for hours over which poem was more suitable: he broke into soliloquies; recited some of the poems out loud for me; in between, he paced up and down the room without saying a word; shuffled his papers not twice but four or five times. And then he looked at me for help with sad, beseeching eyes.

"I know it's difficult to make a decision, but it is three o'clock in the morning, Lesley," I said with frustration. "Choose the poem that expresses your feelings for Lilly in the simplest way."

"That's it!" Lesley's eyes lit up with relief and then he added, "I don't know what I'd do without you, Vartan." And he finally let me go to bed.

The next morning, Ram, who'd been with us for over two years and whose English was getting better every day, was given a new job – that of messenger. He was instructed to carry the envelope to Apcarian and Associates and deliver it to Ms. Lilly and under no circumstances to anyone else.

"Lilly, Lilly. You got that Ram?" Lesley kept on repeating.

"Leave him be, Lesley. Ram is as stubborn as a mule. I've observed him on many occasions. If he has to do something or if he decides to do something, nothing or no one can stand in his way. He'll deliver your envelope to Lilly," I said. "Forgive me for prying, but did you include a note with the poem?"

"I certainly did! A short one just for her to understand my intentions are honourable and in no way disrespectful of her. I signed the note using my initials, L. A. I hope that's sufficient for her to guess who the author is," Lesley frowned and then added, "I'll go and see her at the firm in two days' time. Do me a favour, Vartan. Pray for me at your church."

I was anxious myself that evening. I had left work early and was waiting at home for Lesley's return from Apcarian and Associates. He eventually showed up and I jumped on him the moment he stepped in, surveying his face.

He gave me a broad smile and said, "I'm the happiest man on earth!"

"Tell me what happened!" I said with impatience.

"I was received by the usual senior clerk upon my arrival. I immediately asked to speak to his superior, Ms. Apcarian. There were a couple of things in the contract I needed to clarify, I said. He was a bit surprised since I had asked him a whole load of questions during my previous visits, but he nevertheless led me to her office. The minute she saw me, her eyes lit up and she got up from her seat, and I tell you, I thought she was beauty personified. 'Thank you, Mr. Francis,' she said taking my papers from the clerk; she invited me to sit down and promptly closed the door behind her. 'Do you have any particular queries, Mr. Atkinson?' she said. I told her my only wish was to sign the contract immediately and in her presence alone. She showed me where to sign, placing her finger elegantly on the precise spot. When I had finished, she said that my papers were all in order and, looking straight into my eyes, added, 'Thank you, Mr. L. A.' I could barely breathe. Our conversation continued:

'You have an Armenian business partner, I understand. You must therefore be familiar with our conservative oriental values,' she said.

I nodded in such a way as to assure her I was perfectly aware of them.

'That doesn't mean I can't appreciate what you write,' she said softly.

'Then you wouldn't mind me sending you more of my poems,' I blurted out.

'So long as they are delivered to me directly,' she said.

'It will be my pleasure to do so – but on one condition,' I responded.

'And what would that be?' she asked.

Plucking up my courage, I said, 'You would have to forward me a return missive.'

She didn't respond in words but gave me a sweet, shy smile.

A knock on the door disturbed us. It was the senior clerk to say Lilly was needed in her father's office. She got up and said, 'I must dash. Please excuse me Mr. Atkinson. And thank you for your confidence in our firm' and left the room like a fluttering butterfly.

My dear friend, I am lost in love for Ms. Lilly Apcarian."

✥

CHAPTER 17

"NOW LOOK HERE, LESLEY. LILLY'S one smart young lady. She's already made inquiries about you and even knows about me. She's also tried to make you aware that it's not going to be easy to have access to her in the way you might have easy access to someone like Ms. Whittaker," I told Lesley.

"I understand perfectly well. But please believe me, I would not hesitate to ask for her hand in marriage this very minute," Lesley said with determination.

"All I'm saying is that we need to come up with a strategy for you to be able to do just that. Remember, you're an Englishman, and I am certain that's not going to go down too well with the protective father. By all means do write to her but not too often and we'll see if she responds. And by the way, don't ever follow her when she's leaving work for her residence. I can assure you she will always be chaperoned and if anyone spots you hovering around her, you might as well kiss our strategy good-bye. In the meantime, give me a couple of weeks and I'll try to find out more about Lilly's father and the best way to approach him for a delicate matter like this," I said.

I immediately set out to learn more about Apcar Apcarian's personality. Everyone I spoke to, discretely and without mentioning my true purpose, said he was a stern man and very protective of his daughters. One person told me about how his older daughter's engagement to his associate was of Apcarian's making as his gratitude to the person who had saved him from ruin was immeasurable. The associate was twenty years older than Apcarian's older daughter, and the man said it was certainly going to be an arranged marriage. Seth corroborated the story, and being very observant and quick-witted, said:

"Don't tell me you're interested in the younger daughter."

And, purposely not waiting for my response in order not to embarrass me, he continued:

"He's a tough guy to deal with. My advice is find one of the Armenian community notables who is close to Apcarian to act as a go-between. Your 'khoja' title and your position in our community in Madras should give you an advantage over others," he concluded.

I then realised how difficult it was going to be for Lesley to ask for Lilly's hand. If it was difficult for an Armenian to approach her father, it would be a lot more difficult for Lesley. And I didn't have the heart to tell him straightaway for I had never before seen Lesley so happy.

Lesley was madly in love. In order not to arouse suspicion, and instead of attempting to see Lilly in person, he sent her letters and poems only every three or four days. Ram would deliver the letter or poem to her at around 10 o'clock in the morning, every time. Lilly would discretely slip a little note into Ram's hand in return. In time, Lesley's and Lilly's love blossomed and I knew there was no turning back for them.

"I'm ruined, finished!" cried Lesley barging into my office.

"What's the matter?" I said with surprise. I'd believed everything was going well with Lilly and he.

"Here, read it," he said, and handed me a short note from Lilly.

"She says Apcarian and Associates are moving to Penang, to Georgetown."

"She's going to take my heart with her. I have to do something right now. I can't lose her, Vartan."

"Calm down, Lesley. We'll have to think this through."

"What can we do?" Lesley said in a high-pitched voice, indicative of his frustration.

"Alright, listen. Before you met Lilly, we discussed the matter of moving the business to somewhere more opportune. If you recall, you said let's give it a few more months. Those months are now over and our trading results are not any better. Now is the time to take the decision. Obviously Apcarian and Associates have come to the same conclusion. I was hoping we could move to this new settlement, Singapore, but if you want to follow Lilly, Georgetown it will have to be."

"I must ask for your forgiveness, Vartan. I have been neglecting the business lately and have been oblivious of our affairs. How long do you reckon we need to finalise things here and move to Georgetown?"

"If we work fast, and you help me out with the bureaucracy, I would say two weeks."

"That's excellent! I'll be at your disposal – totally. I'd rather be in Georgetown, near Lilly, sooner than later."

"We won't be able to set up premises and the like before our arrival in Georgetown as we would have done under normal circumstances, but we'll just have to make all those arrangements when we get there. Come to think of it, when we're settled and you're near your beloved Lilly, I wouldn't mind spending some time in Burma procuring rubies, as Sarkis suggested. And it will be easier to travel to Burma from Georgetown."

"Good idea. I agree," said Lesley, adding, "I've got to do something urgently. I've got to figure out how to tell Lilly of our plans."

The following morning around 10 o'clock, the three of us were standing close by the premises of Apcarian and Associates. The purpose of my being there was to give Lesley cover whilst he sent Ram to Lilly with a note saying he was coming over to see her. Ten minutes later, Ram was back.

"Lady Ma'am Lilly there. She very happy with note," he said with a grin on his face and left us.

As we parted, I said, "I'm going to find us a ship to take us to Georgetown. I'll meet you back at the house around 6 o'clock this evening. Now act with caution. And good luck, my friend!"

That evening, Lesley recounted his meeting.

"I walked straight to the senior clerk's desk and told him I needed to see Ms. Lilly concerning the status of my contract since I had heard the firm was moving to Georgetown. He immediately complied and ushered me into her office. Lilly wasn't at her desk but turned up a few seconds later. She didn't close the door behind her this time but as she slowly walked towards her desk, her eyes didn't leave mine. I had butterflies in my stomach, like I do now just thinking of her. Let me tell you the rest:

'I knew you would come today,' she said almost in a whisper. 'It's my last day at work here. We're leaving for Georgetown next Friday on the *Governor Petrie.*'

'Sweet Lilly, I will follow you to the end of the world,' I said.

'I know,' she said shyly lowering her eyes.

But before I could say anything more, a young lady poked her head through the door and, as if to warn her, said, 'Lilly, father's coming'.

'That's my older sister, Manoushag – Violet in English,' and then, looking towards the door again, she said, 'Father!'

A bald man with a thick moustache and stern face walked in. He was quite tall, a little portly, and was wearing an impeccable set of trousers and coat.

'I was just telling Mr. Atkinson here that he needn't worry about his insurance contract with us. Since we will be keeping a permanent small branch of the firm open in Madras, we will honour our engagements,' Lilly said.

'Will you please excuse Ms. Apcarian,' her father said looking at me. And then, addressing her, he said, 'You have to leave with Violet right now. Your mother needs you at the house to start the packing.'

He then gently grabbed my arm and ushered me out of the room without even giving me the chance to say goodbye to my sweet Lilly.

'Is there anything else I can do for you, Mr. Atkinson?' he said when we were nearing the hallway.

'No, thank you. Everything was clarified by Ms. Apcarian,' I said, adding, 'I'm very pleased to have met you, Mr. Apcarian.'

He seemed slightly surprised for a moment at that declaration but quickly offered me his hand and gave me a strong handshake before I left the premises. He does seem to be a no-nonsense man – tough to deal with, I imagine. I'm just petrified at the thought of asking him for his daughter's hand," Lesley concluded.

I felt this was the right time to tell Lesley everything I had been told about Apcarian.

"Is there anyone here in Madras who can act as a go-between before they leave then? We don't have much time," Lesley inquired.

"I'm afraid not. Not as much as we need to impress Apcarian," I said.

"In that case, I shall sail on the *Governor Petrie*, too, and maybe I can strike up a friendship with Lilly's father during the voyage. That way, I can eventually ask for her hand in marriage directly from her father."

"You will do no such thing," I said. "The whole thing might blow up in your face. It's just too risky. Look, this is what I suggest. We will sail on the *Anahid* to Georgetown. Melkon Khan is here. I saw him this afternoon. He's sailing a week after the *Governor Petrie*. It will take us longer to get to Georgetown but at least we will be able to get there not long after Lilly. Trust me, Lesley, this is the best way. It seems to me you have an ally in her sister. That is important and we have to keep it in mind. But what I'm going to tell you next is what you really want to hear. I know just the right person in Georgetown who can act as our go-between."

Lesley moaned and groaned for not being able to get letters to Lilly during the short period before she left Madras, but as soon as she was gone, he did everything in his power to hasten our departure from Madras. We tied up loose ends with clients and said farewell to our acquaintances. We were almost ready to depart, save for packing our personal belongings, when Ram caught us early one morning before we left for some errands.

"I come to Georgetown with sirs," he declared.

We knew Ram was an orphan like both of us, and in his case from birth. He had absolutely no one in this world save for us. Both Lesley and I agreed that we could not leave him behind.

On the set date, our crates of precious stones and the other goods that we owned were loaded onto the *Anahid*. We reckoned we had enough stock to last us a fair few months in Georgetown, at least until we settled comfortably. We also thought we had made the right decision to have Ram come with us. We would certainly need the extra pair of hands to help us with all the daily chores that awaited us. Although 19 years old now, Ram was as excited as a boy of 10 as we boarded the ship. This was a true adventure for him. He smiled incessantly and, with a child's curiosity, inspected everything on board the *Anahid* intently, completely oblivious of us. By the time the *Anahid* set sail, he had already made friends with Bab and Maam, and all through the voyage we had a hard time finding him if we needed him.

Although getting on in years, Melkon Khan was gregarious as always and on top form. I noticed he had better clothing on than usual. I thought this sartorial improvement matched the look of his renovated beloved *Anahid*.

"I bought myself a new set of clothing to celebrate the capture of the *Corne Noire*. Last month, she had an ill-fated encounter with a heavily armed British vessel. She was half destroyed before they captured her. Most of the pirates were killed, and the rest of her ended up in a scrap yard," Melkon Khan said.

"That is the best news I've heard in a long time," I remarked.

Every evening during this journey we would sit down with Melkon Khan and have a long chat about this and that and reminisce about the 'good old days' when my uncle was alive.

"So you're going to operate from Georgetown soon," Melkon Khan said one evening after supper.

"Yes, that's the plan. Perhaps you can advise us on where to stock our goods in Penang," Lesley said.

"I know a few good places near the harbour – and not very expensive."

"Melkon Khan, I have a favour to ask of you," I said. "Do you re-member you introduced me to Agha Caloustian once in Georgetown? We would be grateful if you could arrange for us to visit him when we get there. I'd like Lesley to meet him. And since we will be trading from Georgetown and are newcomers, it would be a wise move to make contact with the doyen of the Armenian merchants there. I recall you saying he is an important man to know."

"Certainly, Vartan, it would be my pleasure," Melkon Khan said. "I don't mind paying Agha Caloustian a visit myself. I always appreciate his hospitality, especially that wonderful brandy he offers his guests. He's such a generous man, you know. And despite his elevated position in the community of merchants, his wealth, experience, and knowledge, I have never found him intimidating or condescending. That's because he has never forgotten his humble origins. Now that's what I call a great man!"

I looked at Lesley and he winked at me. We both understood that if ever there was a man who could help us with Apcarian, it was Agha Caloustian.

CHAPTER 18

⚜

IT WAS A DARK EVENING with a heavy monsoon rain drumming down as we docked at the harbour in Penang.

"There's nothing much you can do at this time in Georgetown. Stay on board the *Anahid* tonight and, God willing, at daybreak you can sort yourselves out," Melkon Khan said.

I could feel that Lesley was desperate to get ashore and discover the whereabouts of Lilly. He didn't sleep much that night. I was drifting in and out of sleep and I was aware he was doing the same.

By dawn, we were already up. Melkon Khan took us to the cluster of warehouses that was the go-downs and we rented one. With the help of Bab and a couple of crewmen, we quickly transferred our stock there, together with some of our belongings for storage until we could find permanent lodgings in town. By 9 o'clock, we were done.

"I won't be able to put my mind to anything else, Vartan, until I find out where Lilly is," Lesley said, whispering so no one would hear. I nodded in sympathy.

"Melkon Khan, we intend to go into town and find lodgings as soon as possible. But first, we urgently need to get in touch with business associates who moved here not long ago from Madras. What's the best way of discovering their whereabouts?" I inquired.

"I would say your best bet is Mr. Manookian, the lawyer. At this time of the morning he'll still be at the Chinese inn he's been lodging at for the last six months, having moved here himself from Madras. He knows everyone in town and in particular all the newcomers from Madras. The Chinese inn is easy to find. It's located on one of the streets to the south of Armenian Street."

We thanked Melkon Khan for all his assistance and said we would be back that evening to collect the rest of our personal belongings and to fetch Ram, who had remained on board the *Anahid*.

We reached Armenian Street in no time but it took us longer to locate the Chinese inn. We succeeded eventually after asking for directions from a couple of passersby and caught Mr. Manookian just in time; he was on his way to a meeting with a client.

"Apcarian and Associates – yes, I am well acquainted with Mr. Apcarian. I had the pleasure of a meeting with him last week. I arranged the signing of the lease papers – the firm's premises and the house. It's a lovely mansion at the far end of Armenian Street with a beautiful, exotic garden. It's very near the Armenian Church," Mr. Manookian said.

"We actually need to know where the firm is located. We require insurance for our goods," Lesley interjected.

"Well, it's not far from Armenian Street – two blocks north, on Jarmine Street. You won't miss it. It's the large corner building. They occupy the top two floors."

"We are very much obliged. You have been very helpful," I said.

"If you need any assistance with legal matters, I'm at your service," said Mr. Manookian as we took our leave.

I succeeded in persuading Lesley that it was unwise for us to just walk unprepared into the premises of Apcarian and Associates on our first day in Georgetown and said we should rather concentrate on searching for business premises and lodgings immediately. Lesley grumbled but soon agreed. We were more than fortunate that day, finding not only suitable premises, but also permanent lodgings within two hours of leaving the Chinese inn and Mr. Manookian. We had been walking around the streets parallel to the Chinese inn, looking for advertisements for rental premises when we spotted a small building. We found the Chinese caretaker, who showed us around. The very spacious ground floor had been a clothing shop and had a large glass front; we thought it could easily be turned into offices. The second floor was a decent-sized apartment. It had been used as living quarters and had a table and some chairs, but nothing else in the way of furniture. A family of four had lived there comfortably according to the caretaker. The back of the house had a modest outbuilding in a small garden which had been neglected for a good while.

"This is just the place for Ram!" Lesley said and quickly added, "He could do wonders with this garden."

"Let's go and fetch him," I said. "We need a week or so to get this place ready for us to move in. In the meantime, we can lodge at the Chinese inn."

"Alright," Lesley said "but I've got to somehow let Lilly know I'm here – by tomorrow morning at the latest."

The following morning, Lesley, wearing freshly pressed trousers and decked out as if he were going to some important function or Sunday mass, left the inn to see his beloved Lilly. A couple of hours later, as Ram was cleaning the apartment upstairs and I was arranging the office furniture I had purchased earlier that morning for our new premises, Lesley returned.

"Well, did you see Lilly?" I asked impatiently.

"Unfortunately not – but it's not all bad news. Let me tell you what happened exactly. When I walked in, I was relieved that none of the clerks recognised me, nor I they, for Apcarian and Associates have retained none of their Madras clerks. I asked one of them if I could see Ms. Lilly Apcarian. I gave him my name and said I was a client of the firm from Madras and an old acquaintance. He said Lilly was not present but that someone else would see me shortly. My heart sank and I dreaded the thought of seeing her father again. A few minutes later, the clerk ushered me into a back office. It was her sister's. The resemblance to my Lilly could not be missed, but Ms. Violet Apcarian has slightly darker hair and looks fuller and taller than my petite Lilly. Let me tell you the conversation I had with her, word for word:

'How can I be of help to you, Mr. Atkinson?' She said in a serious tone.

'My Armenian business partner and I arrived in Georgetown yesterday from Madras and are setting up a trading firm here. And since we have an existing insurance contract with your firm, I was hoping to be able to modify the terms to cover our business transactions in Georgetown,' I said, and I tell you I was completely taken aback by her response. She's indeed as sharp as they say she is.

'Mr. Atkinson, you say you only arrived in Georgetown yesterday and you have hastened to come and see us before you have had the time to start operating from this town. Surely, this is an odd undertaking,' she said.

She had cornered me, so I took the plunge and said, 'Ms. Apcarian, I do not wish to offend you in any way, but my true purpose in coming here today is to inquire after Ms. Lilly's health and to inform her that I am in Georgetown.'

'I appreciate your frankness, Mr. Atkinson. My sister has not been working here since our arrival. She's been looking after our mother who is in poor health and whose condition has been aggravated by the rough sea voyage.'

'I'm very sorry to hear that, Ms. Apcarian,' I said.

'And for my part, let me be frank with you too, Mr. Atkinson,' she said. 'Lilly will be very pleased to hear you are in Georgetown.' And her face changed momentarily and I caught a glimpse of a smile.

'Would it be imprudent of me to send her a letter then?' I inquired.

'Do not deliver your letter yourself, Mr. Atkinson. Send it to me with a messenger and I shall see that Lilly gets it. Let this be a matter known only to the two of us for the time being. My father is not a man easily fooled, and you will have to deal with him sooner or later.'

"And that was how she spoke – frankly and clearly. Then she bid me farewell," Lesley said.

"I told you she was an ally," I said. "Now, back to business, Lesley. Meeting with Agha Caloustian is our next priority."

❧

"Don't forget to mention his contribution to the building of the Armenian Church in Georgetown. He'll be most pleased with that," Melkon Khan advised as we walked to Agha Caloustian's prestigious offices, which occupied all four floors of a centrally-located mansion.

Upon arrival, a personal assistant ushered us into the same reception room where I'd had my first piece of chocolate all those years ago. Looking around at the fine furniture and decoration, Lesley whispered, "I didn't quite expect this."

"Shush, Lesley, he'll be here any minute,' I said.

"*Voghchuyn tzez*," said Agha Caloustian, greeting us in Armenian and making a grand entrance with his personal assistant in tow.

He then switched to English and said, "Welcome my friends. May I offer you some aged French brandy of excellent quality?" Without waiting for our response, he gestured to his personal assistant that that was what was needed, and urgently.

Melkon Khan's grin didn't go amiss, for Agha Caloustian remarked, "Melkon Khan is a man after my own heart – always appreciative of a good vintage." Then, turning to me he added, "Your good reputation precedes you Khoja Vartan. I am honoured by this second visit of yours after so many years."

"It is I who am honoured and am but your humble servant," I said.

"Come, come, no need for such modesty. Khoja Asadur of Isfahan, the doyen of all we Armenian merchants, was here only a couple of weeks ago and mentioned you affectionately. He said you had written to him a few months ago telling him about your possible move to Georgetown.

I told him he needn't worry. You will have all the backing you need from me, especially since you're a business associate of Sarkis Manuk of Burma who, by the way, also mentioned you."

"In actual fact, I have not met him personally yet. It is my business partner, Mr. Lesley Atkinson here, who is a good friend of Mr. Sarkis Manuk."

"Atkinson. Yes, indeed, I do recall. Sarkis mentioned you on several occasions and spoke very highly of you. I knew your father very well, may his soul rest in peace. It is my pleasure to have met you at last."

"The pleasure is all mine, Agha Caloustian," Lesley said.

The French brandy arrived and was dispensed generously to each of us.

"He's such a jewel of a man, that Sarkis. He spent two years here during the Anglo-Burmese War. I was sad to see him return to Burma. I had enjoyed his company almost on a daily basis," said Agha Caloustian and, taking a sip of his brandy, continued, "So, have you found business premises yet?"

"Yes, we have, on Orchid Street. The Atkinson and Vartan Trading Firm will be open for business as of tomorrow morning," I declared.

"In that case, I shall be referring clients to you immediately. There are dubious Chinese precious stones dealers in town and I have not been able to recommend them to anyone. If you'll permit, one of my senior clerks will visit you tomorrow and give you the details of prospective clients," Agha Caloustian said, taking another sip of his brandy.

"We are very grateful to you for being worthy of your consideration," Lesley responded.

At this point Melkon Khan winked at me, reminding me of the Armenian Church.

"The Armenian community as a whole must be very grateful to you, Agha, for having completed the building of the Armenian Church in Georgetown. And, indeed, for leaving no stone unturned to have it consecrated in such a short time," I said.

"One has to do what one can do," he said with a smile, clearly pleased I had mentioned the church.

When we got up to leave a short while later, Agha Caloustian wished us good luck with our new venture, and added, "Do not hesitate to knock on my door anytime you need me." And addressing Melkon Khan, said, "Come visit me again one evening before you leave Georgetown. We can share a bottle of brandy and play a game or two of backgammon, like we used to in the good old days in Isfahan."

"You two didn't really require my presence there. He already knew who you were," said Melkon Khan and this was the only comment made as the three of us walked back in silence to our lodgings in the dead of night.

Melkon Khan was proud that he was treated as an equal by a man who owned ten ships and more, compared to his one; I was satisfied that I had the backing of a powerful ally, for I did not yet know if our business was going to prosper in this new town, and Lesley was content that he had found the perfect go-between to obtain his heart's desire.

In this complex and difficult world, who could not but wish for more men like Agha Caloustian?

CHAPTER 19

✤

AS OUR BUSINESS ACTIVITIES BEGAN to multiply during the following month, so too did the letters that were exchanged between Lesley and Lilly.

We developed a good client list with the help of Agha Caloustian's senior clerk, and soon the orders for our precious stones started coming in. A Chinese clerk and an Armenian book-keeper who was recommended by Mr. Manookian, the lawyer, joined our staff. We decorated the apartment upstairs as best we could. And our living quarters, together with an equipped kitchen, were more than adequate for two bachelors.

Ram brought order to the back garden and his own quarters in no time. He managed to save a dying pineapple tree and also began growing some plantain. He was working on saving another tree from certain death when one morning I asked him what kind of tree it was.

"Orange," he replied.

"Don't tell me stories, Ram; I don't believe orange can grow in this tropical climate."

"Ram promise orange will grow!" he said with conviction.

To my great surprise and joy, he proved me wrong; whatever he saved, planted, or cared for, bloomed and gave fruit all year round.

It didn't take me long to notice Ram's happiness at resuming his role as the messenger of the two lovers. He understood his role perfectly well and acted with utmost caution when delivering the letters to Lilly's sister, and from Lilly via her sister at the firm. Once I heard him say to Lesley, "Father of Lady Ma'am was in office. So, I wait outside and give letter when he leave."

Lesley was getting very impatient. He had not yet seen Lilly – not even once – since our arrival. In his letters, he continually asked her if there was any way they could meet. Her reply was that it was virtually impossible since she was house-bound, caring for her ill mother. And whenever she went out for errands, she was accompanied by either her sister or father.

"I'm going to lose my mind if this carries on," Lesley told me one night after work.

"I think it's time now for me to visit Agha Caloustian and ask for his assistance," I said.

The following morning I promised Lesley I would go and see Agha Caloustian that very same afternoon. He wrote a letter to Lilly telling her that we would be seeking the help of Agha Caloustian in approaching her father to ask for her hand in marriage. He gave the letter to Ram to deliver to her sister at the firm. When Ram returned an hour later, he still had Lesley's letter in his hand.

"What happened?" Lesley said, horrified.

"Firm closed – big paper on door. Doorman say Lady Ma'am mother dead," reported Ram.

"The mourning period will last at least three days. That's the Armenian custom," I told Lesley when he inquired.

"How about attending the funeral in your church? That way I could at least see my Lilly, and my being there would console her." And then a few minutes later, he added, "I don't think that's appropriate. She may not appreciate my being there. Why don't you go in my place and offer her my condolences?"

"I don't think that's appropriate either, Lesley. Neither of us has been formally introduced to the Apcarian family and my attending the funeral might look odd. Why don't you write to Lilly and maybe we can have your letter delivered somehow in a few days. She may even be back at the firm by then. And I think it would be a good idea to postpone my meeting with Agha Caloustian for a couple of weeks until the mourning period is truly over," I said.

Lesley agreed. We busied ourselves in work and succeeded in mounting the 'Atkinson and Vartan Trading Firm' plaque in big letters on our glass shop window.

About a week later on a Saturday evening, Lesley and I were discussing business matters alone in the office when, suddenly, Lesley jumped out of his seat and flew out into the street. I followed him.

A young lady in a carriage was looking intently out of its window. When her eyes settled on Lesley, she gave him a sweet smile. But the carriage didn't stop and in a matter of a few minutes had turned the corner at the end of our street.

"That was Lilly – my Lilly!" Lesley shouted. He could jump for joy, he said, for he had finally seen her after over two months of yearning for even a glimpse of her.

"A beautiful girl – you have exquisite taste, my friend," I said, adding with a smile, "You must have given her our address in one of your letters."

Lesley nodded, "I knew she would do something like this. I knew she longed to see me too – all the more because she hasn't been able to write to me lately. But why today, and what message did she intend to give me?"

"My best guess is she's telling you that she'll be back at the firm," I said matter-of-factly.

"In that case, I shall give Monday a miss but I'll be at the firm like a shot first thing on Tuesday morning. It is high time we revised the terms of our insurance contract with Apcarian and Associates," Lesley said with determination in his voice. He then grasped my arm tightly and begged me to go and see Agha Caloustian immediately.

I sent a note to Agha Caloustian with Ram, explaining that I urgently needed to see him on a personal matter. Half an hour later, Ram was back with a note from Agha Caloustian. He had a dinner engagement later in the evening, but if I could make it to his offices within the hour, he would gladly see me.

Agha Caloustian was in his office seated at his great, gleaming rosewood desk. I guessed he must have been very busy that day and did not have the time to receive guests in his reception room.

"I apologise for barging in on you like this, Agha Caloustian."

"Don't apologise, Khoja. I meant it when I said you could knock on my door at any time. Tell me, how can I be of help?"

"Well, it is about a delicate personal matter that I have come to see you. It concerns my partner, Mr. Atkinson," I said, and recounted the whole story as concisely as I could.

"It is indeed quite a delicate matter," Agha Caloustian said, rubbing his chin. "I know Apcar Apcarian very well. We go back a long way – to my days in Calcutta – and I still have business dealings with him. He is not an easy man, but his concern about the well-being of his daughters cannot be swept aside. He has just lost his poor wife, who had been suffering for years, and I don't know how positively disposed he would be at the moment to a marriage proposal. His older daughter, Violet, is engaged to be married to one of his business partners but, from what I hear, they keep on postponing the wedding as the fiancé is always travelling here, there and everywhere on business. Unless Violet marries first, I do not think Apcarian would consent to his younger daughter marrying. And one other important concern is the question of how he would behave if the marriage proposal came from a non-Armenian."

"Sadly, that is a main concern of mine, too," I said.

"But, Khoja Vartan, I don't mean to discourage you or your friend, especially as the young lady is consenting," he said.

"What would you advise us to do?" I asked.

"Let's take matters one at a time. Apcarian is suspicious of anyone, and I mean anyone, he is not acquainted with. To begin with, Mr. Atkinson needs to be introduced to Apcarian formally and socially; having you as a friend and partner would be to his advantage. I tell you what – I am invited to a luncheon at the Apcarian's tomorrow after Sunday mass. Let me see how I can bring about an introduction. Come by on Monday evening after work and we'll talk again about this," Agha Caloustian concluded.

I reported everything Agha Caloustian had said to an apprehensive Lesley upon my return.

"What a mess I've put myself in," he said. "But I'm hopeful and will gladly suffer in order to win my Lilly."

"In your hour of glory, don't forget this poor soul who's been suffering with you and working diligently on your behalf," I said, and for the first time in weeks I managed to make Lesley laugh.

On Monday morning, I was just about ready to start looking over some of the week's orders when a messenger turned up with a note in Armenian and waited for my response:

Respectful Khoja Vartan Bantukhtian,

It is my pleasure to invite you to a meeting at 2 p.m. today at the premises of Apcarian and Associates to discuss a matter of utmost importance to our family.

I would be honoured if you would grace us with your presence.

Sincerely,

Manoushag Violet Apcarian

I told the messenger I would be there at the required time. I then spent the whole morning cursing Lesley for having put *me* in this mess. He had left early that morning for the go-downs to retrieve some of our goods and I knew he would not be back before late afternoon. I agonized over what the 'important family matter' could be and hoped I wasn't being led into a trap. I could not knock on Agha Caloustian's door at this time of day either; our agreement was to meet in the evening after work.

So it was with great apprehension that I arrived at the firm a few minutes before 2 p.m. As I walked towards the desk of one of the clerks, I caught a glimpse of Lilly walking out of one of the side offices. She stopped, smiled at me discretely, and then disappeared into another office.

Her smile reassured me and my anxiety slowly began to dissipate when the clerk walked me to what I expected to be the office of her sister. As the door opened, a young lady greeted me.

"Welcome, Khoja Vartan Bantukhtian. I'm Manoushag Violet Apcarian."

My heart missed a beat.

"Please, Khoja Vartan, do take a seat," she said, and with a delicate gesture indicated an armchair.

My heart was pounding hard but I did not know why I had lost control over the way it functioned.

"I apologise for having given you such short notice. My dear mother passed away recently and…"

"Allow me to offer you my sincerest condolences, Ms. Apcarian."

She looked at me. There was a long pause, and sensing the awkwardness of the moment, she resumed the conversation.

"I, I thank you – but please call me Violet." She smiled at me. My knees weakened.

"Certainly, Ms. Violet, how can I be of help?"

"As I was saying, my mother passed away recently, and my family would like to have a tombstone erected on my mother's grave in the Armenian Cemetery. You were recommended to us by Agha Caloustian. He is in awe of your exquisite Armenian calligraphic skills."

"I am humbled by Agha Caloustian's opinion of me. And I would be honoured to use my modest skills for such a worthy deed."

"It's just that we're in somewhat of a hurry. Since there are no Armenian stonemasons here, a close friend of the family has offered to go to Madras, have the calligraphy carved on a tombstone by the Armenian stonemason there, and have it shipped to Georgetown. But he is scheduled to leave for Madras on Friday."

"I understand. I can have the calligraphy ready by tomorrow," I said.

"That's not necessary. Wednesday would be fine, Khoja Vartan," she said. She then produced a piece of paper and handed it to me. It had the epitaph for her mother's tombstone in her own handwriting.

"My father is of the opinion that you should be compensated for the work."

"Ms. Violet, let me make one thing clear to you. It is true that I am a merchant, a trader, but I have never before profited from my calligraphy nor have I the intention of doing so in the future. I was taught by a priest who selflessly served his pupils and, when needed, I will serve my people likewise, including yourself and your family," I said in a gentle but firm tone.

"Forgive me, Khoja Vartan. I did not mean to offend you," she said with a frown.

I immediately regretted that I had upset her, but our eyes met as she smiled. I smiled back, saying, "No harm done, Ms. Violet. I shall have the calligraphy ready on Wednesday."

"Would you like me to send a messenger to pick it up or would you honour me with another visit, Khoja Vartan?" she said with a look that meant she preferred the latter.

"It would indeed give me great pleasure to visit you again, Ms. Violet," I said and got up to leave.

She walked with me to the door. And as we parted, I was already longing to see her again.

CHAPTER 20

✤

BEING IN NO MOOD FOR work after my encounter with Ms. Violet, I walked the streets, lost in a reverie. I was overwhelmed and could think about nothing else but her. I just couldn't comprehend what had happened to me. My world had suddenly changed – turned upside down. My heart was in revolt, constantly pushing me towards a sweet numbness that came with the thought of Ms. Violet.

Finding myself at our premises at around 5 o'clock in the evening and drenched in sweat, I freshened up and left for my evening meeting with Agha Caloustian.

When I returned, Lesley had long been back from the go-downs and had just finished supper.

"At last! I've been waiting for you on tenterhooks. What did Agha Caloustian say?" he asked.

"This is going to be a long story," I said. "Let me begin with this morning."

As I recounted the day's events, Lesley peppered me with questions.

"At the Sunday luncheon, Agha Caloustian had told the Apcarians to come to you for the calligraphy so you would be introduced to the family that way. What a quick thinking, clever man! I can't wait to ask, Vartan, was Lilly there at the firm?"

"Yes, she was. I am certain she knew I was coming. She came out of an office just as I arrived and greeted me with a discrete smile."

"Do you think it will be alright to pay her a visit tomorrow morning then?"

"Yes, I do. And, as we agreed, do it under the pretext of talking to her about our current insurance contract with the firm."

I then told Lesley about my meeting with Violet. His eyes widened when I said I felt attracted to her and awkward in her presence, but I left out the fact that I had been thinking about her constantly since.

"My friend, I think you're hooked, as I was on that first day I met Lilly."

"I *can't* be. She's engaged to be married, for God's sake!"

"But she's not *actually* married yet, is she?"

"No, but the sooner *she* gets married, the sooner *you* can marry her sister. So let's not talk about Violet anymore, my friend, I beg of you. What's important now is arranging your introduction to Lilly's father. Agha Caloustian is certain I will be invited to the Apcarian home because of the calligraphy. And he told me to make sure the invitation includes *you*. And if and when I get the invitation, to be certain you are included."

Early next morning, after finalising a few business matters with the clerk, I went upstairs to work on the calligraphy. Lesley left soon afterwards to see Lilly. I sat myself at the table thinking I would finish the calligraphy in an hour or two, but no sooner had I begun than my mind strayed. I imagined myself in Violet's office and recalled my encounter with her over and over again. I thought of her delicate gestures and her thick, shiny hair, plaited and gathered on the crown of her head. I thought of her beautiful round face and peach-coloured cheeks and lips. Lesley's description of her was correct; she had a fuller figure than her sister's. I loved the way she moved, almost on tip-toe. She wore a black dress, like her sister – they were still in mourning – but I thought it suited her perfectly since it matched her raven-coloured hair and highlighted her smooth and fair complexion. Her huge dark eyes, with long dark lashes, were what had fascinated me most. Lilly's big dark eyes were open, round, innocent; Violet's, although sad, were alluring and mysterious.

I dared imagine that she was drawn to me too. That was what I'd felt in her presence. I desperately yearned to find out the depth of her feeling, but I also knew I had to tread with great caution for, after all, she was still promised to another.

"Stop fantasizing! Have you written only two words in all this time?"

Lesley startled me. He said he'd been standing behind me a good few minutes, watching me, and I hadn't even felt he was there.

"I've got marvellous news – on three accounts!" he said.

"And which three accounts are those?"

"To begin with, since it was my first opportunity in months to see Lilly face to face, I told her I adored her and asked her to marry me."

"And what was her reply?"

"Yes! Of course! I told her we are not sparing any effort to approach her father to formally ask for her hand in marriage."

"That's excellent news, congratulations!"

"Second, she tells me, my friend, that you made a terribly good impression on her sister. Violet's been trying to find out more about you. Lilly said she told her whatever she knew – that is whatever I had written about you in my letters."

"And?"

"Third, she said the family's going to invite you over, and Lilly is hoping you'll be able to bring me along. Aren't you happy?"

"Yes, I suppose it's all good news. Let's hope tomorrow's going to turn out to be as good as today."

"I've got to run. I have something in mind to purchase for Lilly."

"And what is that?"

"An engagement ring!" shouted Lesley and was gone in an instant.

I re-started the work on the calligraphy with enthusiasm. I reasoned if Violet hadn't felt at least a little for me, she wouldn't have asked about me. I finished writing two large copies in less than an hour. It was my habit to do two copies for the stonemason in case he damaged one of them whilst working. After I'd read and re-read the copies, I felt satisfied with what I had written:

In memory of
Anna Apcarian
Born in the Year 1776 in New Julfa
Died in the Year 1826 in Georgetown
Loving spouse of Apcar Apcarian
Mother of Manoushag and Shoushan
May the Lord illuminate her soul

I didn't wait to share supper with Lesley. He was still not back and I'd decided to go to bed early. Anxiety suddenly gripped me when I thought about the next day. But then my anxiousness turned to a yearning to see Violet again. And, I was amused to find that I had left her handwritten paper in my pocket – just as Lesley had kept Lilly's handwritten receipt after *their* first encounter.

Wednesday noon came and I was still struggling to make up my mind about what to wear. I finally settled on a pair of brown trousers and a large green-coloured cravat with purple stripes that I had recently purchased.

When I got to Violet's office, she was waiting for me. She smiled broadly, flashing her beautiful, pearly teeth, and said, "Khoja Vartan, what a pleasure to see you again."

"I'm happy to see you again, too, Violet…I mean, Ms. Violet," I said nervously.

"You may call me Violet, Khoja Vartan, since I am certain we soon will become well acquainted," she said, looking at me with her mysterious eyes.

I didn't know how to respond, so I blurted, "You may call me Vartan. Khoja sounds old-fashioned even to my ears," and gave her the calligraphy.

"I am sure you understand how important this is to my family. We miss our mother dearly but she had suffered for too long," she said sadly, and then looking at my work added, "I have never seen such marvellously stylised Armenian. I am forever grateful to you."

As she looked up from my calligraphy, our eyes met. I didn't turn my gaze away, savouring the beauty in her eyes for as long as I could.

There was a long silence and then she said, "I was told you are originally from Erzerum, and a widower."

"Yes, I lost my beloved wife and infant daughter to a dreadful epidemic in Isfahan almost four years ago."

"I am truly sorry. I cannot begin to understand such a tragedy," she said, lowering her eyes; and then she looked up again and said, "Forgive me for prying but have you not thought of re-marrying? You're a very young man."

"Frankly, I didn't feel the need to re-marry until..." and then I checked myself and continued, "You are engaged, I understand."

She touched the gold ring she was wearing and said, "Yes, to Bedros Alexanderian, who is one of the two partners of my father. He's been away on a long business trip to Borneo."

"And when is the wedding to take place?"

"In around three months' time, when he returns," she said. Her eyes darkened and lost their glimmer. For a moment, she looked away into the empty space in front of her. And then she resumed the conversation.

"My father's other partner is Catcheres Sarkis. Both he and my father expressed the desire to meet you. I hope you will honour us with your presence on Sunday for lunch at our home," she said in a jolly tone.

"Thank you, but I have promised my business partner, Mr. Lesley Atkinson, to lunch with him on Sunday."

"I beg your pardon, but I really meant to invite Mr. Atkinson as well. I believe he is well acquainted with my sister Lilly. I would be grateful if you could convey to him that she thinks the world of him and that I would hate for her to be disappointed. I must also mention that Mr. Davis and his associate, Mr. Palmer, will be attending. They are well-known lawyers in Georgetown; so, inevitably the conversation will be in English rather than Armenian. All the guests, including Agha Caloustian, will be arriving at midday."

I was just beginning to understand how much cleverer the two sisters were, compared to Lesley or myself. Perhaps I needn't have been so anxious about getting Lesley introduced to Apcar Apcarian. It seemed both sisters had already figured out the best way to do it and had left nothing to chance.

"I am certain Lesley will be as delighted as I am to attend; he is indeed very fond of Ms. Lilly."

"I look very much forward to seeing you on Sunday…"

Our eyes met again.

"...Vartan," she said.

"And I you, Violet."

❧

"I gather from what you just said that there will be quite a number of people at the Apcarian's on Sunday," Lesley remarked.

"I expect so, and you'd better be careful not to show too much familiarity with Lilly. Concentrate on making a good impression on the father. Remember, that is your main aim. In any case, if I know Agha Caloustian, he will do his best to promote you, and I'll do what I can."

"Thank you, my friend. You have already been of great assistance. Did Violet mention Lilly at all in her conversation?"

"She said Lilly thought the world of you and if you didn't turn up on Sunday Lilly would be very disappointed. You're very fortunate, Lesley, to have Violet on your side. She knows Lilly is in love with you and she will help you, for the sake of her sister first and foremost."

"What you say is true. There's something puzzling me though – why are you avoiding telling me how you feel about Violet?"

"Look, Lesley. I told you I was attracted to her and I believe she is attracted to me in a certain way. But she's engaged. She is to be married in three months' time and I can't see any way around that. So why pursue the matter?"

"But Vartan, I know you pretty well and I sense you're in love with her, although you won't admit it. For all I know, she might have fallen in love with you, too. She's to marry someone who is twenty years her senior. Do you think she's in love with him? You yourself told me it is an arranged marriage. Vartan, how can you just ignore the matter? I am paying Lilly a visit at the firm tomorrow. She will have the revised insurance contract for us. I'll quiz her regarding Violet's feelings towards you. If she knows anything, she will surely tell me."

My mind wanted me to tell him not to do it, but my heart desperately wanted otherwise. So I didn't give him a straight response, but said, "Let's assume Violet is in love with me. How do you expect her to break off the engagement? Can you not see that even she, with all her intelligence, won't be able to carry out such a thing? I cannot expect her to betray her father and the man who saved him from ruin just for my sake. And, my dear Lesley, can you not see that if such an event occurred, it would jeopardize your plan to marry Lilly? So let's focus on getting her father's approval." And steering the conversation away from Violet, I continued, "I thought you were going to show me the engagement ring you bought for Lilly."

Lesley produced a little red velvet box and handed it to me. It contained a gold ring in the shape of a flower with a single large diamond in the middle.

"That is a magnificent ring, Lesley! I can see it's an item of exquisite workmanship. I'm sure Lilly will love it," I said.

"Are you superstitious, Vartan?"

"I have faith in our Lord Jesus Christ, so I shouldn't be. But I suppose sometimes I am, instinctively," I replied.

"Exactly my thought," he said. "Then I shall not show it to her just yet. I shall give it to her on the very day I am engaged to be married to her."

CHAPTER 21

❦

ON SUNDAY MORNING I WAS as anxious as Lesley. We both fussed endlessly about our choice of clothing; we were worried that we might look too serious for the young ladies and not serious enough for their father. Lesley changed his cravat at least four times and we finally agreed on the most suitable one: silk and sober without being sad.

"You look truly dapper!" I said, for Lesley did cut a fine figure. He was tall and thin with wavy blond hair and well-trimmed sideburns.

"You don't look too bad yourself with that fine head of brown hair," he said, winking at me.

A few days earlier, upon his return from seeing Lilly at the firm, Lesley had reported to me what Violet had told her sister about me.

"Lilly repeated to me Violet's exact words: 'I find Khoja Vartan most charming and pleasing. If only I weren't engaged…' Lilly believes Violet really and truly admires you. I wish we could do something about this engagement of hers."

To that I had replied, "That would be a tall order, Lesley. Let's see what happens on Sunday first."

By 11:30, we were ready to depart and Ram found us a carriage for hire. As we got in, Ram said, "I come with sirs to Lady Ma'am house."

"What are you talking about? You will do no such thing," Lesley said sharply.

"Why do you want to come with us, Ram?" I intervened.

"Gardener in Lady Ma'am house my friend. He say I come too."

"And how do you know this gardener?" Lesley hissed.

"I meet him in market. He speak my language – from Madras."

"Let him ride with us, Lesley."

"You're such a devil, Ram! Come on then!" Lesley gestured.

We watched Ram as he made himself comfortable in his seat, put one arm on the side of the carriage window, fixed his hair with the other, and gave us a smile that meant he was ready for the journey.

"I told you before – you can't fight his obstinacy," I said to Lesley and we both burst out laughing.

Twenty minutes later, we were at the Apcarian mansion. The large gate was open. There were two men standing at the gate. Jumping out, Ram immediately greeted one of them. The other pointed us to the pathway. This was flanked by two very spacious tropical gardens with bushes and flowers, and tall trees beyond. Ram and his gardener friend began chattering at a great rate as they walked off into the lush vegetation.

Lesley and I had walked a good few minutes up the pathway before the grand three-storey mansion came into view. A veranda stretched all along the ground floor. As we approached the house, we could see some of the guests had already arrived and were being served beverages. We were greeted by Lilly, but Violet promptly took over and said, "Let me introduce you to my father and our other guests."

"It is indeed a pleasure meeting you at last, Khoja Vartan. Please accept my heartfelt gratitude for your assistance and your gift of wonderful calligraphy to the family," Apcar Apcarian said, and turning towards Lesley, "I recall we met in Madras – such a pleasure seeing you here in Georgetown, Mr. Atkinson."

We were then introduced to Catcheres Sarkis, Apcarian's partner, and Messrs. Davis and Palmer and their spouses. Mr. Manookian, the lawyer, was also present. The last guest to arrive was Agha Caloustian; he was accompanied by his newlywed daughter and son-in-law. It was only on that day I discovered Agha Caloustian was a widower; Lilly mentioned that he had lost his wife just a year prior to our arrival in Georgetown.

Lunch was served indoors in a large and opulent dining room. Besides the butler and housekeeper, I counted three domestics. I thought that the Apcarians must also certainly employ a good number of kitchen staff, and at least four gardeners if one considered the size of the lush gardens surrounding the property. This is when I panicked. Lilly was the daughter of a very well-to-do man and I didn't know how Lesley's financial status would be regarded by her father. The sight of Agha Caloustian very quickly calmed my nerves, for I knew he would come to Lesley's rescue on that score.

The seating arrangements at the table had been cleverly worked out by Lilly and Violet. They had their father and Catcheres Sarkis at opposite ends of the table, thus dividing the guests into two groups. To the right of Catcheres were seated Mr. Davis and Mrs. Palmer, and to his left, Mrs. Davis and Mr. Palmer with Mr. Manookian between them. This was purposely done, I was certain, to ensure that neither Mr. Davis nor Mr. Palmer had the chance to monopolise the conversation with Lesley at the table. On the left of their father were seated Lilly and Lesley, and on his right Agha Caloustian and myself. Violet sat next to me, facing Agha Caloustian's daughter and her husband. The newlyweds were too engrossed in conversation to care where they were seated.

"Mr. Atkinson is the son of the late John Atkinson, Apcar. I'm sure you remember him," began Agha Caloustian.

"Difficult to forget a man like John Atkinson – he had an imposing personality and was a brave man, too. He was one of the first to break away from the East India Company and set up on his own in Madras. I met him on several occasions in Calcutta." And turning to Lesley, he added, "I am honoured to have his son at my table."

"It is my privilege to be seated at such an honourable table," Lesley responded.

"Lilly tells me you have renewed your insurance contract with our firm since your move to Georgetown, Mr. Atkinson. May I ask what type of business you are involved in?" Apcarian inquired.

"Mainly precious stones, Mr. Apcarian, and Khoja Vartan is my partner – apart from being my closest friend," Lesley said smiling in my direction.

"Without his expertise in the precious stones business, I would not have taken the plunge," I quickly added.

"Yes, indeed, the precious stones business is very lucrative so long as one knows what one is dealing with," Apcarian said and focused his gaze on me. I do not know if he meant it, but the way he looked at people was intimidating. I was sure Lesley would agree with me.

"I knew your late uncle very well. He had the reputation of being an honest and dependable man. Agha Caloustian mentioned that you inherited his title of 'khoja', and with the blessing of none other than Khoja Asadur of Isfahan himself. I suspect you have many other talents, still modestly hidden from us, apart from your excellent calligraphic skills. I wish you and Mr. Atkinson successful trading in Georgetown," Apcarian said.

"God willing! Don't forget these two young men are closely associated with Sarkis Manuk of Burma. Sarkis indeed thinks very highly of Mr. Atkinson," Agha Caloustian butted in.

"Sarkis Manuk is a serious trader and is not in the habit of associating himself with anyone he could not trust with his own life," Apcarian said in a stern tone. "I am truly impressed, Mr. Atkinson."

Lesley thanked him and glanced at me. We both understood that now at least he had a better chance with Lilly's father.

After lunch, we all retired to the drawing room. Catcheres Sarkis continued a conversation he had started with Mr. Davis and Mr. Palmer about trade and the insurance business. In a corner of the room, Mr. Manookian was doing his best to charm the English ladies, causing them to burst into animated laughter now and again.

"Let's walk in the garden," Lilly said, turning to Violet.

"Let the young ones go for a walk in your beautiful grounds, Apcar," Agha Caloustian suggested, adding, "And let us old folks play a game of backgammon, and perhaps you can offer me a water-pipe?"

The newlyweds were out of the drawing room as soon as they heard this. Lilly and Lesley followed them and I left the room with Violet.

The grounds were so vast and lush with vegetation that the newly-weds soon disappeared. As we walked further into the bushes, I heard Lilly giggle a couple of times, but both she and Lesley were soon out of sight.

I stood there alone with Violet. She was wearing a black dress, but not of the conservative type I'd seen her in at the firm. This one had a plunging neckline that showed the upper part of her ample bosom. The neckline rose up in two puffed-up short sleeves, through which cascaded a sheer black fabric covering her arms and ending at her tiny wrists. I don't know what came over me but I grasped her small hand and held it tightly. She didn't try to release it but looked at me, surprised. Her hair was parted in the middle and gathered in curly locks at either side of her beautiful face. She looked heavenly. And then those dark mysterious eyes met mine.

"I'm in love with you, Violet."

She did not respond. She then let go of my hand, and took my arms and slowly placed them around her waist. I drew her close to me and her sweet scent overwhelmed me. Still looking straight into my eyes, she raised her delicate fingers and touched my face gently. I could hear her breath and the pounding of my heart. Closing her eyes, she planted a soft kiss on my lips. We stood there motionless, holding each other tightly for a long while.

Suddenly, she started, "I can hear voices."

I let go of her, and as she turned towards the house, I stopped her.

"I..."

She placed her fingers on my lips. "Don't say any more, Vartan."

I gently took her hand and kissed it. We headed back to the house in silence and in joy.

⚜

It was past four o'clock in the afternoon when Lesley and I returned home. Ram joined us again for the ride back; he had been waiting for us at the gate with his gardener friend.

Neither Lesley nor I said a word as the carriage rolled away. We just kept smiling at each other.

"Sirs very happy, yes? Ram very happy too; good friend, nice talk, gardener friend give me very nice food," he said with a big smile.

"You're a rascal, Ram, you know that? If anyone heard you, they'd think we treat you badly and don't feed you properly," Lesley said with a stern face.

"Sir angry with Ram but Ram very happy with sirs," Ram said with a puzzled face.

"I'm only joking, Ram. You go and see your gardener friend whenever you like," Lesley said.

"Sirs are happy when Ram is happy," I added.

Ram relaxed and laughed warmly, as indeed all three of us did all the way to Orchid Street.

A client who had just arrived from Madras was waiting for us at the door. Obliged to take care of this unexpected visitor, we invited him to stay for supper. By the time the client left, it was past 10 o'clock. Neither

Lesley nor I felt like going to bed that night. So we made some more tea and sat in our respective armchairs. Lesley nursed his tea in silence for quite a while.

"I can't keep it to myself any longer. I've got to tell you – I kissed Lilly," he said earnestly.

"And how did she react?"

"She blushed at first but then kissed me back. And she told me she loves me dearly. She's a real angel, my friend."

"And you're the devil incarnate," I said, and leaning back in my armchair, gave him a contented smile.

"Don't tell me you kissed Violet!"

"In fact, she kissed *me* when I told her I was in love with her."

"I knew it! I could sense you had fallen for her, and she for you."

"She didn't actually tell me that."

"She wouldn't have kissed you if she hadn't. We must overcome the obstacle of her engagement."

"I am thinking about it every single minute of the day, Lesley. I will deal with it when the time is right. Now, tell me, what did you think of Agha Caloustian's performance today?"

"The man was brilliant! He had not only prepared the ground for us, but his interventions were spot on."

"I must admit he did present you to Apcarian in the best possible light. He had even thought of mentioning Sarkis Manuk to convey to your intended father-in-law both your financial viability, which we had completely ignored, and your good character."

"Indeed. You didn't do too badly yourself with Apcarian either, Vartan."

"You must agree with me that Apcarian is not an easy character. He's shrewd and intimidating, but deep down I think he's a correct and reasonable man. I am paying Agha Caloustian another visit at the end of next week. You need to come along this time and give him the go-ahead yourself. As I told you before, he is willing to act as the go-between because he knows if you went straight to Apcarian to ask for his daughter's hand, you would surely fail."

"I am ready and willing, my friend. I'll do anything for my Lilly. I cannot imagine life without her."

I couldn't imagine my life without Violet either. But unlike Lesley, I couldn't ask Agha Caloustian to intervene on my behalf – to sow disruption in the family's best-laid plans by breaking off her engagement.

CHAPTER 22

❧

A COUPLE OF DAYS LATER, having finished our chores in the office, Lesley and I sat down to plan how we might discretely get in touch with Lilly and Violet, and see them if possible. Lesley didn't think it wise to turn up at the Apcarian firm to see Lilly. He could not think of yet another pretext if he came face-to-face with her father. I was certain Violet would not make the first move, even if she wanted to. So we decided that, until after our meeting with Agha Caloustian, the best strategy for now was to write to them. We were getting ready to lock up and go upstairs for supper when we heard a knock at the door. It was none other than Apcar Apcarian himself.

Lesley quickly opened the door and said, "Good evening, Mr. Apcarian."

"Good evening, Mr. Atkinson."

"To what do we owe this honour, Mr. Apcarian," I said.

"I apologise for disturbing you like this but I have come to ask a favour of you once more, Khoja Vartan."

"Please do take a seat, Mr. Apcarian," said Lesley.

"And allow us both to thank you again for your hospitality. I assure you we welcome a visit from an honourable man like yourself. We are always at your service," I said.

"I don't want to take too much of your time, so let me get to the point straightaway. I shall need to be away on business for three weeks and just got word that my departed wife's tombstone will be arriving from Madras within the next ten days. As I am leaving the day after tomorrow with Catcheres Sarkis, and Violet's fiancé is away, too, as you know, I am loath to leave Violet to deal with the matter on her own. In fact, it was her idea that I come to you. She thinks you would also be eager to inspect how your calligraphy has turned out in carved form. I hope this important family matter will not take much of your time as I know you are a busy man. But I would be much obliged if you could oversee the transfer of the tombstone from the vessel and deal with the priest with regard to having the tombstone installed at the cemetery," Apcarian said earnestly.

"With your permission, Mr. Atkinson is better suited than me to overseeing the transfer of the tombstone from the port since he manages all our harbour activities. I shall gladly deal with whatever else is required," I said.

"I do not wish to impose on Mr. Atkinson as well," Apcarian said, looking at Lesley.

"It gives me great pleasure to be of service to you, Mr. Apcarian," Lesley replied.

"I am very thankful to both of you. I shall ask Violet to contact you when the tombstone arrives. A very good evening to you, gentlemen," he said and took his leave.

Through our shop window, Lesley and I saw him get into a carriage parked on the other side of the street. We realised it had been waiting for him. As it started to move, we could just barely discern the silhouettes of Lilly and Violet, seated next to their father. We were sure the two had been watching us through our window all the while their father was talking to us. As soon as the carriage was out of sight, Lesley let out a cry of excitement.

"Here we were racking our brains as to how we were going to see the girls and, out of the blue, their father offers them to us on a silver platter!"

"Don't be crude, Lesley."

"It's the perfect pretext for seeing them and being around them! Aren't you happy, Vartan?"

"Yes, of course. I couldn't be happier…"

The next two weeks were the happiest weeks of my entire existence. I was completely consumed by my passion for Violet, a feeling I was experiencing for the first time in my life. And every day that passed made me long for her even more. The arrival of the tombstone was the God-sent excuse that allowed both Lesley and I to spend long hours with Lilly and Violet. Lesley oversaw the transfer of the tombstone to the Armenian cemetery. My calligraphy was very well executed in carved form, and that pleased me greatly. I met with the Armenian priest and within a matter of two days the tombstone was placed on the grave of Anna Apcarian.

Lilly and Violet invited us to the Apcarian house on two occasions – on a Sunday and the following Saturday afternoon – in appreciation of our assistance, they said. Since we were the only guests, Lesley and I could not have been better rewarded. On both occasions, Lesley suggested that we take a walk in their vast grounds, but neither Lilly nor Violet was keen on the idea. We suspected that they had agreed in advance to avoid a repetition of what had happened during our first Sunday lunch there for fear of being seen by the domestics. Instead, we spent both afternoons on their veranda, chatting. Violet asked me about Erzerum, my years at the monastery, and my life in Istahan. I, in turn, asked her about her childhood in Calcutta. I savoured every iota of information I gleaned from her and cherished those long conversations, for I had her all to myself and hoped that she would get to know me better and come to love me as much as I loved her.

As they had still not seen the tombstone, Violet and Lilly were impatient to visit their mother's grave. So we arranged to accompany them to the cemetery on the following Sunday afternoon.

"Shall we invite them over for tea afterwards?" Lesley asked as we stood nearby watching the sisters praying in silence at their mother's tomb.

"I don't know if they will agree to that, but let's try."

Lilly was most keen on the idea and Violet finally gave in to her. When the carriage stopped in front of our premises, Violet and Lilly hastened indoors for fear of being spotted by someone who knew them. Once indoors, we invited them to our secluded little garden, which was shaded in the afternoons. Both Violet and Lilly admired it. Ram had indeed done wonders with the small space that we had. But, it being Sunday, his day of rest, he was not present to receive their compliments.

"I completely forgot Ram is not here. If you'll excuse me ladies, I'll go upstairs and make the tea myself," Lesley said.

"I'll come and help you," Lilly said with enthusiasm, and they were both gone.

Violet sat in one of the wicker armchairs and I, still standing, gazed upon her radiant looks in silence for a long while. She looked at me now and again, but didn't say a word.

"You are so beautiful, Violet," I said finally.

"You shouldn't say that to a woman who is engaged to be married."

I went over and knelt in front of her. Taking her soft hand in mine, I kissed it. She looked at me and then, turning her face away from me, she said in a soft, defeated voice, "I cannot fall in love with you."

Before I could respond, Lilly and Lesley were back with the tea. They chirpily chatted away. Perfectly suited to each other, both in temperament and looks, I thought. Just then I caught Violet looking at me – a look that said she concurred.

When Lilly and Violet had left, Lesley said, "Their father's arriving tomorrow. I can't wait any longer. I've got to marry Lilly as soon as possible."

"Well, Agha Caloustian promised he would talk to Apcarian the day after his return. So let's keep our hopes high," I said, trying to be as positive for Lesley as I could.

Deep in my own heart I was troubled, still wondering if Violet could ever love me as much as Lilly loved Lesley.

❧

It was the end of the week and Lesley and I were anxiously waiting in front of Agha Caloustian's colossal rosewood desk for the verdict.

"I saw Apcarian yesterday evening, but I'm afraid to tell you his answer was a clear 'no'," Agha Caloustian said.

Lesley's face darkened and sweat beads formed on his forehead.

"But I don't understand. Why will he not give his consent?" Lesley said in his high-pitched nervous voice.

"Mr. Atkinson, I understand your frustration but, as I told Khoja Vartan before, there is no telling how a man will react in these circumstances, even if he's a man who is otherwise open-minded and forward-looking. And let me tell you this, too. He has great admiration for both of you gentlemen – in every way. He mentioned this to me several times in my conversation with him and wanted me to convey that message to you. His decision has got nothing to do with whether the older sister is married or not. I shouldn't say this to you, for he asked me not to, but he will not give his consent simply because you are not an Armenian. He is terrified of the thought that his beloved daughter might be hurt or maltreated in some way if she marries outside our community."

"I would give my life for her, Agha Caloustian. I would never allow her to be hurt in any way," Lesley said indignantly.

"Perhaps Mr. Apcarian is testing Lesley's resolve in order to ensure Lilly will be in good hands," I interjected.

"Well said, Khoja Vartan. I wouldn't lose hope if I were you, Mr. Atkinson. Let's give the consenting lady a little time to soften her father.

He now knows she wants to marry you. And I promise I shall talk to Apcarian very soon again and give it another try," Agha Caloustian concluded.

Lesley was thoroughly depressed by the time we left Agha Caloustian. He could not sleep that night and neither could I. We were both at a loss as to what our next step should be.

The news from Lilly the next day was not good. We received a note in the afternoon through Violet's messenger. The short note was written by Violet, and in it she said that her father had confronted Lilly and chided her for daring to embark on an amorous relationship with Lesley. He had banned her from going to the firm and confined her to the house. He had also accused Violet of having aided Lilly and reprimanded her for not having warned her sister of the negative consequences of her actions. She ended the note with these words: "Lilly is a fragile creature and I'm afraid for her health."

"My poor Lilly...And I am incapable of helping her. I'm going insane, my friend. I can't just sit idly here. I have to do something," Lesley said almost in tears.

"I'll tell you what – let's close early. We'll go upstairs, have something to drink, and think this thing through," I said.

Ram came up to get us some tea and to prepare supper. I sat Lesley down.

"Alright – are you certain you want to marry Lilly immediately?"

"Of course I am, Vartan. What are you getting at?"

"Are you certain Lilly would not be having second thoughts about marrying you? She may have had a change of heart after the pressure exerted on her by her father?"

"I am as certain as my own name that she would not falter."

"And considering the current situation, what do you think her father's response would be if Agha Caloustian approached him again with your marriage proposal?"

"His answer would be negative."

"And if it is negative, then it would be a long while before he changes his mind. You'll have to reconcile yourself to the idea and be prepared to wait until things settle down before you make any further attempts."

"This has gone on for far too long as it is. I am not prepared to wait any longer," said Lesley scratching his head roughly. "The only alternative I have, and I was hoping it would not come to this for I dared not mention it before, is to elope."

Both Lesley and I looked at each other, surprised at where our conversation had led us. I resumed the conversation.

"That would definitely ruin all our previous efforts. Are you prepared to take that responsibility, Lesley?"

"I am. It's just that I need to propose it to Lilly first; unless I have her consent, it cannot be done."

"If she agrees with you wholeheartedly, then I will do all I can to help you both, as I too can see no other alternative."

"In that case, I need to write to her immediately. But how am I going to get the letter to her? We need to be extra cautious now, Vartan."

"I don't think it's fair to impose on Violet. I could take it to the house myself if you agree. I'll have to think of a good excuse for going there," I said.

"Ram can take letter to Lady Ma'am Lilly," Ram said, poking his head out from behind the kitchen door.

"How long have you been standing there listening to us?" Lesley said.

"Ram has gardener friend – Ram can take letter," he said, rolling his eyes as if to say he was obviously the best person to do it.

CHAPTER 23

LESLEY GAVE RAM THE LETTER the next morning and asked him to wait for Lilly's reply.

"Lesley sir not worry – Ram very careful," he said as he left.

Two hours had passed and Lesley was starting to fidget.

"Don't worry. Ram is smarter than you think. He may have had to wait in order to get to Lilly. In any case, he went there on foot and it's going to take him a while before he returns."

"I wish we'd sent him in a hired carriage," Lesley said.

Four hours had passed and still there was no sign of Ram. By this time, I too was somewhat alarmed. I told Lesley I would hire a carriage and go towards the Apcarian house and maybe I would see Ram on the way.

"If I don't, I'll try and find his gardener friend who might know his whereabouts."

And just as I was leaving, Agha Caloustian's messenger turned up to say that Agha Caloustian wanted us to go to his business premises immediately – Ram had had an accident. We jumped into a carriage with trepidation in our hearts and were at Agha Caloustian's in just ten minutes.

"Is Ram alright? What happened?" I said.

"Well, there was an accident at the Apcarian house," Agha Caloustian said calmly.

"What sort of accident?" Lesley said anxiously.

"Please, gentlemen, do sit down and I shall tell you," Agha Caloustian said in a reassuring tone, trying to calm us down.

"I was told you sent Lilly a letter with your messenger, Ram, to the house because her father had confined her there and had banned her from getting in touch with you, Mr. Atkinson. Am I right?"

Lesley nodded.

"In this letter you were trying to persuade Lilly to elope with you," Agha Caloustian said.

"That is not wholly correct. I was asking her if she agreed to such a plan since we were unable to get her father's consent to get married," Lesley replied.

"Alright – Lilly was sitting on the veranda when Ram got there. He gave your letter to her. She read it and wrote you a quick reply. I was told all this by someone who witnessed everything. One of Apcarian's gardeners, who is a friend of Ram's, I believe."

Both Lesley and I nodded.

"Unbeknownst to Lilly, her father hadn't yet left for work and he caught her red-handed, so to speak. Seeing Ram, he quickly put two and two together and guessed that you had sent him. So he grabbed Ram by the collar in order to snatch Lilly's letter from him. Ram managed to release himself from Apcarian's grip and get away. Unfortunately, he tripped and fell over the fencing of the veranda. When he fell, his head hit one of the border stones of the garden. They tried to revive him but he remained unconscious. Apcarian panicked and quickly sent for Dr. Smith, and then sent someone over to fetch me. When I got there the lad was still unconscious, but Dr. Smith said he was alive."

"Is he alright now? Where is he?" I said.

"Khoja Vartan, I'm afraid he's still unconscious, although he doesn't have any apparent head wound – just a scratch. Dr. Smith calls it 'coma', caused by concussion. He asked us to move the lad to a comfortable place. I volunteered to take him here."

"All this is my fault. I should never have sent him to the Apcarian house," Lesley said, clearly distraught.

"If it's any consolation, Dr. Smith believes the lad should regain consciousness in a few days but he can't be certain. Put your trust in God," Agha Caloustian said affectionately.

"Can we see him?" I asked.

"Yes, certainly. We placed him in a room that I use if I am too busy here to go home," he said, and led us to a back room which was in fact a fully decorated bedroom with a large bed. Ram was lying there. He looked peaceful, as if merely sound asleep. Sadness and guilt engulfed both Lesley and I.

"Do not worry, gentlemen. Dr. Smith will be coming to check on him every day, and he will be looked after 24 hours a day by Maria, my late wife's personal maid, whom I still employ. You may visit him every day and at any time that suits you."

"We are indeed very grateful for your kindness, Agha Caloustian," I said.

"Come, let me offer you something to drink – I have something else to tell you," he said, and led us to his reception room.

He then told us that we had just missed Lilly's father who had turned up to check on Ram's condition.

"The man was distraught. He said he was very sorry and felt he was responsible for what had happened. He asked me to convey to you his sincere apologies."

"It was clearly an accident and he didn't mean to hurt Ram," I said.

"This is between you and me, gentlemen; he admitted Lilly had written that she was willing to elope with you, Mr. Atkinson."

"It would be heartless of me to think about elopement now when Ram is between life and death."

"I understand, but hear what I have to say, Mr. Atkinson. Lilly's father knows there is nothing he can do to change her mind and he is aware of how determined you are. But I warned you about him before. He is a stern man with an ego the size of Mount Ararat. He told me in no uncertain terms, again, that he will not give his consent willingly. Even if he expects Lilly to elope with you, he will not make it easy for you."

We were terribly upset about Ram's condition and could think of nothing else. We visited him every evening after work and prayed for his recovery. On the third day, at lunchtime, Agha Caloustian's messenger turned up to say that Ram had come to. So we rushed over to see him.

When we got there, Agha Caloustian told us Dr. Smith had just left and Ram was conscious and doing well.

"Dr. Smith checked his eyes, ears and everything else. Everything's in perfect order, he said. So put your minds to rest. He just wants the lad to stay in bed for a week to recuperate; he might as well stay where he is and Maria can continue looking after him," Agha Caloustian said.

"We do not want to abuse your kindness," I said.

"Nonsense! Let's go and see him," he said in a jolly tone.

The minute Ram saw us he gave us a huge ear-to-ear smile and said, "Lesley sir, Vartan sir, Ram very well." Then, he cast his gaze around the room as if to say he couldn't be in a more comfortable place.

"You had us worried to death, you rascal," Lesley said.

"But you're alright now. You've come back from the dead, just like Lazarus," I said.

"Who Lazarus?" Ram inquired.

Agha Caloustian laughed, and looking at the young Indian lady standing next to Ram's bed said, "Ask Maria. She's a true Catholic, and from Madras, and she speaks your language!"

A week had almost passed and we were desperately looking forward to Ram's return, for, in truth, we were rather helpless around the apartment without him. Then, we got an urgent message from Agha Caloustian to pay him a visit.

"Please do sit down, gentlemen," Agha Caloustian said as he ushered us into his office himself and dismissed his personal assistant.

"Let me ask you first what your plans are regarding the elopement," he said.

"We've been doing all the preparation work. I've already contacted the Anglican priest since Vartan found out the Armenian priest will not marry us without Lilly's father's consent," Lesley said.

I added, "We've also been refurbishing the apartment that we reside in now so Lesley and Lilly can have a decent home to go to after their wedding – at least as a temporary measure. I have already found lodgings – two rooms – right next door to our premises."

"Good. I meant to tell you that, legally, since she is 21 years of age, Lilly is free to choose whom she marries. Nevertheless, if her father attempts to contact the authorities in order to have the marriage annulled or create problems for you, he will not be able to go far as I have my own contacts in high places at the Governorate," Agha Caloustian said with pride.

"Thank you for reassuring me, but we still haven't worked out a strategy for the elopement because we can't get in touch with Lilly," Lesley said.

"I guessed that much. It's not going to be easy to get to Lilly. The reason why I asked you to come here today is because Violet, her sister, sent me a letter this morning saying that even she was being closely watched and the only way she could communicate with you was through me. She said that she urgently wanted to tell you that Lilly is no longer at the house. Her father sent her to Glugar, on the north coast. Don't be alarmed. It's not that far from here. She is staying with a cousin of Catcheres Sarkis who has a house there."

"That changes things quite a bit. I was still hoping we could get in touch with Lilly through Violet," Lesley said with an air of disappointment.

"I think we need a couple of days to devise a fool-proof plan," I said. Lesley nodded in agreement.

"I agree, too," said Agha Caloustian, and then added, "I have something else to report to you – concerning Ram."

"Is anything the matter?"

"Is he alright?"

"No worries, gentlemen. I can see why you're attached to him. He is indeed a likeable soul. Your Ram wants to marry my Maria!"

Both Lesley and I looked at each other with surprise and utter disbelief.

"I went round to see him this morning to tell him that he'll be returning to you tomorrow. He said he won't leave unless Maria comes with him. I tried to reason with him: I said she was older than him by a good four or five years; I told him she was a fervent Catholic and she would never become a Hindu; I told him he'll have to marry her in her church. And you know what he said? 'Please sir, Ram will do what you like, what Maria like. Don't care. Ram loves Maria.' And he kept on repeating these words until I told him I'll have to speak to you first."

"In this world, there is no one more obstinate than our Ram!" Lesley said.

"Agha Caloustian, we are very sorry for repaying your kindness with this headache that Ram is causing you," I said.

"No, no, no! Don't get me wrong, gentlemen. If you have no objections, and I have none, they can get married right now if God permits. I spoke to Maria and it is clear she has developed a soft spot for your young man, no doubt about it. She came here as a teenager, fourteen or so, and served my wife with loyalty for a long time. After my wife passed away, I did not truly need her services but I kept her as she had grown up in my household. It would give me immense personal joy to see her happily married. Come to think of it, she would be a perfect helper for Lilly. After all, she will need one when she marries you, Mr. Atkinson. So what do you say, gentlemen?"

"Isn't tomorrow a Sunday? I'm certain we can find a Catholic priest to marry them," I said.

"That lucky rascal is going to get married before me!" remarked Lesley.

Ram and Maria were married the following day. On our third attempt, we found a Catholic priest who didn't object to Ram not being baptized. With a little coaching from us, Maria, and the priest, Ram was ready to face the wedding ceremony.

He was all smiles as Maria shyly followed him to the altar. Lesley and Agha Caloustian, whose eyes had watered by now, were their two witnesses. And I was the only invited guest. When the wedding ceremony was over, the priest blessed the newlyweds and requested their full names in order to record the marriage.

"Maria Pedro," said Maria in a whisper.

The priest then turned to Ram, waiting for his response. Poor Ram. Having never had a family, he'd never had a family name either. We'd failed to anticipate this as we coached him. A hushed silence fell over us as we waited to see what he would say. The priest repeated his request. Again, Ram hesitated. Then, turning around to look at me, eyes smiling, he seemed as if inspired. Turning back to the priest, he declared confidently:

"Ram Lazarus!"

CHAPTER 24

❀

AFTER LEAVING THE NEWLYWEDS IN the care of Agha Caloustian, who had insisted on providing 'a honeymoon nest for the love birds', Lesley and I headed for home. Lesley promptly began to devise the elopement plan.

"So, what do you think?" he said, after elaborating.

"I think that's a very good plan. I suggest we find a place where you can lie low after the wedding. You'll need to spend a couple of weeks there until such time as things have calmed down with the father and you can bring Lilly home to the apartment," I said.

"That's a very good idea. The only loose end in the whole plan is Violet. It is imperative we find out if and when she's going to visit her sister, which I'm sure she will at some point, and also whether she will be able to do so on her own, unaccompanied by her father," Lesley mused.

"We must tell Agha Caloustian about the plan tomorrow and ask him to get in touch with Violet immediately," I said.

"I'm hoping I'll be wedded to Lilly by next Sunday," Lesley said with conviction.

Agha Caloustian got a quick response from Violet on Tuesday morning. In her note, she said that she would be going to visit Lilly in Glugar on Thursday afternoon at 3; she needed to take some clothing over that Lilly had asked for. She also thought she could manage to leave work early and visit Lilly again on Saturday around 2 o'clock in the afternoon. Her father had an important meeting with clients at that time and would not miss her.

Upon our instructions, Agha Caloustian's written response to Violet stated that we would be following her carriage on Thursday to learn the exact location of the house in Glugar where Lilly was staying. Agha Caloustian also asked Violet to stop her carriage at a point of her choice before she reached Glugar so we could give her a letter of instructions for herself and Lilly to follow for the elopement, which was to take place on Saturday.

On Thursday afternoon, just before 3, Lesley and I had our carriage parked opposite the main entrance of the Apcarian and Associates' building. A little after 3, we spotted Violet coming out of the building and getting into a carriage. We followed. A good 15 minutes later, her carriage stopped at a junction just outside of Georgetown. We got closer and stopped our carriage next to hers. She already had the window open and she looked straightaway at me first. She was wearing a straw hat with black ribbons coming down from either side, framing her beautiful face. My heart started beating fast – I had so missed seeing her.

"Thank you, Violet," Lesley said and passed the letter to her from the window.

"I have a small suitcase to give you. It contains a few things that Lilly might need on Saturday. And her wedding dress – my mother's," she said anxiously.

I quickly jumped out of the carriage, went round the other side of hers and opened the door. As she leaned over and handed me the suitcase, our fingers touched.

"I wish I could attend the wedding, but I doubt it very much. Whatever your plan is for Saturday, I have to be back at the house by 5 o'clock so my father doesn't become suspicious."

"I wish with all my heart you could be there. I miss you terribly, Violet."

Her eyes suddenly welled with tears. Without saying another word, I let go of the carriage door. Her carriage started to slowly move on and we continued to follow.

"She's thought of everything Lilly might need, even the wedding dress," Lesley said a while later.

"Lilly's the only sister she's got," was my reply.

A good half hour later, we were in Glugar. Violet's carriage finally stopped in front of a large house painted all in white and standing at the edge of the seashore. She got out, quickly glanced in our direction to ensure we were there, and carrying another small suitcase, headed towards the door. She disappeared inside. Her carriage waited for her.

About an hour and a half later, the door opened. Violet came out first, followed by Lilly. A few minutes later, Violet was in the carriage. Lilly, who was standing at the door, waved at her but she was looking in our direction. As soon as Violet's carriage moved off, she went back in and closed the door.

"I can't believe Lilly's so close and I can't speak to her," Lesley said with sadness when we had lost sight of Violet's carriage.

"Patience, my friend. Let's inspect the area to make sure nothing goes wrong on Saturday," I said.

The area was very quiet and the few houses in the vicinity of the white house were a good distance away.

"Holiday homes belonging to the wealthy families of Georgetown – they come here to breathe the fresh sea air. Further down the coast people own plantations," Lesley remarked.

We asked the carriage driver to take us towards the back of the white house. We spotted a private two-wheel carriage parked at the other end of the house.

"I'm guessing this is why Violet thinks she won't be able to make it to the wedding. Whoever is in the house with Lilly now is perfectly capable of driving into Georgetown on Saturday and informing Apcarian that Lilly has disappeared; they may even be able to follow our carriage, all the way to the church. When Lilly joins us on Saturday, we must take another route to Georgetown," I said and Lesley nodded in agreement.

He then stopped the carriage and asked the carriage driver if there was another route to Georgetown, an alternative to the main coastal road we had taken earlier. The man said there was and quickly turned the carriage around. He drove back to the main coastal road, but instead of heading east to Georgetown, he took the opposite direction. Ten minutes later, as soon as we passed a large, expensive-looking inn overlooking the seashore, the carriage turned left into a side lane. We gathered it was a shortcut since it led us to an inland road parallel to the main coastal one. The carriage turned left again and we were on our way back to Georgetown.

"I have an idea, Lesley. After the wedding, you and Lilly can stay at that expensive-looking inn that we passed earlier on. No one will ever suspect you are in Glugar," I said.

"That's a brilliant idea. It would be an ideal spot to hide out for a week or two," he said and added with a smile, "We've devised the perfect elopement plan!"

On Friday, Lesley went to see the Anglican priest to confirm the wedding date and time and to ask if the priest could make one of his rooms available just before the wedding for Lilly to change into her wedding dress. He then went over to Glugar to inspect the inn, and, if it proved suitable, to reserve a room.

I went to visit Agha Caloustian to update him on the progress of matters and to find out if there were any messages from Violet. There were none.

"That's rather good news, I should think. It means everything's going according to plan," he said.

"And how are Ram and Maria doing?" I inquired.

"The love birds are doing just fine. I tell you, they are perfectly matched, although I didn't think so at the very start. And of course, they are looking forward to attending Lesley's and Lilly's wedding tomorrow."

"I'm glad to hear that," I said.

"Khoja Vartan, about tomorrow, I hope you and Lesley don't mind if I don't attend the wedding. I shall ask my daughter and son-in-law to attend on my behalf. And Lilly might appreciate a female companion when she's readying herself as I am certain she will be sad her sister is not present."

"Indeed, I'm sure she would be very grateful to you and to your daughter for her companionship. And I understand you may have other, important engagements, Agha Caloustian."

"It's not quite that, Khoja Vartan. I've been thinking ahead. Apcarian is very attached to his daughters. His attachment to them exceeds the usual bond between father and daughters. The reason is very simple. He feels they fill the gap in his heart of the missing son, the son he never had and the one he desperately longed for. I understand him perfectly well for I too have no son of my own. But I do not share his desperation. I am reconciled with my destiny and I thank the Lord for all the blessings he has given me. Apcarian's daughters know exactly what I'm talking about and they have made it their life's mission, so far, to fill the gap of the missing son in their father's heart."

"Is that the reason why Ms. Violet didn't object to her father's choice of the man she is to marry? I understand he's a lot older than her," I dared comment.

"Precisely, and I wouldn't want to be in her shoes. The poor girl will be marrying someone she does not truly love," he said.

I nodded, disguising the torment in my heart.

"And that is why I am eager to help Lilly to elope. Apcarian may be able to employ emotional blackmail to force his older daughter to accept his plans for her. But Lilly will soon be beyond his control. This will teach him a good lesson. He will certainly be very angry with her for having eloped. He'll have wished she hadn't taken such an action. Still, in the long run, he will want to make contact with her again as, despite his stern appearance and authoritarian behaviour, he has a soft heart. I am sure he will approach me to help him with the reconciliation sooner than you think. If ever he finds out I attended Lilly's wedding, he will never forgive me. And that will aggravate an already strained relationship with his daughter, with negative consequences for Lilly and Lesley within our community here."

"As always, you are the wisest of us all, Agha Caloustian," I said.

He responded with a satisfied smile.

Saturday noon was soon upon us and Lesley was ready but I could see he was tense and nervous. I tried to entertain him as best I could until it was time to follow Violet's carriage again. Violet took the carriage, as planned, and headed towards the outskirts of Georgetown. Her carriage stopped at the same spot as previously; we stopped next to her. I was seated on her side of the carriage. She tilted her head and moved it forward out of the carriage window, as did I. Our faces almost touched.

"There are a number of Catcheres Sarkis' male relatives at the house. Park your carriage behind mine, but a little further away. I will come out of the house in exactly one hour. Lilly will accompany me to my carriage with the excuse of bidding me farewell."

"Alright, Violet. Understood. When we leave with Lilly, we'll be taking a different route than yours to throw off whoever might try to follow us," I said.

Then she grabbed my arm, squeezed it tightly and looked at me with great apprehension.

"Don't worry, Violet. We'll take good care of Lilly."

She let go of my arm and fell back in her seat. Her carriage moved on again and we followed until she reached the white house and went in. Precisely an hour later, the door opened and Violet came out. Lilly followed her to the carriage. They embraced and Violet gave Lilly a shawl. As soon as Violet was seated in her carriage, Lilly covered her head with the shawl and headed straight towards us hastily. Lesley helped her into our carriage as I watched Violet's carriage depart. I checked the house door, which had been left ajar, but there was no sign of anyone.

"Let's move. Quickly!" I said.

We were soon behind Violet's carriage. She turned left onto the main coastal road, and we swung right to head further inland. I immediately put my head out of the carriage window and looked behind us. I knew Violet would do likewise. She, too, would want to make sure we were safely away with Lilly.

Lilly was shaking like a leaf out of fear and anxiety. Lesley tried to reassure her. He had his arm protectively around her and was telling her everything would work out alright. Lesley cajoled her and then gave her the engagement ring he had kept for so long. He finally managed to relax her, but out of fear of being spotted by someone she knew, especially in Georgetown, Lilly kept the large scarf on her head until they'd entered the church. Lilly was pleasantly surprised to see Maria and Agha Caloustian's daughter already there and waiting for us; the ladies led Lilly to a back room to dress her. Ram gave us one of his big smiles and Agha Caloustian's son-in-law politely greeted us. I followed Lesley to the altar and was almost as anxious as he was, being his best man. We didn't have to wait for too long before Lilly appeared in her wedding gown. She looked lovely indeed, and Lesley whispered, "This makes it all worth every bit of trouble and suffering."

The wedding ceremony was the shortest I had ever witnessed. I could not be sure if that was because it was the Anglican way of weddings or if it had been abridged purposely by the priest since he was aware it was a case of elopement. But it didn't matter, for the brevity suited all of us present, who were relieved that the whole affair had finally come to a happy end. There was now not a trace of the previous fearful and anxious Lilly. I kissed her hand and congratulated her and called her 'Mrs. Atkinson'.

"Thank you, best man," she said and glanced at Lesley lovingly.

Lesley gave me a huge hug and said, "We did it! Thank you, my dear, dear friend."

Lesley and Lilly were soon off to the inn in Glugar. As all five of us stood in front of the church waving at their moving carriage, I quietly became aware once again of my own longings. I returned home alone and began earnestly praying that I would soon be united with Violet. If only God Almighty would hear my prayers.

CHAPTER 25

⚜

"YOU CANNOT IMAGINE THE UPROAR Apcarian created last night, Khoja Vartan," Agha Caloustian told me the next day after he'd sent word for me to come around.

"Tell me everything that happened, Agha. I have been instructed to report all to Lesley and Lilly. I'm to go and see them in a few days at their hideout."

"I'll start from the beginning then. When Lilly had not returned from saying goodbye to Violet, Catcheres Sarkis' relatives had quickly understood that Lilly had eloped. A couple of them hastily rode into Georgetown and went straight to Apcarian's house with the news. Luckily for her, Violet had reached home by then. Apcarian had a fit of rage when he heard the news. He immediately sent someone to fetch myself and Catcheres Sarkis. I was horrified by what the messenger recounted and feared Apcarian would have a heart attack any minute and drop dead on the spot, so I went to the Apcarian house as quickly as I could. When I got there, I witnessed his fury unleashed on Violet. He accused her of aiding her sister to elope. Frightened, she vehemently denied it and said the last time she saw Lilly was when she was waving her goodbye, and began to cry. Hearing this, Apcarian turned to Catcheres Sarkis and said that if it wasn't an arranged elopement, then Lilly must have surely been kidnapped by Mr. Atkinson and taken against her will. He threatened to go to the authorities. When

Catcheres Sarkis attempted to calm him down, he began blaming his relatives and held them responsible since Lilly was in their care, he said."

"I can't believe what I'm hearing," I said. "That is the most un-gentlemanly type of behaviour I have witnessed in this town. These people were just doing Apcarian a favour by lodging Lilly at their residence. He must have completely lost his senses."

"Indeed, so I intervened at this point for I could sense the hostility in Catcheres Sarkis' relatives and thought things could get ugly. I had to tell Apcarian that I had just got word that Lilly and Lesley were married at the Anglican Church. His eyes widened. The news clearly shocked him. He then attacked me. He said that I should be ashamed, being the doyen of the Armenian community in Georgetown. I was a friend of Lesley's and therefore must have known about his plans to elope with Lilly, he said. I had to assure him that I had no inkling and said that the news was reported to me by none other than the lad Ram whom he had almost killed, albeit accidentally. Defeated, Apcarian collapsed in an armchair and kept on repeating, 'How could she? I shall never forgive that bounder Atkinson for taking my little Lilly away from me.' Catcheres Sarkis tried to calm his nerves by saying that he shouldn't be so upset since we knew Lilly was alright and was not in any way harmed. And then, upon a nod from him, his relatives left promptly. I myself thought it was the right moment to say to Apcarian, but in a calm and serious manner, that Lilly was in love with Lesley and that he should be happy for her. And I did."

"What was his response?"

"He just looked at me with glazed eyes and said nothing. When I left, Catcheres Sarkis was still there. We had at least managed to put a stop to his rage."

"Have you heard anything since?"

"Yes, this morning, I got a letter of apology. It was just a couple of lines from Apcarian asking me to forgive him for his un-gentlemanly behaviour of last night. I told you this would happen, didn't I? The road to reconciliation has already begun," he smiled, and I accepted his offer of a celebratory glass of brandy.

It was one early morning a few days later. I had intentionally woken up very early to do a few household chores before I opened the business premises, Ram being still at Agha Caloustian's with his Maria. I had been packing some of my clothing and personal belongings in order to transfer them bit by bit to my new lodgings next door ahead of Lesley and Lilly's return. Around 7:30, I heard a tap-tapping noise. Wondering who it could be at this time of the morning, I went downstairs. And there she was – Violet. I let her in. She was carrying a small leather suitcase.

"I can't stay for long; my carriage is waiting and I have to get to work," she said nervously. "I just wanted to give you this. The last time I saw Lilly we agreed that I would send her some fresh clothing a few days after her wedding if I could. She told me you would be able to deliver them as you would know where she was."

"Come in, for at least a little while," I said, taking the suitcase from her. I led her to the back garden. She didn't want to sit down.

"I certainly will deliver the suitcase to Lilly. They're staying at an inn in Glugar until things settle down here with your father."

"In Glugar? Who would have thought – certainly not my father," she said, and added sarcastically, "You two planned all this down to the last detail."

"We wouldn't have succeeded without your help, Violet."

"Is she happy? Did she look pretty in her wedding dress?" she asked with an innocent smile and glittering eyes.

I came closer and, taking her hand, looked into her beautiful face and said, "She looked angelic, and they are the happiest newlyweds in the world." And squeezing her tiny hand in mine, I whispered, "We could be happy together, too."

She suddenly planted a kiss on my cheek. I leaned over and began kissing her soft neck; she placed her hand on my head and ran her fingers through my hair. I shuddered with joy, such heavenly bliss. Shortly, she gently pushed me away and said coyly, "I hope you're not thinking that I will consent to eloping with you."

"That is one possibility. You can't be hostile to the idea. You just helped your sister to elope with Lesley."

"I would have done anything to make Lilly happy," she said in a serious tone.

"But what about you – us?"

"I told you before. I cannot allow myself to be in love with you. I don't want to be the cause of my father's demise," she said, maintaining her serious tone.

"But Violet, I gather from what Agha Caloustian tells me, your father is already softening up and will eventually come around to forgiving Lilly for what she did."

"You don't understand. Lilly is the baby of the family. My father will forgive her – no matter what she does. I'm different. I carry the mantle of the older daughter."

"The mantle of the heir – the son he never had."

She nodded, sadly.

"Is that why you accepted to marry your father's associate even though you don't love or even care for him?"

"You don't know what you're saying," she retorted. "That associate of my father's is the kindest man I've ever met. Without his loyalty, my father would have remained in utter ruin. And I shall be marrying him next month," she said in a determined voice.

"Please, Violet, don't say that. You cannot brush aside the feelings we have for each other."

"Perhaps it's just temporary infatuation."

"If you're trying to upset me, Violet, you're certainly succeeding. Is that how you feel about us?"

"Alright. Let me tell you this. I don't pretend to know everything about you but I think I know you enough to say that you are incapable of betraying a man who trusted you with his daughters' care, a man who honoured you with the responsibility of placing his wife's tombstone on her grave."

"Well, in that case, since I helped Lesley and Lilly to elope, I should feel terribly guilty," I responded.

"You helped them because none of it involved you or me. You're selfless – like me. We are two of a kind, Vartan," she said, looking at me affectionately.

And coming closer, she placed her head on my chest. I held her tightly and said, "My sweet Violet, my sweet girl."

We remained in each other's arms for a long while.

When she moved away, she was crying. Tears kept pouring down her flushed cheeks.

"Don't cry, Violet, please."

"I want you to look me straight in the eye and tell me you don't feel guilty for having betrayed the memory of your late wife. Tell me you don't feel guilty for having lived, for having loved again."

I wasn't expecting those words from Violet. They left me speechless.

"Now you know how guilty I feel. I can betray neither the man who saved my father nor my father. I cannot fight my destiny – however much I want to," she said despairingly.

Still sobbing profusely, she turned and hastened towards the door.

"Don't leave, Violet."

"I beg of you, Vartan," she said, looking at me one last time. "Forget this unfortunate girl."

She rushed out the door and into her waiting carriage. I watched forlornly as the carriage disappeared.

I was in a daze for days. One minute I felt helpless and the next, angry, rejected, and betrayed. I wanted to forget Violet, as she'd asked me to, but my heart wouldn't allow it. I was constantly reminded of her words and although I wanted to un-love her, I couldn't. My mind was in never-ending turmoil. I could not bear the thought of Violet being married to someone else. In my heart, she was mine. I felt sorry for myself and cursed my fate for the loss of all my family members and my dear Mariam and Anoosh. I had suffered terribly since, and loneliness had been my constant on more occasions than I cared to remember. But the emptiness I felt now was deeper than anything I had ever experienced, for I had lost Violet, the true love of my life.

One evening, I found myself in front of the Armenian Church. There was not a soul in sight as I entered. I stood motionless, facing the altar. The silence that reigned and the smell of the burning incense brought tears to my eyes. I prayed over and over again. When I left the church, I had made up my mind to leave for Burma.

The following day, I visited Agha Caloustian to inquire if any of his vessels were scheduled to leave for Burma soon. He said there was one in six days' time. As I left, he said, "I wish you good business there. Please convey my best regards to Sarkis Manuk. I hope to see you again soon, Khoja Vartan."

I told him I was going to be based there for a good while and would not be back soon but thanked him for his trust and companionship.

Ram and Maria turned up at Orchid Street the next day. The sight of them made me forget my heartache for a moment. I had greatly missed Ram. I welcomed him and suggested that we enlarge his living quarters by adding a room at the far corner of the garden. Ram was pleased, as was Maria, with the idea. I then asked them if they could prepare the apartment for Lilly and Lesley before their return to Georgetown in a few days.

I had been to see them in Glugar twice. Lilly was grateful for the clothing that Violet had sent her. But I didn't have the heart to tell them just yet what had happened between Violet and me or of my decision to leave for Burma. I didn't wish to spoil their honeymoon or their obvious happiness.

"I've figured everything out. It will be good for our business. One of us being based in Burma is the way we'd planned it initially, Lesley," I said the day after Lesley and Lilly had returned to Georgetown and were comfortably settled in the apartment upstairs.

"Why are you doing this? I know you told me that Violet doesn't wish to betray her father, but you're a fool to give up on her like this. We'll think of something to help her break off her engagement. If needs be, I'm willing to kidnap her for you, my friend. Isn't that what they sometimes do in your old country?"

"Don't talk nonsense, Lesley," I said.

"I just don't understand. Why aren't you fighting for her? You are going to lose her forever, my friend. Why are you running away?" Lesley challenged me.

"Lesley, my love for Violet is a love with no future. Don't argue with me, please. I've made up my mind. I'm going to Burma."

On the morning of my departure, I left my lodgings and went next door to say farewell to Lesley and Lilly. They were all there. I said my good-byes to our clerk and book-keeper, and turning towards Ram and Maria, said, "Look after Lesley and Lilly well." They both grinned and bid me farewell. Lilly was standing a little further away, crying. I took her hand, kissed it and said, "Be happy, Lilly." Lesley then took my bag, and we stepped out of the premises.

"I'll get in touch with Sarkis Manuk as soon as I get there and will write as soon as I can," I said.

He nodded, and then said, "I've got something to give you – a note from Violet. She sent it to us last night with a messenger. She told me to make you promise not to open it until you've boarded the ship."

"I promise," I said, and put the envelope in my pocket.

"I hope to see you soon, my dear, dear friend," said Lesley as he gave me one of his big hugs.

I was gone before he could see the tears in my eyes.

I boarded the *Anna*, bound for Burma. My heart was heavy and sadness was now my constant companion. I took Violet's note out of my pocket:

I am condemned by the curse of family duty and loyalty. In order not to betray my father, I have betrayed my only love. Maybe in your heart of hearts you can one day forgive this unfortunate girl. And, wherever you are in this world, remember that she will always carry you in her soul.

CHAPTER 26

As the *Anna* plied the waters north towards the Sea of Burma, I reflected on how this was the first time I had not looked forward to journeying to a new place. I knew that wherever I was going, I was going somewhere akin to hell, for anywhere without Violet was just that.

The further the *Anna* sailed from Penang, the more distraught I became, venturing into the far corners of my mind. I questioned the wisdom of my decision to leave Violet and Georgetown. Was Lesley right? If I had been spontaneous and impulsive like him, I would have perhaps dared to snatch Violet, even against her express wishes. But that was not me. Perhaps Lesley spoke the truth. I didn't fight for her enough. I may have been too proud to challenge her loyalty to her father and to the man to whom she was promised. I had to admit to myself that Violet was right. I did feel guilt at the very beginning when I sensed that I had fallen in love with her. Anoosh was my dear departed wife, the mother of my child. Her memory still had a place in my heart. But Violet was the mover of my heart, the breath of my life. From the first moment I laid eyes on her, I knew my heart would never be the same again. I may have been foolish to leave, but if I hadn't left, would she have realised our souls were bound together for eternity?

One bright sunny morning, as the *Anna* was slowly and steadily approaching Burma, I went on deck for the first time since the start of the voyage. I was lost in thought when I noticed a young man walking towards me. He hesitated for a moment and then said in Armenian, "Khoja Vartan – am I correct?"

"That is indeed my name. But forgive me – I do not recall having met you before. I am nevertheless honoured, sir," I said.

"I was introduced to you some five years ago in Batavia but allow me to re-introduce myself. My name is Tovmas, the younger son of Takoohy Manuk."

"I apologise for not having recognised you, Mr. Tovmas."

"I was only 17 then and I've changed," he said, pointing to his thick sideburns.

"The nephew of Sarkis Manuk! What a pleasure meeting you again. I have fond memories of my trip to Batavia, and in particular of your family there – your brother, mother, and your older uncle and his family. Are you visiting your Uncle Sarkis then?" I inquired.

"I've been assisting him in the business. I've done so for a little over a year now and I'm returning from a business trip to Malacca. I caught the *Anna* just in time and was unable to visit you and your partner in Penang. It was I who was shipping the rubies to you these past months."

"I am most grateful to you. I thought it strange when you addressed me as 'khoja' as I didn't have the title five years ago. What an auspicious coincidence to have met you like this. As it happens I'm travelling to Burma with the main purpose of meeting your uncle. He had advised my partner and me that it would be wiser if one of us was based in Burma to procure the rubies."

"I am aware of that. My uncle talked to me about it and asked me to take care of your shipments temporarily as he is indeed too occupied with his other projects."

"I must thank him for the assistance he has given us and look forward to meeting him in person. But my decision to come to Burma was taken on the spur of the moment and I'm afraid I was unable to inform him about my arrival. I hope this will not be seen as inconsiderate on my part, Mr. Tovmas," I said.

"Do not concern yourself about that, Khoja Vartan. He is not a man who places a great deal of importance on formalities. You will plainly see this when you meet him. In fact, he will be waiting for me when we arrive in Rangoon."

"I do not care for formalities either. So please feel free to address me simply as Vartan," I said.

"And you may call me Tovmas, the one who shall always be at your service in Burma."

Meeting Tovmas took away my apprehension at going to a place I had never been before. This unexpected, pleasant, well-mannered and helpful companion uplifted my spirits during the rest of the journey to Burma.

My expectations of his uncle, Sarkis Manuk, were: that he was an experienced merchant, a dependable and loyal associate, and a shrewd man in his late thirties. Within less than an hour of meeting him in Rangoon, I understood why Lesley and Agha Caloustian thought so highly of him and with such affection, too. Sarkis Manuk was unlike any other man I had ever met. He was an exceptional character and one with whom one made friends immediately and wished to remain so for the rest of one's life.

In physical appearance, Sarkis Manuk was of average height and wore simple but stylish clothes. Not as handsome as Tovmas, he nevertheless had pleasing features and gleaming dark eyes. He was slim but well-built. What struck me the moment I met him were his sun-burnt face and hands. I was soon to discover the reason for this; Sarkis Manuk was a doer, an adventurer, a risk-taker, not a merchant who was content to sit behind his desk.

Unlike Tovmas' mother, his older sister Takoohy, who carried herself in a regal, aloof, and reserved manner, befitting their noble Armenian ancestry, Sarkis Manuk's comportment was that of a simple man of the people. He was friendly, open, and unassuming, brushing aside all manner of formality and even conventional behaviour. So when I met him with Tovmas, shortly after we disembarked at Rangoon, it was as if I was re-united with an old friend, for that is how he made me feel. He called me 'my friend Vartan' as soon as we met, carried my bag all the way to nearby lodgings, told me the essentials of life in Burma, in particular regarding the procurement of precious stones, introduced me to a couple of Armenian merchants that very evening, and even took me to the only Armenian Church in Rangoon. In other words, he put me at total ease on my first day in Burma.

I also learned that although Sarkis journeyed to Rangoon quite often for business, he and his family lived in Ava, where the court of the Burmese king was located. His plan for me was to journey with him to Ava. Once there, he would take care of all the arrangements for me to be based in Amarapura, a nearby town which had been the previous king's capital; it was to this town that suppliers of rubies came first to sell their precious stones. Noticing that I got on very well with Tovmas, and that Tovmas enjoyed my company as he was closer to me in age, Sarkis agreed to let him accompany me and stay with me in Amarapura until I was well settled.

I soon discovered that the people of Burma, who were from the stock of various Asiatic tribes, mainly followed the teachings of the Buddha. Although I had already seen some Buddhist monks in Penang, I was fascinated by the sheer number of them in their red garbs and shaven heads who roamed the streets of Rangoon. The day following my arrival, Sarkis took me to the Maong-Pha temple, the great pagoda of Rangoon. It was larger than I had imagined and was richly gilded. Inside was a huge statue of the Buddha and hundreds of monks were gathered there for prayers. Countless locals then started arriving at the temple with their offerings. These offerings consisted of flowers and fruit for the most part. Sarkis explained to me the difference between Hinduism, with which I was already familiar, and Buddhism. He corrected me when I referred to the Buddha as a god; he said the Buddha was more akin to an ultimate master whose teachings would guide the believer in his quest for self-perfection. Daily prayer, purity of mind through meditation, and purity of body through frugal and simple living were integral parts of their belief.

"It is much like the essence of the teachings of our Lord Jesus Christ," Sarkis said, and added, "But with one main difference. They believe in re-incarnation, a concept borrowed from Hinduism, and we believe in an afterlife for our souls."

When I'd left Penang, I'd been bereft of any of the enthusiasm of undertaking a new adventure. But now, I had to admit to myself that Sarkis had given me back that enthusiasm. My heart still ached terribly when I thought of Violet, which was often, but at least now I knew that Burma would not be quite the hell I had imagined it would be.

⚜

We began our journey north up river to Ava a week later on a Burmese trading boat. It was chartered by Sarkis, Garabed of Shiraz, an older trader and kinsman of the two Armenian merchants I was introduced to in Rangoon, and a Portuguese trader known as de Souza. Other than those I mentioned and Tovmas and myself, there was Father d'Amato, a Jesuit priest and scholar. Sarkis had just met him, and upon learning that he was penniless and had been stranded in Rangoon for over a year, in a typically generous gesture had invited him to join us. Father d'Amato had spent his time in Rangoon studying the Burmese language with Buddhist monks who had welcomed him and provided him with lodging and food. We noticed that the only possessions he had were his ink, quill, and papers. His main objective in going to Ava was to present himself to the king and obtain both permission and a small fund to start an orphanage in the area. The only others on board were crewmen and four mercenary soldiers.

In order to reach the Irawadi River, which would take us all the way to Ava, we had first to navigate the Panlang River, one of the arms of the Irawadi. This required skilful maneuvering along what was but a narrow, meandering channel. I soon discovered the reason why Sarkis had hired the four mercenary soldiers, who were heavily armed. Banditry was rife along these stretches of the river. Without protection, we were an easy target. Sarkis told me that the soldiers, who were of mixed race, Chinese-Portuguese and Christian, had been in the service of the previous Burmese king. I remarked that their experience would undoubtedly make up for the fact that they were no longer in their prime. Tovmas agreed with me and said he couldn't have felt safer – nevertheless, the three of us still carried our Armenian daggers with us at all times. I had stopped wearing mine on my belt since leaving Isfahan. But I always carried it in my leather pouch which also had my notebook and my quill and brass ink pot.

To quench our thirst, we drank water from the river. At the beginning of the journey, when Sarkis gave me some to drink and noticed my hesitation, he said, "Don't be afraid, Vartan. I can assure you, it's perfectly clean, sweet, potable water." And he was right. I did not experience any stomach pain or malaise during the entire trip.

We purchased our food from local villagers. This we did when the river was narrow enough to approach the river bank with ease. The villagers were shy but friendly and their principal activity was the cultivation of rice, fruit, and vegetables. We were thus able to acquire rice, plantain and green, leafy vegetables. Fish was plentiful and so was a local sauce of fermented dried fish which was tasty but with a pungent smell that was truly foul. For the entire journey, and in contrast to Rangoon, we were unable to acquire any sort of meat supplies. This puzzled me since I had seen many water buffaloes, as many as the great number of pagodas and temples that we passed, and even some sheep that roamed in the fields.

"Since the Burmese are Buddhists and believe in re-incarnation, it is a sacrilege for them to slaughter animals. And the bigger the animal, the more revered it is," explained Sarkis. "But strangely, unlike the Hindus who don't eat creatures at all, the Burmese permit themselves to eat fish. In this, the farmer and the prince are equal. They both have the exact same staple diet."

A good ten days after leaving Rangoon, we arrived at a place called Pugan. Father d'Amato, who had been quiet up until then, busying himself every day with his writing, suddenly perked up and asked if we might permit him to visit the ancient city of Pugan. His enthusiasm awakened my interest in seeing this ancient ghost-city, dating back almost a thousand years. Sarkis, who had visited it many times before, encouraged Tovmas to see it as well. Thus, while the others remained on board, Sarkis, Tovmas and I accompanied Father d'Amato. It took us a good few hours to reach Pugan.

The sight of this ancient city was one to behold. Majestic temples, domes, and pagodas, hundreds of them, sprung from the dusty ground of this ghost-city. As we approached it, I noticed that in every structure, alcove or cave, there were intricately carved stone statues of the Buddha in different shapes and sizes. Father d'Amato soon found a Buddhist monk with whom he started a conversation in the Burmese language. He was most pleased when his interlocutor turned out to be an erudite monk, willing to respond to his questions, and thus, he earnestly took notes.

Sunset was approaching fast, and we decided to head back. But before we left the path that had led us to the ancient city, we all turned back to look at it one last time. We were in awe of what we saw. The ancient city was awash in the purple-pink hues of sunset. Just as I'd felt when looking at the crystal waters of the Maluka Islands, I again longed for the skills of an artist to capture such a magnificent sight.

We continued up river on the Irawadi. Although I'd previously travelled on the Pearl River, this was my first ever long river voyage. I'd no inkling how difficult navigation was in these waters, not least because of the numerous small islands that were scattered in the path of the Irawadi itself. This slowed our advancement considerably as it took us longer to navigate around them. We finally reached Ava one early morning, and I was grateful to have Sarkis as my mentor. Without him I would not have been able to venture so far into an unknown land.

CHAPTER 27

✠

THE ROYAL CITY OF AVA was smaller than I had envisioned. It was surrounded by a solid brick rampart that attested to its being a fortified city. The royal palace was a city within the city, where no one was allowed to enter without special permission. It, too, was protected by a solid brick rampart, after the fashion of the main city. King Bagyidaw ruled Burma from here, and I was told that his queen, Me Nu, exercised a great deal of power over him.

On the only two main thoroughfares of the city could be seen all manner of people – Chinese, Europeans, soldiers, workers, shop-keepers, noblemen, and even convicted criminals. These latter were immediately recognisable by the tattoos they bore that stated their past crimes. Crimes were punished severely and executions were commonplace, Sarkis told me.

The Burmese womenfolk in Ava caught my attention, too, as they were unlike their European, Oriental, or Indian counterparts. Although they wore the typical Asian loincloth, they did not cover their hair. Theirs was an easy manner, devoid of the usual female shyness and inhibitions of comportment.

I was amused to hear from Sarkis that the one creature in the city to exact almost as much reverence as the king himself was none other than his royal white elephant.

After our Shirazi companion, Garabed, and Mr. de Souza had left us to go to their homes, the rest of us walked to an inn in the centre of town. Sarkis asked the inn-keeper to lodge Father d'Amato for as long as he required, saying he would pay for it. Despite my protests, he would not let me stay at the inn.

"Don't argue with me. You're my guest and you're staying in my house," he said. I could not but accept since I had by now learned to value his company.

Sarkis' house was made up of several structures around a rectangular courtyard. The main house was of recent build in brick, and incorporated older structures that were now as annexes to the main building. The principal house was very spacious and tastefully but sparsely decorated. As we entered the courtyard, I spotted at least three female domestics. I was offered comfortable lodgings, next to Tovmas', in one of the side annexes.

We were later greeted by Martha Van Grinsen, Sarkis' wife, who was Dutch and the daughter of a pastor from Batavia. Their nine-year-old daughter, Sara, who looked at me shyly, was a replica of her mother. Martha was as tall as Sarkis, and had blond hair, large blue eyes, and pink cheeks. She was gentleness and kindness personified. It was easy to see her devotion to Sarkis. They were a couple who complemented each other. Her calmness and steadiness were a counterbalance to his vibrant and impulsive personality.

When we had retired to our quarters that evening, Tovmas told me how Sarkis had married Martha against the wishes of the Manuk family. Martha was not only Dutch, but also a widow with a five-year-old son when Sarkis first met her. She had previously been married to a Dutch adventurer and hunter in Batavia. He had disappeared during one of his expeditions to the northern jungles of Macassar; no one knew what had happened to him. Sarkis adopted Martha's son when they married and looked after the boy like his own. The previous year, on reaching fifteen, he was sent to Holland for further schooling.

"That is an amazing story. I'm getting to know your uncle a little better now," I said.

"What was important for him was that he loved Martha and wanted to marry her, no matter what. As I told you before, he is unconventional," Tovmas remarked.

"Indeed – that is what makes him so admirable," I concluded.

"A small quantity of rubies are mined in an area close to Amarapura, but the bulk of the mining is done further north in Mogkok, in a valley surrounded by nine mounts," Sarkis explained.

"And you say that Mr. Lee will be my main supplier in Amarapura," I said.

"Yes, because neither you nor I can venture to Mogkok on a regular basis to buy from the miners directly. It is an arduous journey and the effort is not really worth our while. Mr. Lee has his Chinese pickers who roam Mogkok and the area close to Amarapura using a relay strategy. That is how they maintain a constant supply. So, under the circumstances, Mr. Lee is our best man. It is also not prudent for us to be known personally by the king's men. They keep a close eye on the miners since the largest and purest stones are, by law, the property of the king."

"I understand. And the agreement between us is that we split equally whatever I procure from Mr. Lee."

"That is correct. You procure the rubies for us based on the criteria I've explained to you and the samples I've given you, and I shall take responsibility for the proper cutting and polishing of the stones here in Ava. This is a royal city and the best artisans are found here. Tovmas will assist us, especially when I am not in Ava. Once you're settled in Amarapura, he will visit you at the end of every month and transport the stones to Ava. During the month, if you require any assistance or would like to send me or Tovmas a quick message, you will use a local man by the name of Tsaay."

"Who is Tsaay exactly, Sarkis? And who will ship my stones to Lesley?"

"Tsaay is a loyal and competent man who has been in my employment for many years. He will be in your service in Amarapura and will do whatever you require of him for our business. I first hired him when I lived in Amarapura years ago and was doing exactly what you will be doing now. When my business grew, I moved to Ava but still kept my abode in Amarapura and commuted between the two cities. Now, I can no longer do the commuting. I am too busy with my other projects, and in particular my new venture trading in Siamese sapphires. That is no small task and requires a lot of juggling, for there is still great hostility between the Burmese and the Siamese following the Anglo-Burmese War. I presume you know that the Siamese aided the British in the war."

"Yes, I am aware of that. But couldn't you have sent Tovmas to Amarapura in your place?"

"I had initially thought of having Tovmas based in Amarapura, but that idea never materialised because I needed him in Ava to look after things while I was away, which happens quite often. So, my friend, I must thank you for your decision to come to Burma. You have taken a great burden off my shoulders. And regarding your shipments to Lesley, Tovmas will carry on arranging them for you from Ava."

"Sarkis, you mentioned earlier that you had lodgings for me in Amarapura. May I ask further details about it?"

"I told you I had taken care of it, Vartan. My house in Amarapura is at your disposal for as long as you want it. Tsaay has been looking after it all these years and lives adjacent to it in a traditional Burmese dwelling with his wife. Thus, he is close by any time you need him. The house itself is of adequate size and comfortable. It would give me great pleasure if you accept to live there."

"I shall not refuse such a generous offer," I said. "I have one more request. Can you tell me a bit more about Mr. Lee?"

"Certainly, Mr. Lee is a Chinese trader who has been trading in Burma for over 25 years. He is highly experienced and, for a Chinese trader, a correct man, and one who always quotes fair prices. So don't be fooled by his unkempt appearance and short temper. Although at night he is an opium smoker, during the day his knowledge of rubies is unparalleled," Sarkis said with a smile, adding, "Come, my friend, it must be time to join Tovmas and my dear Martha for dinner."

Tovmas and I departed for Amarapura early one morning a few days after my long conversation with Sarkis. It was only an hour's drive by horse-drawn carriage to the centre of Amarapura. Even smaller and less populated than Ava, it was a much calmer city. Nevertheless, it boasted a moat and a royal palace. Its heyday had been during the reign of the previous Burmese king.

Sarkis' house was at the far north end of Amarapura, in a sparsely populated neighbourhood. It was a much smaller house than the one in

Ava, but was a solid brick structure with enough space to lodge at least four individuals. There was a front courtyard and a small garden on the side that led to Tsaay's abode.

When we arrived, Tsaay greeted us warmly, although he seemed surprised at seeing the extent of our baggage: neither Sarkis nor Tovmas had ever stayed there longer than overnight during the last six months. Tsaay immediately introduced me to his wife, Naang. Both Tsaay and Naang inspected me with intense eyes whilst Tovmas conveyed to them Sarkis' instructions. I should mention here that both spoke fairly good English. They had been in the service of an English trader before taking up employment with Sarkis.

I learned from Tovmas that Sarkis had hired four or five Burmese to look after the household and to help him when he lived in Amarapura. But Sarkis could not provide them with accommodation, so they lived nearby. Naang was hired expressly to look after Sarkis' daughter, and Tsaay became his personal assistant. Tsaay and Naang were not married then. That came when Sarkis moved to Ava, just prior to the Anglo-Burmese War. The other employees were let go, but Sarkis wished Tsaay and Naang to continue in his service. It was Sarkis who gave Tsaay the idea of a dwelling for them next to the house, and Tsaay built the traditional Burmese dwelling himself.

Tsaay and Naang were typical young locals in their appearance. They were both very thin and wore the traditional garb: she in a hand-loomed cotton loincloth and vest and he in loose pantaloons and shirt. Both were olive-skinned and had fine and pleasing features. But what distinguished Tsaay from others was the glitter in his dark eyes and his fierce look – a look that said he was not afraid of anything. Naang, who wore her long hair plaited at the back, was truly the most graceful female I had ever come across.

"They seem slightly wary about my being here," I told Tovmas that evening after Tsaay and Naang had brought us some food.

"It's just because you are a stranger to them. They know you're going to live here but don't know what to expect. I wouldn't worry if I were you. They'll take good care of you," he said with a sure tone.

During the following days, Tovmas and I paid Mr. Lee several visits. He was exactly as Sarkis had described him. On our first visit, he seemed in a foul mood, continuously shouting obscenities in Chinese, or so I guessed; these were directed at his assistant, who just accepted the curses without as much as uttering a word. Mr. Lee, who was extremely thin, was indeed untidy in appearance, and his bald head with its singular strands of long grey hair did nothing to improve his looks. Yet, he was very astute. After having made up his mind that I was serious, and sensing my enthusiasm to see the rubies, he brought them all out and helped me sort and choose what I wished to purchase. He was also easy to bargain with. At the beginning, he would give a price swearing that if I asked for a discount, he would lose money on the deal. But, after a little haggling, he would soon fold and agree to whatever the price was I was offering.

Since I bought a fair quantity of stones and he knew I would become a regular customer, Mr. Lee invited Tovmas and me to his opium den one evening.

"Shall we go? I wouldn't mind trying one of those opium pipes," Tovmas said.

But I was wary.

"I don't think it's such a good idea. Your uncle took me to one in Ava to satisfy my curiosity. It was a dark and smoky place with an acrid stench. There were men, half-naked and half-conscious, smoking opium. It's not an experience I would want to repeat. And I would never wish to smoke something that takes away my consciousness either. If you want to go, you'll have to go on your own. I wouldn't want to bear the responsibility of you falling ill or being robbed of your money or God knows what else whilst you're unconscious," I said.

"You're right. Forget what I said. I'd rather we head back home. I'd much prefer to play a game of backgammon with you," said Tovmas with conviction.

Tovmas' week in Amarapura was soon over. I was sad to see him return to Ava as he had been such good company and had helped me greatly. I had spent most of my time with him since our meeting on the *Anna* and had got used to having him around.

"I'm sad to leave, too, Vartan. But I'll be back in a few weeks. I look forward to seeing you then. And as soon as I get to Ava, I will send your shipment and the letter to Lesley. They should reach him within three weeks or a month at most."

The evening of Tovmas' departure was one I would rather forget. I felt all alone in a land that was not yet familiar to me. It had been slightly over a month since I'd left Georgetown. And when I had no company, thoughts of Violet flooded back. Was she married already? It was too tormenting. I so desperately longed to hold her in my arms. But that was never going to happen in this life – never again. I dared to imagine that she might still think of me. And it was that faint hope that was my beacon in the darkness.

CHAPTER 28

⚜

I VISITED MR. LEE ON an almost daily basis as Sarkis had advised. It was the only way of ensuring I had first pick of the rubies that turned up. I'd already spotted a couple of other traders at Mr. Lee's and knew I had to compete with them for the best stones. The rest of my time was spent trying to familiarise myself with the local Burmese way of life.

I discovered that most Burmese locals in Amarapura were of Shan ethnicity, and that included Tsaay and Naang. Their homeland was the Shan States, which covered the territory north and east of Ava and Amarapura. The nine mounts and the Mogkok ruby mines were part of the northern Shan territories; their eastern territories stretched all the way to the Lanna State in the north of Siam. In recent history, the federation of Shan clans had been loyal to the Burmese kings and paid tribute to them in exchange for local autonomy. The Shan chiefs also provided the current Burmese king with the majority of the soldiers for his army. They had fought valiantly against the British during the Anglo-Burmese War, and even though the Burmese king lost the war three years previously and had to give up territory to the British, the bravery of the Shan soldiers was recognised even by the enemy.

But this was all I knew about the Shan people, so one afternoon, having returned from Mr. Lee's early, I thought of finding out more from Tsaay. I also thought this would be a good topic for a conversation with him since I had sensed that he was still very cautious in his daily dealings with me, as was Naang.

Walking through the small garden towards his dwelling, I found Tsaay was tending his vegetable patch. He was surprised to see me. I greeted him and said I'd brought Naang a piece of silk cloth I'd purchased in town. I wished to offer it to her as thanks for the wonderful food she regularly cooked for me. Tsaay immediately invited me in; I accepted his invitation without hesitation.

His small house was raised on four very thick posts, a foot or so high. The roof was thatched. Climbing four steps, I entered what seemed to be a sitting area with floor cushions and a couple of squat tables. The room had bamboo floors and woven bamboo walls. Naang came out of a back room and greeted me shyly. I offered her the silk cloth. She took it with her usual grace and thanked me, although it was clear she hadn't expected a gift from me. Tsaay was unsure about what to do next, so I put him at ease and sat down on the floor, leaning against one of the cushions. After some casual chatter, I asked him about the Shan. His eyes shone with amazement. He was clearly not expecting me to show such an interest in his people. He told me that both he and Naang came from the far eastern part of the Shan States and explained that the Shan States were made up of a number of Shan fiefdoms headed by Shan chiefs. A Shan chief was called a Tsawphaa. Tsaay himself was the grandson of a Tsawphaa. The Shan people mainly occupied themselves with the cultivation of land, but they were poor, not least because they had to pay tribute to the Burmese king.

"Is that why you came to Amarapura to work?" I asked.

He nodded sadly and said, "I came here ten years ago when I was only 17, and Naang came five years ago when she was 19. I miss my people, and Naang does, too. We are so far away from our home."

"Me too, Tsaay, I am also very far away from my home," I said.

That evening, Tsaay and Naang shared their food with me. After the meal, Tsaay brought out a box of betel and offered me some. I accepted, and before placing it in my mouth, I thanked them both for their hospitality.

"You are our first and probably the only guest we will ever have here," Tsaay said.

"Then please consider me as your good friend," I said.

Naang and Tsaay looked at each other and, for the first time in our fortnight together, I saw them smile.

Tovmas turned up at the house barely three weeks after he'd gone back to Ava. It was a Thursday afternoon.

"My uncle said to tell you that you did an excellent job with the choice of rubies. He's very pleased that you're comfortably settled and wants you to come over to Ava every Sunday from now on, whether he's there or not, since I will be there. So, I'm going back on Sunday morning, and I would very much like you to come with me," Tovmas said.

"Alright, but I don't know if I want to go to Ava every Sunday. I promise I will at least come once a month – perhaps on one Sunday of a week when you're not coming over to Amarapura. That way we can see each other twice a month."

"That sounds reasonable. I'd rather play backgammon with you than with that boring Garabed of Shiraz who turns up every so often at my uncle's house."

"Tell me about the shipment, Tovmas."

"No problems there. I sent the shipment to Penang, and your letter to Lesley went with it. He should receive them soon."

Tovmas and I had more or less the same sort of conversation about business every time we met over the next year. We also played backgammon regularly and had long discussions about a variety of subjects. I visited Ava once a month and he came over to Amarapura once a month, but in a different week. I spent long Sundays in the company of Tovmas, Martha and Sara and, occasionally, Sarkis when he was there. He was always gregarious and full of enthusiasm about his trading in sapphires. The other two Sundays of the month I spent in the company of Tsaay and Naang, with whom I had become very close friends.

Dealing in rubies, with me based in Burma, turned out more profitable than either Lesley or I had imagined. Our correspondence mainly dealt with the business. He did mention Lilly in every letter and said they were both doing fine and were very happy. But not once did he mention her father or Violet. At first, I thought it strange that he didn't mention Violet, but then I was almost certain he didn't because she had married and he didn't wish to be the bearer of bad news. I myself didn't dare ask him about Violet in any of my letters, after all, it had been my decision to leave Georgetown and I had to deal with the consequences of that decision alone, day after day, for the rest of my life.

One morning, about a year after my arrival in Amarapura, Tovmas turned up on his usual day.

"I'm sorry I can't stay overnight this time. I'll just have to pick up whatever you have ready for me and I've got to go back to Ava immediately.

My mother arrived yesterday. I still can't believe she undertook the trip on her own, all the way from Batavia. She's such a strong-willed woman. When I left Java two years ago, she swore she would come and visit me in Ava," Tovmas said.

"I'm sure she missed you and would have done anything to see her beloved son again."

"A fierce devotion to her children is indeed one of her character traits. Anyway, you must come next Sunday to Ava to meet her, Vartan. Uncle Sarkis will be in Ava for a while, too, and he's expecting you."

When I arrived at Sarkis' house in Ava on Sunday, there were already other guests there. Garabed of Shiraz was present, and I was introduced to three other Armenian traders, one of whom was accompanied by his wife. I then caught a glimpse of Tovmas' mother. She was sitting in an armchair in the far corner of the room. She was dressed in her trademark black, with a long, single-strand, black pearl necklace. She hadn't changed much at all apart from a few more grey hairs at the temples; otherwise she was the same regal Takoohy.

I approached her, "I'm so very pleased to see you again, Madam Takoohy."

She offered her hand, and I bent over and kissed it.

"Khoja Vartan, the pleasure is mine – after so many years. It is a small world, isn't it?" She said, indicating for me to sit next to her.

"Indeed. I hope the journey from Java was not too tiring for you."

"I took my time getting here. A woman of my age has to travel in stages and in comfort."

"I'd be most interested to hear about your travel route."

"I'd be happy to oblige. From Java, I first sailed to Singapore, the new English settlement. My son, Thaddeus, Tovmas' older brother, has been living there for the last six months and needed to consult with me regarding new business opportunities."

"From what I've heard, Singapore is fast becoming the new trading hub of the region."

"You have heard right. I spent a month there and things look very promising," she said in a serious tone, and then continued, "I knew the journey to Rangoon from Singapore would be too long for me, so I decided to break it at Penang. It gave me the time I needed to send word to Sarkis. That way I could time my arrival in Burma for when he was in Rangoon and have him accompany me on the river journey to Ava. He had informed me beforehand that it might be exhausting for me."

"And was it?"

"Well, not quite. Sarkis and I were lucky to catch one of those new steam boats. I forget what they're called. My memory is not as good as it used to be."

"Steam-paddle boats, Madam Takoohy."

"That's right. We sailed on the only one operating on the Irawadi. And I can assure you, they are the future of river travel; the journey was so much more comfortable than the old boats we're used to."

"May I ask how long you spent in Penang?"

"All of three months! I had to. I was waiting for Sarkis to arrive in Rangoon. Mind you, I have no complaints – I was lodged at Agha Caloustian's in Georgetown. He's such a kind and generous man."

"He was always generous to me when I lived in Georgetown. He is a very good friend, too."

"He mentioned you on several occasions and sends you his best regards. Whilst at Agha Caloustian's, I also saw Lesley, your business partner, on two separate occasions. I was surprised to see that he has an Armenian wife."

"You can consider him a true Armenophile now."

"An Englishman with an Armenian business partner and an Armenian wife – that's very interesting. I believe the father was against the marriage and they eloped."

"Yes, and I helped them elope. They were very much in love and there was nothing else to be done."

"Hmm…I see. They look so very happy together. Agha Caloustian said that thanks to his behind-the-scenes interventions, Lesley's father-in-law finally softened and made the first move by paying an impromptu visit to see his daughter. They were thus reconciled."

"I'm very glad that they are all finally reconciled."

"Unfortunately, Khoja Vartan, a month later the father had a stroke that left him paralysed. Agha Caloustian said his older daughter, who goes by the name of Violet and who is married to the father's partner, has taken over the running of the insurance firm that they own. I'm sure you've met her."

"I know Violet very well, Madam Takoohy."

"Well, Agha Caloustian said she is doing a great job of it all, considering her father is ill and house-bound and her husband is away in Borneo. There's a lady I admire. It must be as hard for her as it was for me when I began in business as a young woman. People didn't believe I could do the job. But I proved them wrong!"

"You are a pioneer, Madam Takooky – one of the first women to succeed in the trading business in this part of the world, and probably the first ever Armenian woman to do so."

"I'm glad that at least someone realises women are as smart – if not smarter – than men."

Just at that moment we heard Sarkis saying lunch was being served and I accompanied Madam Takoohy to the feast table.

Before I left Ava that evening, Madam Takoohy said, "Don't deny me your company, Khoja Vartan."

I promised her that I would travel to Ava every Sunday from then on.

On my return journey to Amarapura, I had visions of Violet, visions which kept recurring even after I arrived home. I imagined her at her desk, all alone, without the support of her father. Why was her husband not beside her? I wondered what sort of a husband would leave such a lovely creature on her own to fend for herself.

In my mind's eye, I could see her eyes, her hair, and her tiny hands. The memory of her kiss intoxicated my soul. I ended up with a good many tear drops on my pillow, expecting them to lull me to sleep, but sleep never came.

CHAPTER 29

⚜

IT WAS A SUNDAY, a month later. I was preparing to head to Sarkis' house in Ava and looking forward to my conversation with Madam Takoohy when I heard the sound of a carriage pulling up in front of the house. Walking outside, I was surprised to see Sarkis.

"I've come on a grave matter. We need to talk. Can I come in?" he said in an urgent tone before I could greet him. I ushered him in.

"Do you know someone called Khoja Markar Shahmir?"

I paused for a moment and then, in a sardonic tone, replied, "Is that what he calls himself now? He is no 'khoja', I can assure you. Khoja Shahmir of Isfahan, my late uncle's partner, was his father and that is as near as he comes to being a 'khoja'!"

"Well, you won't like what I'm going to tell you. He is in Ava, accompanied by a minor Russian nobleman. It seems they've been in Burma for a while trying to ingratiate themselves with the Burmese courtiers in order to make I don't know what sort of business deals. I am unaware of what he's got against you, Vartan, but he has found out from the other Armenian merchants that you're here. Garabed of Shiraz happened to be present at one of their gatherings and this Markar told everyone that they should be careful in their dealings with you. He told them that you were in the service of the British Crown and were planted here to spy on the Burmese. Garabed reported this to me straightaway, saying he sensed this Markar was completely untrustworthy. He found himself unnerved by him."

I told Sarkis I was shocked by the news of the unexpected reappearance of Markar in my life. I then recounted the details of what had happened between me and Markar in Isfahan. When I told him how Markar had tried to have me killed, he was taken aback.

"This is more serious than I had imagined. I thought it was just a matter of some personal differences. The spying accusation is an extremely grave one. If it ever gets to the Burmese, well, let me put it this way, the punishment for such a crime is execution. And the Burmese will take great pleasure in claiming that they've caught a British spy; they still feel great humiliation for having lost the war. Look Vartan, I don't know how much this Markar has found out about you and your circumstances here, but he is dangerous. I did my own asking around about him, and both he and his Russian nobleman friend seem to be very well acquainted with the barrister at court, the Shene. That is not good news as the Shene is closely associated with Prince Sarawaldi, the king's brother. According to rumours circulating in Ava, Prince Sarawaldi heads the group of Burmese nobility opposed to Queen Me Nu's influence at the court. There's no telling how this spy story may be used within the realm of palace intrigues. And, mark my words, although Prince Sarawaldi may be the enemy of the queen, they do have one thing in common – utter contempt for the British."

"So what do you suggest I do, Sarkis?" I asked, still in shock.

"I beg of you, my friend, to heed my advice. Lay low for a while. Do not go out, not even to visit Mr. Lee. Stay at home until you hear from me. In the meantime, I shall figure out what this damned Markar is up to."

He got up to leave but then stopped for a moment, as if a thought had just crossed his mind. Then, he rushed out, shouting, "Where's Tsaay? I need to talk to him," as he headed towards Tsaay's house. I watched from a distance. He found Tsaay and started to explain something to him in Burmese. The conversation between them was animated, and Sarkis was using a lot of hand gestures. It was a good twenty minutes before Sarkis walked back towards me.

"I've asked Tsaay to purchase three horses immediately. A carriage will not do if you have to escape. You have to be prepared for every eventuality. Don't look so worried. Tsaay knows exactly what to do."

"I'm not worried about myself, my dear friend Sarkis. I'm just concerned about you. I wouldn't want you to be involved in this, especially since the Burmese might sooner or later find out about our association."

"If I don't help you now, Vartan, who will? Do not concern yourself about me. I speak their language and know exactly how the Burmese think. I know how to handle the situation. Promise me not to venture out of the house until I contact you again."

I thanked him. He gave me a firm handshake and was gone.

Tsaay left immediately to buy the horses. Naang brought me some food later, but I had no appetite.

After Markar's banishment from Isfahan, I had thought that he was out of my life for good. Now, he had re-surfaced, and I was sure he would not stop until he got his revenge; in his mind, I was the cause of his humiliation and exile from Isfahan. From the moment I'd met him, I'd wished not to have any dealings with him and yet our paths kept on crossing. He was out to ruin my life and hurt my friends and the people I loved. I was filled with a rage that would not dissipate.

It was nightfall when Tsaay returned with the three horses and some basic provisions.

"I did exactly as Sarkis asked," he said.

I helped him unload the provisions and feed the horses.

"Please Vartan, go and get some sleep. You look tired," Tsaay said, "No harm will come to you. I promise I will take care of you."

I tried to sleep but couldn't. I got up and sat at the threshold in the dark. Just then I spotted the silhouette of a man in the moonlight. It was Tsaay at the entrance of the courtyard. He was guarding the house and me.

⚜

It was already dark when a carriage pulled up in front of the house the following day. It was not Sarkis' carriage. I was alarmed, so did not go out until I heard Tsaay's voice. He greeted someone in a soft, polite manner. I quickly opened the door to find Madam Takoohy standing by the carriage.

"Sarkis sent me," she said in a serious tone. "I've come to warn you."

"Come in, please, Madam Takoohy."

She came in but wouldn't sit down.

"There's no time. I've got to get back to Ava. It's already late."

"But why did Sarkis send *you* over?"

"I suggested it to him. The Shene's men came to interrogate him this afternoon. You are in real danger. They accused you of being a British spy. Sarkis told them that he was certain the accusation was unfounded. They said they had a witness who would testify against you."

"Markar Shahmir," I said.

She nodded.

"They asked Sarkis about his relationship with you. Quick thinker that he is, he said that you are a compatriot of his, like many others in Burma, and that he had done his normal duty towards a newcomer by allowing you to stay in his Amarapura house."

"Were they satisfied with that answer?"

"Yes, because they said they knew you were in Amarapura. Obviously they wanted to test Sarkis to see if he was going to tell them the truth. They also wanted to know the purpose of your stay in Amarapura. Again, Sarkis told them the truth. He said all he knew was that you were purchasing rubies here. As soon as they left, Sarkis wanted to come over and warn you, but I stopped him, and Tovmas, as well. I told them both it could be a trap, and they might end up accused of being accomplices."

"That was wise, Madam Takoohy. I wouldn't want them involved in this unfortunate affair, especially young Tovmas."

"So I convinced Sarkis to stay at home with his wife and daughter. I asked Tovmas to take me to Garabed's house in Sarkis' carriage, and we left the carriage right in front of the house in case we were being followed. Half an hour later, I asked one of Garabed's trusted domestics to hire a carriage for me and have it waiting for me at the back of Garabed's house. As soon as it got dark, I slipped out through the back garden gate and into the carriage. And here I am."

"And you will be returning to Garabed's house the same way."

"Yes, and then Tovmas and I will go back to Sarkis' house as if I never made this visit."

"I am so worried about your safety, Madam Takoohy."

"Don't be. Now, this is the message I am to give you from Sarkis. You need to depart before daybreak. He reckons the Shene's men will be here tomorrow morning. He said he has already told Tsaay what to do. Tsaay will help you escape from Burma through the Shan States, to Siam. That's the only way you have out of here," she said, looking concerned.

She then handed me a small note.

"They are instructions from Sarkis about who to contact in Siam."

She paused for a moment, looking perturbed. She brought out a handkerchief and patted her moist brow.

"And there's one more thing. I know you have some rubies here with you. Place a palm-full in a bag and give them to me just before I get into the carriage. Make sure the carriage driver sees you giving me the bag. That way, in case the Shene's men have spotted me and want to know the purpose of my visit to you, I shall tell them that the rubies belong to me and I wanted to retrieve them before they caught the spy," she said with a half smile.

"I am so thankful to you Madam Takoohy. But I am ashamed to have put a lady of your position in such a dangerous situation."

"Khoja Vartan, I may be a lady of means and one who loves her comfort, but I am of noble Armenian lineage – which means I never abandon my own," she said in a firm tone, and then added, "I'll be waiting at the carriage."

"I'll fetch the rubies," I said.

I brought the bag of rubies and made sure the carriage driver saw me giving it to Madam Takoohy. I helped her into the carriage.

"I hope to see you again one day," she said.
"And I, you."

"May the Lord illuminate your path," were her parting words as her carriage moved off.

The three of us left with the first light. We had been ready since midnight but could not start the journey while it was still pitch dark outside.

Naang sat behind Tsaay on one of the horses, and I rode the other. I pulled the third horse, which had a few of our belongings and some food and water. Since the house was located at the northern edge of Amarapura, we did not have to go through the city. We were out in the wilderness in a matter of a half hour. I say wilderness, for the country-side was uninhabited for the most part and wild animals still roamed there freely. Tsaay had warned me of this and had given me one of Sarkis' pistols. I also had my dagger at hand. Tsaay carried his own pistol and his Asian dagger.

"What if the Shene's men decide to follow us after they fail to find me at the house?" I said.

"I'm taking a different route than the usual northern route out of Amarapura," Tsaay reassured me. "We will soon be heading south through hilly terrain and after that we will be heading east. I don't think the Shene's men will venture this way unless they have an expert Shan tracker, which I very much doubt."

We travelled a good half day, skirting the Amarapura area and then took a southerly direction through a hilly area, which slowed us down, taking us two days to cross. During those first three days, we were tense; we wanted to get out of the areas close to Amarapura as fast as possible. We had agreed not to cook, so as not to attract attention, and to not stop for water for too long. Prior to our departure from Amarapura, Naang had cooked rice and placed small portions in neat parcels made of plantain leaves. That is all we had to eat. We stopped only when it got dark. Tsaay and I took sentry turns while Naang slept.

On the fourth day, we spotted a lone villager returning from his field. Naang and I hid behind thick bushes and Tsaay went over to talk to him to ascertain our location. He came back a short while later and said something to Naang in their language. Naang almost jumped with joy and gave me a big smile.

"We're on the right track. We're only 10 miles from Lawksawk. We're in the heart of the Shan territories now and both Naang and I are over-joyed that we will soon see our village of Mong Pa, and our loved ones," Tsaay said, and then added earnestly, "When Sarkis asked me that day to help you if you had to escape from Amarapura, I told him if we were successful in reaching my village, I would not go back to Amarapura. I thought he was going to get angry with me for wanting to leave him for good but do you know what he did instead? He said that everyone de-served to go back to their homeland and thanked me for being loyal to him. He even sent me some money with his sister that night; for my long years of service, she said. I shall never forget Sarkis. I shall never meet another one like him."

I nodded and breathed a sigh of relief, not only because we were finally in Shan territory but also because I needn't have felt guilty for imposing the burden of my escape from Amarapura on the shoulders of Tsaay and Naang. I realised that apart from sincerely wishing to help me escape, Tsaay and Naang had found the perfect excuse to return to their village after so many years of absence.

CHAPTER 30

⚜

WE CONTINUED ON OUR ROUTE but with great caution, skirting Lawksawk and the surrounding villages for fear of anyone seeing me since I was easily identifiable as a foreigner. We had enough rice for a few more days, so we pressed on. But by the time we reached a village called Hopong, we had almost run out of food. We also had trouble feeding the horses. Tsaay and Naang decided to go into Hopong to get supplies. I hid in a secure spot on the outskirts of the village until Tsaay and Naang returned in the afternoon with all that we required.

"Are we beginning our eastward leg tomorrow then?" I asked Tsaay.

"Not yet. I have to go into Tawngi tomorrow. It's the biggest village in this area – more like a small town. It's not far from where we are. It's the only place where we may be able to find the herbs and leaves Naang needs to prepare her concoction. You'll soon see why she has to prepare it. Just look after her, and I'll be back before nightfall," he said.

The next day before dusk, and true to his word, Tsaay was back from Tawngi with a large knife, resembling a machete. It was about a foot long and slightly curved.

"We'll need it to cut through the jungle vegetation," he said.

He had also bought a bunch of strange looking leaves and several types of herbs that were unrecognisable to me. Naang put them all together in a small pot with a little water and cooked them on the open fire for at least an hour until the mixture turned into a gooey pulp. When the concoction had cooled down, she mixed in a sort of waxy oil and poured the preparation into a bamboo receptacle, securing its lid. She then gracefully placed the receptacle in her small basket with her personal belongings.

The next evening, as we were advancing eastwards, I discovered why the large knife and Naang's concoction were crucial. We were entering an area that could only be described as a dense jungle. At certain spots, the overgrown vegetation had to be hacked away to let us and the horses through. I was aware of a number of wild animals lurking and saw four different types of monkeys moving about in the tall trees. Mosquitoes there were aplenty.

"No need to fear, Vartan. We won't get lost, if that's what you're thinking. I know the area very well," Tsaay reassured me upon noticing my apprehension.

We finally reached flat grassy terrain and decided to camp there for the night. The insects and mosquitoes were impossible to bear. That is when Naang produced her concoction and asked me to apply it on my face, neck, hands, and any part of my body that was not covered by clothing. I immediately followed her instructions. I knew then that I would certainly catch malaria if I was unprotected since I hadn't brought the netting that hung over my bed in Amarapura. After applying the concoction on herself and Tsaay, she applied a tiny amount on each horse's head and tail.

"Our traditional Shan medicine, passed on from generation to generation," Tsaay said.

Feeling protected by Naang's oily potion, I fell sound asleep under the watchful eye of Tsaay.

For what seemed an eternity, we continued our advance into the jungle. Two very heavy downpours had left us completely sodden. But despite our discomfort, our spirits remained high. Tsaay and Naang were joyful in the anticipation of finally seeing their closest kin. As for myself, how could I fail to be happy as, with each step, I drew further away from Markar.

At one point, we had dismounted and were skirting around a vast gorge on foot when Tsaay suddenly stopped me in my tracks and gestured not to make a sound. I was just a few steps away from a very long, dark snake that had slithered in front of us.

"This type comes up from the gorge. We must be careful. It's very poisonous," Tsaay said once the snake had disappeared into the bushes. Apart from this incident, we were fortunate not to come across any other dangerous animals, such as the wild cats in that area Tsaay had warned me about.

We reached a short waterfall and Tsaay began to laugh.

"We're very near Mong Noi. We'll soon be entering our clan's territory," he said happily.

The jungle vegetation gradually became sparser, and I could see cultivated lands in the distance.

"Mong Noi," Tsaay said and crouching, drew me a map with a stick in the muddy soil. Mong Noi was the first village, east of which was Mong Pa, and then Mong Tong further east. The three large villages and the lands around them constituted his clan's fiefdom.

"Mong Pa is my village. That's where I was born," Tsaay explained.

"And how far is the Siam border from your village?" I inquired.

He showed me on the mud-map:

"Mong Noi, Mong Pa, Mong Tong," and then he drew a short line southwards from Mong Tong.

"Mayna, Siam," he said, pushing his stick into the mud at that precise point.

The villagers of Mong Noi greeted us warmly, and especially when they recognised Tsaay. They brought us food and gave us all the comfort we needed after such a long and arduous journey.

"We leave for Mong Pa tomorrow morning. You can rest as long as you like in Mong Pa," Tsaay said.

I understood his impatience to get there, being so close to his home village. By the afternoon of the following day, we had reached Mong Pa. The villagers greeted Tsaay and Naang with open arms and some even danced enthusiastically. Many approached me out of curiosity, but with unmistakable friendliness. We were soon taken to the dwelling of the Tsawphaa, the chief, Tsaay's grandfather. The Tsawphaa had a young face, but I couldn't guess his age for the skin on his arms and hands resembled an ancient leather parchment. He had very dark skin and soft eyes. Tsaay knelt in front of him and the Tsawhpaa placed his hand on his head affectionately. Soon, both Naang's and Tsaay's parents and their brothers and sisters were greeting and hugging them. All three of us were then taken to a flat expanse at the edge of the village where a celebration was just beginning.

"The deer ceremony," Tsaay explained as we sat on the humid grass.

The local musicians started playing their string instruments and drums. And then, out of the bushes appeared a giant creature. It looked amazing. It had large deer horns on its head and a face that looked like one. It was clad in shaggy deer skin that, in reality, was made of thousands of leaves. I guessed the creature was manned by four men. One must have been standing on the shoulders of the other since the creature's head and neck were the size of two men in height. The other two were the creature's legs and body with a long tail. When I pointed this out, Tsaay nodded in agreement. The creature began moving and dancing, and it did so for a long time. Some of the villagers joined in with excitement. Some were aping the creature's movements while the village children were running around it in circles.

"You're not really Buddhists, are you?"

Tsaay didn't answer my question directly but said, "This ceremony is part of our ancient Shan beliefs."

When the ceremony ended, the creature disappeared behind the bushes but the villagers were still dancing and laughing. We were offered copious amounts of food – rice, meat, and fruit – which were presented to us by the young girls of the village. I noticed the young females wore the same type of clothing as Naang and had their hair in a single plait at the back of the head. The older females wore their hair in a bun but some wore a very large head cloth, the size of a folded blanket. I was surprised to see some of the older womenfolk smoking from tiny pipes. Unlike the women in their loincloths, the men wore a pair of loose cotton trousers and a loose, collarless shirt. Some of them also had turban-like headdress.

After weeks of travelling, my own clothes were soiled and my shirt had a few rips in it. Tsaay read my mind and said:

"I'll have to get you brand new clothing – like that which you see the men wearing."

Just then Naang approached me and said, "Your house is ready. Let me take you there."

I accompanied her to a small dwelling, similar to the one they had in Amarapura. It was on short stilts and was made of bamboo. By the time she finished showing me where things were and where to get water, Tsaay had appeared with the new set of clothing he'd promised. I thanked them both and bid them goodnight.

Later, after having a good wash, I sat on the bamboo floor in my unusual new clothing and soon felt at home.

It was three weeks after our arrival in Mong Pa when I was awoken in the early morning by the sound of villagers running past my bamboo dwelling. I quickly dressed and went out to ascertain the cause of the brouhaha. Pandemonium reigned. Villagers, men, women and children were hastily heading out of the village. I searched for Tsaay and Naang but couldn't find them. So I followed the villagers. After walking a fair distance out of the village, we reached the flat terrain where other villagers had gathered. They were all looking up towards a small raised piece of ground. A tiny elderly woman was standing in front of a rock and moving her body once to the right and once to the left, as if she were performing a dance. I spotted Tsaay in the crowd and he quickly joined me.

"What's happening? And who is she?"

"She's our Sayama, our female shaman. Look carefully at the rock facing her. Can you see the snake?"

I made several attempts and, finally, spotted the cobra. It had raised the upper part of its body and was looking straight at the Sayama. Suddenly, it puffed up its head in an attack position.

"Why is she standing so close to the cobra? It's going to attack her," I said with fear.

"You don't understand. This is our belief. She has to kiss the cobra three times in order to bring safety, prosperity and fertility to us, to our land."

The next scene sent shivers down my spine. Silence reigned in the crowd. The Sayama performed her ritual movements again. She performed these with the agility and grace of a young woman. The cobra remained in its attack position but seemed to have frozen. With the same agility, the Sayama put her head forward and kissed the cobra once, and then twice, and then three times. Slowly, she took a few steps back. The cobra, mimicking her movements, moved its head first to the right and then to the left and then began to retreat. In a few seconds, it had vanished into one of the crevices of the rock.

The crowd watched the Sayama descend slowly from the high ground. As if in a trance, she looked at no one in particular. Her eyes were frozen. When she reached the lower ground, she didn't stop. She carried on walking towards the village. It was only then that the villagers, in unison, let out a shout of joy. With that, they too began to head back to the village.

"I'm glad you witnessed what happened here today. The Sayama has brought you the same blessings," Tsaay said, sure of his words. I nodded and smiled.

All through that day and into the evening the village was alive with celebrations. There were songs and dancing, and a great deal of food, which I was invited to share with Naang and Tsaay.

"I shall remember what you told me today, my friend. I shall also pray to my God so He will bless you and Naang and your village always," I said to Tsaay before I left them.

I had not prayed once since my escape from Amarapura. So when I got to my bamboo house, I immediately knelt down, held the triangular pouch that contained my mother's prayer of long ago and that I always carried with me, and prayed. I thanked the Lord for the good friends that I had encountered in Burma. Without Sarkis' and Madam Takoohy's help, I would have been unjustly executed as a spy. They had both put themselves in danger for me. I prayed for their safety and well-being. I prayed for Naang and Tsaay, too. Without them I could never have succeeded in escaping from Amarapura. When I finished my prayer, I sat down and thought of the Sayama and the cobra. I remembered the conversation I'd had with Lesley about superstitions. It occurred to me that perhaps Tsaay was right. Perhaps I was meant to witness what happened on that day and to receive blessings from the Sayama. In a strange way, had I not already received them – and three times? I had been saved from murder twice and I had surmounted the urge to take my own life after losing my wife and daughter.

My destiny had been like the destiny of my own Armenian people. Like my people, I had to struggle to survive, even if my life seemed small and insignificant. No matter how dangerous, how long, and how difficult the journey, I was determined to make it to Siam and then to Penang and the people I loved.

And then it was, in that Burmese village, it finally dawned on me that I had made the biggest mistake of my life. In my mind I had blamed Violet's husband for having left her on her own when, in truth, it was I who was to be blamed for having abandoned her to tend for herself. Instead of standing by her and fighting for the love we had, I had left because of my foolish pride. I should have known that she would never, alone, have been able to stand up to her father. She was now married to someone else, but my love for her was still alive in the depths of my heart. I had to go back to Penang for her. Now it did not matter if she were never mine in this life for all I wanted was to love her from a distance and know that she lived and breathed not far away from me.

CHAPTER 31

✤

"ARE YOU CERTAIN YOU HAVE rested enough? It's going to be a longer journey from here to the royal city of Siam."

"I'm ready to leave, Tsaay. I won't rest until I'm out of Burma."

"In that case, we can depart tomorrow for Mong Tong. The man who will take you to Siam is waiting for us there. I sent word to him with one of the Tsawphaa's messengers when we first arrived here. He'll be able to furnish me with the details of your route when we meet. There's one problem though. Riam, for that is the man's name, doesn't speak a word of English," Tsaay said.

"I will have to manage without English. I have no other choice," I told Tsaay.

By the following evening we were in Mong Tong. Naang had come along with us. We were received at the village elder's house and I was soon introduced to Riam. He was a small, dark man with thick, black hair and huge teeth which were frequently visible because he smiled and laughed a lot. We quickly made friends since my sign language made him laugh.

"Riam knows all the trails leading to Mayna. He's a small trader in this and that and makes the journey to Siam very often. He also knows the Lanna Fiefdom like no other. The people there speak a similar language to ours and he has good contacts. Many of his relatives live there," Tsaay said to reassure me.

"So when we reach Mayna, we would already be in Lanna."

"Yes. And the fiefdom of Lanna pays tribute to the Siamese king and is, therefore, part of his territories."

"I understand. How far will Riam accompany me?"

"He will travel with you through Lanna southwards until you can take a river boat or barge to take you to the south of Siam, to the king's city."

"To Bangkok. Once I get there, Sarkis told me who to contact for my trip to Penang," I said.

"Just do what Riam does, since you don't speak our language. He is a good man. He is as good as gold, which is what his name means. He will look after you," concluded Tsaay.

Two days later, in the morning, I was ready to depart. Riam had already packed his small horse and I mine. He had refused to travel with a third horse in tow, saying it would only slow us down, and I certainly didn't wish to argue with him. Tsaay and Naang had helped us prepare the provisions we needed to get us to Mayna. They were both waiting to say their farewells. Naang approached me first and gave me her bamboo receptacle containing 'the insect concoction'.

"You will need it during the journey," she said, and bowed gracefully. I bowed back and thanked herself and Tsaay for saving my life. Tsaay shook my hand and then turned his fierce eyes on me for a moment. I looked at him with sadness. We both knew we would never see each other again.

"I shall always be grateful for your friendship," I said, and mounted my horse. I rode off and didn't look back – it pained me so to leave them.

It took us three days of trekking over difficult terrain to reach Mayna. Without Riam I would not have covered even ten miles in that time. He knew every nook and cranny in the area, which route to take and which to avoid. At one point, we had to cross a river. Luckily, the water was not too deep and the horses bravely struggled through to the other sides.

Early one evening, after we had descended a small hill, Riam said, "Mayna. Lanna." He kept on repeating these words and would not stop until I had repeated them back to him. I quickly gathered that he wanted me to repeat them to assure him that I understood we had reached Siamese territory.

We continued our journey for another four weeks, heading south. Passing through several villages, we stopped at the big towns of Chiang Rai and Chiang Mai, where we stayed with his relatives. After that, and at every town or village that we went through, he would say its name and ask me to repeat it. When I did, he would laugh and tap me on the shoulder to say, "Well done!" As we journeyed further south, we shared little huts to sleep in every night, and when Riam bought our food, usually rice, fish and some vegetable or Asian beans, he would not begin to eat until I had taken my first mouthful and nodded that it was alright.

One evening, we stopped in a relatively large town with a very long name which I cannot, alas, recall now. Riam gestured that I should go to the small inn where we were to sleep, and he left. An hour later, he came back with a typical set of Siamese men's garments and urged me to wear them. I pointed out to him the Shan outfit I was wearing and he shook his head as if to say he didn't approve. I opened my small parcel and showed him my soiled European trousers and my shirt, but again he shook his head and urged me once more to wear the Siamese outfit. It consisted of large, straight pantaloons that were shorter than the Shan ones I'd been wearing, and a shirt that came to the waist. I tried them on and Riam showed me how to tie the rectangular piece of cloth that acted as a belt around my waist. I kept on the soft straw and cotton shoes that Tsaay had given me. Riam then checked me out and laughed approvingly. I finally understood that we were no longer in Lanna but in Siam proper and it would be a lot easier to travel in local garments. I also knew that we would be parting ways soon.

A few days later, we came to a village near the banks of a fairly wide river. Both Riam and I spotted a barge on which fruit and other goods were being loaded. Before I knew it, Riam had gone over and was talking to someone on board. He came back and pointing at the barge repeated the words "Bang Makok."

"Bangkok, Bangkok," I responded.

Riam let out one of his long laughs and then, still laughing, took my stuff off my horse and headed towards the barge. This was it. This is where we parted, and the barge was to take me to Bangkok. Riam put my things on the barge and signalled me to board. At this point, he went over to the man he had talked to earlier, one I took to be the man in charge of the barge, and paid him some money. I quickly guessed that, for my own safety, he didn't want anyone on the barge to think that I had money on me. He next rushed to a small food market on the river bank and got me some dried fish, rice and fruit and gave them to me. He then placed a local straw hat on my head. He was as good as gold, this Riam, for he had not only helped me escape from Burma, but had also looked after me during all the weeks we had travelled together in Siam. I bowed to thank him and he bowed back and gave me his usual tap on the shoulder and laughed. The barge started to move away, but he stood there on the river bank until we could see each other no more.

As the barge advanced slowly down the river, I was enveloped by loneliness. Not because I was frightened but because I was unable to speak to any of my new travel companions on board. Apart from the man in charge, there were a dozen men who took turns to row. Riam had been successful in disguising me as a local, and as we passed village after village, I remained incognito to anyone looking at the barge, but not to my travelling companions. I sensed that they would have liked to have asked me questions or converse with me but couldn't. I found them a lot friendlier that the Burmese, less shy, and more gregarious. If only I could understand their language. During the full week that I was with them, and perhaps to compensate for the fact that they couldn't communicate with me, they fed me instead. However well they treated me, by week's end, the long journey was taking its toll on me and I was beginning to feel tired to the bone.

One mid-day, the barge stopped at a convergence of canals. I thought I had finally reached Bangkok but the man in charge shook his head and pointed to a direction further south. A couple of the barge men then shouted to a canoe that was passing by, and after exchanging a few words with the canoe owner, they gathered my belongings and threw them onto the canoe and pushed me over into it. I had to sit down so as not to lose my balance. I looked back up at the men on the barge and lowered my head in gratitude and they bowed in reply.

The canoe owner turned his canoe around and took the direction southwards to Bangkok. A short distance later, I was able to distinguish several side canals converging into a larger mass of water, which I assumed to be the main river of the city. After we'd travelled for another few miles, I spotted large buildings on either side of the river and very ornate temples. "Bangkok?" I said to the canoe man, and he nodded, "Bangkok." I had finally arrived but had never imagined the Siamese king's city to be this way – a city with very few roads. It was simply a city built on canals with a large river flowing through it. Soon, the river traffic began to intensify. There were boats and canoes of all types and shapes moving up and down the river. This was the way people commuted in this city. And then panic gripped me. I didn't know how to explain to the canoe man where I wanted to go.

I then instinctively scanned the people in the nearby canoes to see if anyone could help me. I first spotted a couple of Chinese men, and then a Malay-looking man, and then my eyes rested on a young man who looked English; at least, he had the same type of hat and jacket as Lesley.

"Sir, I beg your pardon, do you speak English?" I shouted.

The man turned and looked at me.

"I need help with directions. I'm trying to get to the Oriental Inn," I said.

"First time in Bangkok?"

I nodded.

"I'm going there myself," he said. "Just follow me."

The man Sarkis had asked me to contact upon my arrival in Bangkok was an Isfahan Jew by the name of Solomon Yahud. He part-owned the Oriental Inn and lived there on a permanent basis.

"Any friends of Sarkis are friends of mine. Welcome to my inn," he said in Persian. He was a short man in his forties with dark skin, thick dark eyebrows, sharp little eyes, and thin lips. He wore European clothing and was flamboyant in manner. I was soon to find out the reason for his flamboyancy. Solomon Yahud was not only a successful businessman but also an accomplished singer. He played the traditional hand-held drum as he sang his Hebrew and Persian love songs. His delivery was of such beauty and sensitivity that he brought tears to the eyes of all who heard him.

"I can't believe what I'm hearing. You actually came from Burma overland? I was wondering why you were wearing those funny clothes," he said, without being inquisitive about the reason for such a journey.

"Well, I was hoping you could tell me where I could get a new set of European clothing and shoes," I said, slightly embarrassed.

"That's not a problem. The shop you need is right next door to the inn. I am a partner in that, too," he said with a self-satisfied smile.

"Are there many foreigners who live here or trade from here?" I asked, changing the subject.

"There are many Chinese and English merchants and Khmer workers, and others. I don't know of any Armenian merchants who operate from here other than our very dear friend Sarkis, who comes over now and again for the sapphires. There are a small number of Jewish traders, too. I myself settled here and opened the inn and the shop with a partner a couple of years ago. That was when the new king, Rama the Third, allowed free trading and greatly reduced taxes. Of course, the British and their trade ships arrived first and were followed by others."

"I wasn't expecting a city built literally on water. It was a complete surprise to me."

"This city has God knows how many names – 'Krungthep', 'Bang Makok', 'Bangkok', 'Rattanokosin', 'the City of Angels', 'the Residence of the Emerald Buddha', I could go on and on. It has as many canals as it has names and that's what I loathe about this place. I hate getting in and out of canoes. The only alternative one has is to negotiate the narrow alleyways, and that's even worse! God, how lucky I am to have this inn on one of the few proper streets in the city!"

"On my way into the city I noticed the ornate temples and a very grand palace. The Siamese art of decorating temples and buildings seems superior to that of the Burmese. The Siamese that I came across also looked happier than the Burmese, and their monks were not as shabby in appearance."

"True. The court culture is very refined here, and that's the main reason. It trickles down to the monks and the populace."

"I do not wish to burden you with my request, but I have no one else I can turn to for help. I need to find passage to Penang as soon as possible."

"Leave it to me, young man."

"I possess Spanish dollars and was wondering if they are accepted currency here; I need to pay for my stay and the trip to Penang."

"Any money is good money in this place, my friend," he said knowingly and added, "You must be very tired. You shall have the best room in the inn."

The room Solomon Yahud offered me was lavishly decorated and the bed was the most comfortable I had slept in for years. The next day, and with great flair, he sold me a pair of black trousers, a well cut jacket, a shirt, and a pair of fashionable shoes made of the softest leather. He even sang to me in the evening; I told him I was amazed to be listening to his beautiful rendering of a Persian love song in such a faraway place as Siam. When, two days later, he told me that he had found an English vessel to take me to Penang, I couldn't have been more pleased.

CHAPTER 32

I LEFT BANGKOK ON BOARD the *Exeter*, a large merchant vessel, an East Indiaman that carried both passengers and cargo. She had *trompe l'oeil* cannons painted on her outer hull to ward off pirate ships; she was the first of her type I'd ever seen. She sailed smoothly downriver out of Bangkok until we reached a place called Paknam at the mouth of the sea. Paknam was busy with scores of small boats and Chinese junks, all anchored there waiting for the flood-tide to turn. When it did, we were soon out on the open sea and finally I could sigh with relief at having succeeded in my escape from Burma. It pained me that I was considered a criminal, a spy no less, in that country and could never return. The business of rubies had been profitable for both Lesley and me, but I had left Burma with virtually nothing. Other than the clothes on my back, I had only my leather pouch with my personal papers, my dagger, Sarkis' pistol, and an amount of rubies, so small I could hold them in the palm of one hand. I reasoned that none of this mattered; as long as I was alive, I could work again and would soon think of something else to trade in.

One long day dragged into the next aboard the *Exeter*, with only short stops at Singapore and Malacca to relieve the tedium. My impatience to get to Penang intensified. I longed to see Lesley, Lilly, Ram, and Maria again. Of course, I also thought of Violet constantly and wondered how she would react when she saw me again after nigh on two years absence.

As the *Exeter* approached Penang, my anxiety grew at the thought of seeing Violet again, but it disappeared as soon as I had disembarked and hired a carriage to take me into Georgetown. The familiar neighbourhoods, roads, and buildings had a soothing effect on me. When I reached Orchid Street, it was early evening. I looked through the glass window of Atkinson and Vartan Trading Firm and saw Lesley and Lilly intensely scrutinizing a document. For a good few minutes, they didn't feel my presence. Lilly was the first to notice me.

She flew to open the door, shouting with joy, "Oh my God! Vartan!"

Lesley followed her and gave me one of his big hugs and said, "My dear friend! We thought we had heard the last of you."

"Never! I'm back, safe and sound," I said.

"We were worried sick about you," Lilly said.

"Yes, we were. Takoohy Manuk was here about six weeks ago with her son Tovmas. She told us what had happened in Burma and how you escaped. She said not to worry, but we hadn't heard from you in months so we really didn't know what to expect and, so, we imagined the worst," Lesley mumbled.

"There was no way I could have communicated with you from where I was. I shall recount the details to you once I've rested. But tell me, is Takoohy Manuk still here?"

"No. She only stayed a week. After what happened to you, she decided to leave Burma as quickly as possible with Tovmas. They planned to join her elder son in Singapore."

"Did she say anything about Sarkis? Is he still in Burma?"

"Yes. After your escape, she said, neither she nor Sarkis was bothered by the authorities about the matter."

"That's such a great relief. I was filled with dread that they might have got into trouble because of me."

"You've been through such a perilous journey. It is hard for us to imagine what it was like," Lilly said.

There was a moment of silence, and then I said, "Is Violet alright?"

Lilly and Lesley looked at each other. And Lesley said, "Come, at least sit down and we'll tell you."

It was Lilly who began:

"After you left, Violet was in a terrible state and fell very ill. She stopped eating and she became so weak, she didn't have the strength to get out of bed. The doctor had told my father that there was nothing wrong with her physically. So my father interpreted it as a kind of depression and a direct result of my elopement, since Violet had not been allowed to see me or get in touch with me. Agha Caloustian intervened at this point and had long chats with my father. My father had to swallow his pride and come here to see me. We had a tearful father and daughter reconciliation, and he begged me to take care of Violet. I stayed at the house for ten days and Violet's condition improved considerably, especially when she knew that my father had forgiven Lesley. Lesley visited us every day and stayed for a long while, chatting with my father. That encouraged Violet to get out of bed and join them. At the end of those ten days, Violet was ready to go back to work at the firm. But two weeks later, her fiancé returned from Borneo and said he had organised his business there in a way that allowed him a few months of free time. He was ready to go ahead with the wedding. Lesley and I were terribly worried about Violet and how she would react," she said, and looked at Lesley.

Lesley took over from there:

"I can assure you, my friend, she's a very strong lady. She put a brave face on it and went ahead with it although, as Lilly and I knew, she was aching inside. The wedding took place at the Armenian Church a week later."

"I knew she had got married. Takoohy Manuk told me," I said, not daring to meet Lesley's eyes.

Lesley continued:

"Not long after the wedding, her husband took her on a trip to Calcutta. His old mother and sister still live there and he wanted to introduce his bride to them. By then we had received word from you of your safe arrival in Burma. I told her this discretely when we were saying goodbye to them at the harbour and she burst into tears. I panicked but realised that her husband thought she was crying because she was so sad to be leaving her sister and father; he knew she'd never been away from them before."

I sighed.

"I must confess to you both, here and now, that I made the biggest blunder by leaving. I should have listened to you, Lesley. I should have stayed and fought for Violet. I have been to hell and back, physically and in my heart and mind."

"I believe you, my friend. But hear the rest of it," Lesley said.

Lilly now took over:

"When they returned from Calcutta, Violet's husband stayed another month. They lived in my father's house. The plan was for her husband to go back to Borneo and, when he returned six months later, he would take Violet with him to Borneo. But things didn't turn out the way he'd planned. Shortly after he left, my father had a stroke that left him paralyzed and unable to work. So Violet more or less had to run the firm all on her own since neither her husband nor Catcheres Sarkis were in Penang. I couldn't help her myself. I had to go over to the house every day to make sure my father was being looked after properly and to keep him company, to alleviate his sense of frustration and helplessness."

"Takoohy Manuk did tell me of your father's illness and how Violet was running the firm on her own. What I don't understand is why her husband has to be away for so long," I inquired.

It was Lesley who answered me:

"He had established a branch of the firm in Borneo because of the lucrative antimony and diamond mining that has developed there in recent years but couldn't find enough competent staff *in situ* to sell the insurance policies; so he had to stay there for longer stretches of time. He did come back for Violet six months later. But seeing that Catcheres Sarkis was away on a long trip that took him to Calcutta first and then to Singapore, and considering the condition Violet's father was in, they both decided that it would be better if Violet stayed in Penang to look after the business. He returned to Borneo for at least another three months. A short while later, Apcarian had another stroke but didn't survive this time. Both Lilly and Violet were devastated. He was still only in his fifties."

"I'm very sorry to hear that, Lilly," I said. She lowered her eyes and nodded.

"And what happened next, no one expected," Lesley said, continuing:

"It was barely two weeks after Apcarian's funeral when we got the terrible news of Violet's husband's demise in Borneo. He had gone to one of the remoter mining areas for a few weeks to see some clients, and he caught malaria. Three days later, he was dead, poor man. His acquaintances there could do nothing to save him, and the unfortunate man had to be buried in Borneo. You can just imagine Violet's mental state. Although she didn't shed a tear on hearing the news, we knew she was deeply shaken. She respected him and thought him a fine man."

"Yes, she had told me how much she respected him. That is a very tragic end to a life. I wouldn't wish it on anyone. How is Violet faring. Is she alright?" I said.

Lilly was the one who answered, and said:

"Forgive us for not writing any of this to you. It was Violet's wish. She begged us not to let you know that her husband had passed away. After his death, she just buried herself in work, and for months we hardly ever saw her. I couldn't go back to the firm to help her. Our Armenian book-keeper had left us and had gone back home to Calcutta. I had to take over from him to help Lesley, and that's what I've been doing ever since. And then Violet turned up here one early morning in a panic. It was the day after we'd met Takoohy Manuk and her son at Agha Caloustian's and she'd told us about your dramatic escape from Burma. Violet stood where you're sitting now and said, 'Something terrible has happened to Vartan. I know it. I feel it.' She kept repeating this over and over. We tried to calm her down but had to eventually tell her what Takoohy Manuk had reported to us and that we hadn't heard from you in months. She broke down and cried and said she was cursed, for she had lost not only her father and her husband in a short span of time, but the love of her life, too. We tried to reason with her but she had lost all sense of reasoning. And then she collapsed. We had to move her upstairs and call for the doctor. He said she displayed the typical symptoms of a nervous breakdown. He asked us to look after her and make her stop work. He said she desperately needed to rest. Lesley and I did our best and within two weeks we were able to lift her spirits sufficiently to get her back on her feet again."

"Of course," said Lesley, "We told her we continued to nurture the hope that you were still alive and that she should certainly do likewise. She agreed and slowly came around to our way of thinking. She herself admitted that she'd had enough of work and welcomed the much-needed rest. A few days later, she said she wanted to go to Calcutta to see her late husband's mother and sister. She wanted to comfort them. She said they had lost their loved one, whose grave they will never be able to visit. We encouraged her to go. At least she had given herself a purpose, a reason to carry on with life. And that's where she is now, Vartan. We are expecting her to be back within a month."

"That is indeed good news," I said. "I pray with all my heart that I will see her again soon. I have caused her such immense pain and suffering. I hope she can forgive me."

I found lodgings a few buildings away from our business premises and applied myself to working with Lesley again. Lilly helped us, with great enthusiasm.

"We had very good returns with the rubies," Lilly said one morning, showing us the ledger.

"I'm sure we had, but that's over now, I'm afraid," I said.

"We didn't do badly with supplying spices to Minas in Isfahan, either. But things are slowing down here in Georgetown," Lesley remarked.

"We'll think of something to boost our returns. Perhaps Sarkis can supply us with sapphires from Siam," I said.

"Takoohy Manuk mentioned it to me and I think that might be a good idea but that alone may not be sufficient. I'm thinking of a more drastic change. I recall, Vartan, you were toying with the idea of a move to Singapore a while back, before we moved to Penang," said Lesley and, turning to Lilly, added, "He gave up on the idea when I met you and wanted to follow you to Penang."

"I'm still keen on it. A lot of traders are moving to Singapore and I got first-hand information from Madam Takoohy, who spent some time there considering the possibilities. She has moved there now, you tell me. She confirmed my intuition that it is likely to be the new trading hub of this region and will overtake Penang," I said with conviction.

"The problem is we don't have enough funds to confidently throw ourselves into a new venture. We may have to wait a while before we move," Lesley said.

"I have an idea for securing funds quickly. When Violet returns, I shall ask her if I could sell my share of my father's firm," Lilly intervened.

"We'll see. We'll discuss this again when she returns," Lesley said.

Just then Ram walked in with our tea. On the day of my arrival, Ram had almost thrown himself on me in welcome – something he had never done before. He had understood from Lesley's and Lilly's conversations that I had been in danger of losing my life, he told me. Maria was also pleased to see me and kept hovering around, asking if I needed anything. And they had both been keen on my having a look at their modified lodgings. As usual, Ram had applied his handiwork to the extension at the far end of the garden and had transformed the space into comfortable lodgings for himself and Maria.

"What do you think of coming to Singapore with us Ram?" Lesley said as Ram was pouring the tea.

Without raising his eyes from the cups, he said firmly, "Ram will go to Singapore with sirs. Ram will never leave sirs."

When he left the room, Lilly told me that Maria had become pregnant right after I'd left Georgetown, but had lost the baby – stillborn. She, being a fervent Catholic, had dealt with the tragedy in her own way, through her prayers, seeking consolation from God. But Ram had taken it quite badly. After a while, he managed to surmount his grief through work. The Chinese clerk we employed had left just then and Lesley began giving Ram chores to do in the office. With Lesley's help, he had applied himself to improving his reading and writing skills in English and was now able to manage small amounts of paperwork.

"So you see, we've all had our share of misfortune whilst you were away," Lilly concluded.

CHAPTER 33

✤

THE FOLLOWING WEEKS WERE SPENT anxiously awaiting Violet's return. Some six weeks after my arrival, I turned up for work one day; Lesley and Lilly were at their desks. They both smiled, and Lilly said, "She's upstairs, resting. She arrived very early this morning."

I rushed upstairs and found her in the room that used to be my bedroom. She hadn't changed a bit. She was as beautiful as ever.

"My Violet," I heard myself saying.

She looked up in astonishment. She got up from her seat and walked towards me. My eyes followed her.

"I thought you were dead," she said in a sad voice.

"Can you ever forgive me?"

She came closer, gazing gently into my eyes, and touched my face delicately with her fingertips. She then placed her cheek next to mine. I held her tightly in my arms and heard her whisper, "Don't ever leave me."

Violet and I were married at the Armenian Church in Georgetown three weeks later. Lesley was our best man, and, as is the tradition in our church, Lilly was our best woman. Ram and Maria were present. Agha Caloustian was also present with his daughter, his son-in-law, and his first grandchild, a lovely boy of one. The only other person in attendance was Catcheres Sarkis.

My marriage to Violet was the start of a new life, a happy life that I had never imagined possible since leaving Isfahan. Violet was the one my heart had chosen, and every day for the rest of my life I would thank the Lord for uniting us.

And so it was that the three orphans, who had left Madras for Georgetown, now left Georgetown for Singapore. But they were no longer alone. The six of us embarked on a new journey to a new settlement with new hopes and expectations.

I had read somewhere before our departure that although Singapore was a new English settlement in the Malaya States, and was now administered by none other than Colonel Farquhar himself, there had been other settlements there a thousand or more years ago. The ruins of an ancient town, around which the new Singapore was built, attested to this. I imagined a thousand years ago, people like us had embarked on a similar journey. And perhaps others will in the future, to a place that nurtures new hopes and new beginnings.

Thus, Lesley and Lilly, Ram and Maria, and Violet and I sailed to Singapore in the new year of 1829. We sailed safely on the *Exeter* through the Straits of Malacca and eventually reached the Channel of Rabbit and Coney, the Western entrance to the Straits of Singapore. This is when I wished I had a draftsman's skill of drawing for yet a third time in my life. For what greeted us were some sixty small, green, wooded islands of magnificent beauty. I had no doubt we had made the right decision. Violet held my hand and squeezed it gently; looking at me with tears of joy welling on her lower eyelids, she smiled.

Singapore opened its arms wide to us and we were settled within two weeks of arrival. We found two large go-downs near the water for our future stock. The floor above the go-downs was large enough to turn into three independent living quarters. We had pooled our money. Violet and Lilly had sold their share of their father's insurance firm to Catcheres Sarkis, and it was this money that we used to purchase the go-downs. The money Lesley and I had saved was put into the business. About a month after our arrival, we resumed our trade in precious stones, but also began importing woven loincloths from the Celebes and white cotton vests and shirts from the Coromandel Coast. These were the type of garments both male and female natives wore all over the Malaya States. Soon, our business prospered, and not least because we had the help of Lilly and Violet, who, indeed, were better with accounts and paperwork than Lesley and I could ever be.

Over the years, I have often found myself thinking of the Sayama and the three kisses of the cobra. I am now convinced that she must have conferred upon me not just three blessings, but three and a fair few more.

Almost thirty years have passed since my arrival in Singapore, and I am an old man now. The reader of these memoirs, be you my close kin, or dear friend, or precious descendant, you may be curious to know what has become of all those I met during my life's journey.

I shall recount by starting with my arch-enemy, Markar. A few years after I had settled in Singapore, I got news of Markar's death. It was Sarkis Manuk who reported it to me. After my escape from Burma, Markar remained there with the Russian nobleman, both of them embroiled in the intrigues of the Burmese court. They switched allegiance and became staunch supporters of the powerful Queen Me Nu and her brother, who rewarded them with lucrative business deals. Unfortunately for Markar, in 1837, the brother of the king, Prince Sarawaldi, had gathered enough support from the Burmese nobility to topple the king. The usurper prince had the queen and her brother executed, and the king was put under house arrest. Markar and his Russian friend were also executed. This was done on the express wishes of the usurper prince who considered them as traitors and wanted to take revenge. It is sad to say that they both died a terrible death, disembowelment being a common method of execution in Burma.

Minas, my friend and business partner in Isfahan, is alive and well, and his son, Asadur, has taken over the running of the business. True to his caring self, Minas looked after Mr. Ashod in his last days, until he passed away some ten years ago. Minas' daughter, Mariam, is married with three children. She writes to me now and again and, to my great joy, tells me that she always visits the tombs of my loved ones in Isfahan. I wrote to her a few months ago and told her that if the Lord gives me the health and the strength I require to make a long journey and a pilgrimage to Jerusalem with my Violet next year, I shall visit Isfahan on my way to the Holy Land and finally meet her.

Agha Caloustian died peacefully in his sleep eight years after we left Georgetown. During his last years, he visited us twice in Singapore, and both Lesley and I felt honoured by those visits and were able to offer him his favourite brandy. He left his vast fortune to his only daughter. After his death, his daughter, her husband and their son moved to England permanently.

Melkon Khan, who had no family of his own, did not live for very long after he was forced to sell his *Anahid*. Without her, he had no purpose and lost his enthusiasm for life. I have heard that she was scrapped about the same time as his passing in Madras. She had become too old to brave the high seas.

Tsaay and Naang had two children, a son and a daughter, and still live in their village. Their news was relayed to me by Sarkis Manuk. Since I left them all those years ago, I have never forgotten to mention them in my prayers. Recently, another Anglo-Burmese war has broken out and I worry for the safety of my friends and their people.

Sarkis Manuk, with his family, joined his sister and her two sons in Singapore in 1837. With the harsh rule of the usurper Burmese king, he didn't feel safe in Ava. He continued his business activities from Singapore and travelled to Siam regularly. Eventually, both he and Madam Takoohy decided to return to Batavia for three reasons: Sarkis' wife, Martha, longed to return to her birthplace to be closer to her Dutch family, his daughter, Sara, had married a Dutchman who wanted to settle in Batavia, and Madam Takoohy's elder son wished to start a new business venture with one of his cousins there. Tovmas, though, still lives in Singapore and imports European crockery and cutlery. He is married to the daughter of one of the first Armenian merchants to settle here. They have two daughters. Tovmas visits me at least once a month and we always end up playing a game of backgammon, just as we did in the old days in Amarapura.

Little Arakel, or Archbishop Nareg as he is now known, took over from Father Sahag and became the headmaster of the Armenian School in Erzerum. But, tragically, he had to flee the city with the other Armenian folk, including my kin, to the relative safety of Echmiadzin when the Russians invaded in 1827. Father Sahag died in exile, heartbroken, shortly after their escape from Erzerum. Another, more recent conflict, the Crimean War, which took place between 1854 and 1856, has destroyed what remained of my birthplace. In 1828, Little Arakel started a makeshift school near our Mother Cathedral in Echmiadzin for the children of the Armenian refugees from Erzerum. This makeshift school has now become one of the most reputable educational establishments in the area. It would not surprise me if my Little Arakel someday ends up being ordained the catholicos of the Armenians. Indeed, his dedication to his people is still the main focus of his life.

Ram and Maria had five children in Singapore – three sons and two daughters, all now grown up. With Lesley's encouragement and their father's enthusiasm, Ram's three sons are the proud owners of two grocery stores and sell foodstuff to the local Chinese population, which has grown considerably over the last twenty years.

Lesley and Lilly are as affectionate towards each other as they were when they first met. Although they have not had children of their own, they have never complained about their lot. And apart from having each other, they have doted on our children. I could not have wished for better kin and friends than Lesley and Lilly.

Violet gave me four cherished sons, all born within the first seven years of our arrival in Singapore. We were unable to baptize them. The Armenian Church in Singapore, the founding of which had taken place in 1826, was not completed and officially consecrated until 1836. That is the year Father Yohannes, our resident priest, baptized all four of them on the same day. Lesley and Lilly are godfather and godmother to all four. Our eldest son we named Jacob, after my father. My second son is named after my uncle, Gregory. My third son is named after my first teacher, Sahag, or Isaac as people call him here; and my youngest son is named after my Little Arakel. All four attended the small Armenian School the merchants established in Singapore and were schooled in both Armenian and English. All are now young men and have been helping Lesley and me in the business of trading. Both Violet and I are eager to see them marry and have families of their own before we depart this world.

The love of my life, Violet, is ever present with her attentiveness and love. And I pray that the Lord will take me first, for I could not stand life without her. She has been my anchor in exile. And although I have prospered in this welcoming land of Singapore, and have been fortunate to put my calligraphic skills in the service of my church and countrymen, and still do in my old age, I have a heavy heart when I think of my homeland. I often think of the Armenian merchant's tomb in Malacca and remember the words carved on his tombstone – words that still bring tears to my eyes. Like him, I will not witness the freedom of my homeland. My four children may end up at the four corners of the Earth, in exile like me. But I pray to the Saviour that one day deliverance from exile will come to my children's descendants, and my people's suffering will come to an end, a time when we are finally free of the chains of foreign rule.

I praise the Lord for giving me the strength and the ability to write this, the story of my life – may He have mercy upon me.

EPILOGUE

MISS FLORA NEVER GOT TO read the memoirs in English translation. She passed away in her sleep just three months after our meeting. I had kept in touch with her during that period, informing her of the progress I'd made with the translation of the memoirs. She had also offered to leave Olivia and myself half her personal wealth. She wished to leave the other half to a youth organisation in Macau. Both of us declined the offer, but in the end, she persuaded us to accept the inheritance on behalf of Joey. The last time I spoke to her over the phone, she had said:

"So, what are your plans for the future?"

"I've decided to go to Armenia and donate Vartan's manuscript to the Madenataran."

"That's the old manuscripts' museum, isn't it? I do envy you. Soon, I won't be around and will have lived my life without ever having been to my forefather's homeland, or what remains of it. I'd never thought of it that way before, but now that I'm old, that's my only regret in life. Anyway, you will tell me all about it on your next visit, won't you? That would be good enough for me, I think," she'd said.

Miss Flora would have approved if she'd known that not only was I going to visit Armenia, but that I had decided to live and work there for some time.

Two events had occurred on a business trip I undertook to New York shortly after Miss Flora's death. The first was that, through work associates, I had met one of the directors of a world-famous financial institution who had offered me a post in Armenia to oversee the implementation of a new project there. I was elated and could not pass up the opportunity.

The second event was not as joyful as I had anticipated it to be. On arrival in New York, I contacted the Armenian Archbishop of the Eastern Diocese of America and asked for assistance in finding the Bantukhtians.

"We'll have to go through the prelacy files. It's going to take a few days," Archbishop Karekin told me. I was surprised to get a phone call at my hotel from the Archbishop himself a couple of days later.

"There's only one Bantukhtian on our files presently. Her name is Lucy, but she doesn't use her maiden name. She's married to Hrant Missakian and they live in New Jersey, I'm told. You should be able to trace them easily if they're listed."

I thanked Archbishop Karekin profusely and promised to attend Sunday mass as it was he officiating on Palm Sunday.

When I called her, Lucy was astonished, but somewhat suspicious of my intentions when I said I'd be happy to visit her in New Jersey to save her the trouble of coming to New York.

"Oh, no!" she said. "Hrant works there, in Manhattan, and I can meet him after work and we can come and see you."

I met the Missakians in my hotel lobby the following evening. Our initial meeting was, naturally, a bit awkward as I did not know where to start and they seemed overly reserved. After we'd exchanged pleasantries, they were more comfortable and became more open and talkative.

Hrant owns a rug and carpet business and is doing very well, and Lucy, who is in her early forties, used to be a school teacher.

"I gave up on that. I've got three young children to look after. That's a full-time job."

I agreed and asked her about her family. All she knew was that they had come to the United States in the late 19th Century and that they initially sold oriental carpets.

"I was never aware of my Armenian roots. I grew up as an American," she said. "I'm glad I married an Armenian, though." She gave Hrant a tender look. "We met in the 1990's when I joined an Armenian club for the first time for folklore dancing."

As the evening progressed, I realised that I was disappointed in them. They were nice, decent, hard-working people, leading a quiet, suburban American life. But they were not genuinely interested in Vartan's memoirs or the family history, or the history of the Armenian people in general. They listened to Vartan's story, the events leading to the meeting with Miss Flora, and my descriptions of her and Olivia with polite nods, but with discernable indifference.

"They'll probably send me a Christmas card and that'll be that!" I said to myself after they had left. But when I went to bed that night, I was no longer sad. "That's life," I said, and thought of Yow and Olivia. How they had bombarded me with questions when they had received the English translation of Vartan's memoirs and how excited they were and inquisitive about everything. They'd become family to me now, and yet, I had never actually met them in person.

Today is September 1st and I'm taking the flight from Beirut to Yerevan, the capital of Armenia. Most of the passengers are Armenian tourists from the Diaspora visiting the 'homeland'. September is the best time to visit Armenia. The harsh heat of the summer is over and it's the grape harvest season. Soon, the heavy vats would be filled to make that wonderful Armenian brandy so much appreciated by Winston Churchill.

Last night, I spoke to Yow and Olivia, and they both vowed to come and meet me in Armenia for Christmas. I told them both they would need proper warm clothing. I'm told winter can be bitterly cold in Armenia.

SOURCES

While writing this novel, I benefited from consulting the following works:

Aslanian, S. D. (2011). *From the Indian Ocean to the Mediterranean: The Global Trade Networks of Armenian Merchants from New Julfa.* Berkeley, CA: University of California Press.

Bedrosian, R. (2000). *Soma among the Armenians.* http.//rbedrosian. com/soma.htm

Bournoutian, G. A., trans. (2010). *Arak'el of Tabriz: Book of History.* Costa Mesa, CA: Mazda Publishers.

Crawfurd, J. (1828). *Journal of an Embassy from the Governor-General of India to the Courts of Siam and Cochin-China.* London: Henry Colburn.

Crawfurd, J. (1829). *Journal of an Embassy from the Governor-General of India to the Court of Ava in the Year 1827.* London: Henry Colburn.

Jeyaraj, D. (2012). *Embodying Memories: Early Bible Translations in Tranquebar and Serampore.* www.martynmission.cam.ac.uk/media/ documents/HMCseminars2012/

Kevorkian, R. H., ed. (1996). *Arménie entre Orient et Occident: Trois Mille Ans de Civilisation.* Paris: Bibliothèque Nationale de France.

Lang, D. M. (1988). *The Armenians: A People in Exile.* London: Unwin Hyman.

Najmuddin, S. Z. (2006). *Armenia: A Resume (with Notes on Seth's Armenians in India).* Oxford: Trafford.

Seth, M. J. (1895). *History of the Armenians in India: From the Earliest Times to the Present Day.* Calcutta: Author.

Wright, N. (2003). *Respected Citizens: The History of Armenians in Singapore and Malaysia.* Victoria: Amassia.

The translation of the epitaph on the Armenian merchant's tomb in Malacca is an amalgam of the two versions that appear in Wright's and Seth's books. The modifications are mine, based on my reading of the calligraphy on the Malacca tomb.

Although I have strived to be as historically accurate as possible and have mentioned a number of real historical personalities, this novel is a work of fiction and its main characters are fictional.

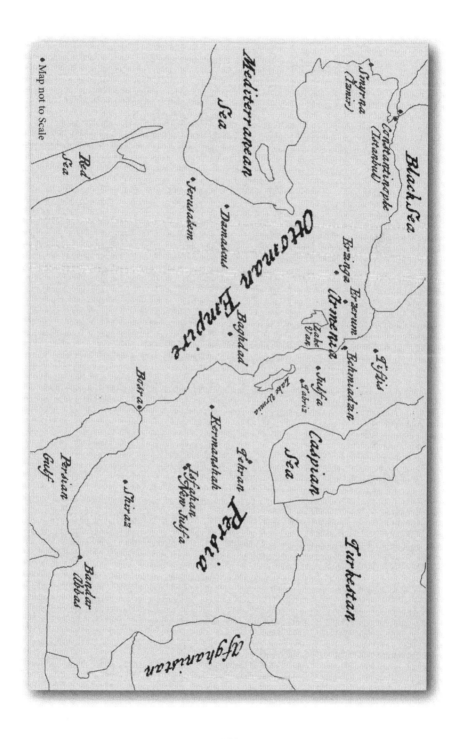

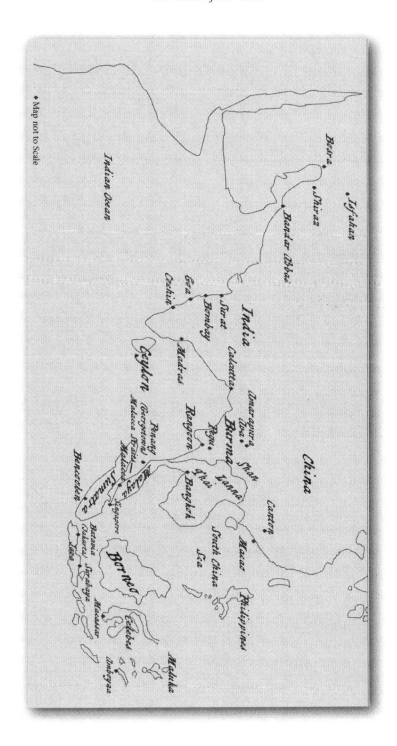

Made in the USA
Charleston, SC
02 February 2016